This Side of Sad

Also by Karen Smythe

Stubborn Bones (stories)
Figuring Grief: Gallant, Munro, and the Poetics of Elegy (criticism)

This Side of Sad

KAREN SMYTHE

GOOSE LANE

Excerpts from "The Verb to Be" by André Breton, translated by Bill Zavatsky and Zack Rogow, in *Earthlight* (2017). Used with permission from Black Widow Press, Boston, Massachusetts. Excerpts from *Waiting for God* by Simone Weil, translated by Emma Craufurd, translation copyright © 1951, renewed © 1979 by G.P. Putnam's Sons. Used by permission of G.P. Putnam's Sons, an imprint of Penguin Publishing Group, a division of Penguin Random House LLC. All rights reserved. Excerpt from *Man's Search for Meaning* by Viktor E. Frankl, copyright © 1959, 1962, 1984, 1992 by Viktor E. Frankl. Reprinted with permission from Beacon Press, Boston, Massachusetts.

Edited by Bethany Gibson.
Cover and page design by Julie Scriver.
Cover image from the series *Femina Plantarum*, copyright © 2013 by Elsa Mora. www.elsamora.net
Printed in Canada.
10 9 8 7 6 5 4 3 2 1

Library and Archives Canada Cataloguing in Publication

Smythe, Karen E. (Karen Elizabeth), 1962-, author
      This side of sad / Karen Smythe.

Issued in print and electronic formats.
ISBN 978-0-86492-985-3 (softcover).--ISBN 978-0-86492-986-0 (EPUB).--
ISBN 978-0-86492-987-7 (MOBI)

I. Title

PS8587.M994T45 2017   C813'.6   C2017-902823-5
                                       C2017-902824-3

We acknowledge the generous support of the Government of Canada, the Canada Council for the Arts, and the Government of New Brunswick.

Goose Lane Editions
500 Beaverbrook Court, Suite 330
Fredericton, New Brunswick
CANADA E3B 5X4
www.gooselane.com

RECYCLED
Paper made from
recycled material
FSC
www.fsc.org   FSC® C103567

For J.H.

I know the general outline of despair. A very small shape, defined by jewels worn in the hair. That's despair.... I know the general outline of despair. Despair has no heart, my hand always touches breathless despair, the despair whose mirrors never tell us if it's dead.... I don't remember anything and it's always in despair that I discover the beautiful uprooted trees of night.... In its general outline despair has no importance. It's a squad of trees that will eventually make a forest, it's a squad of stars that will eventually make one less day, it's a squad of one-less-days that will eventually make up my life.
    — André Breton

There is both continuity and the separation of a definite point of entry, as with the temperature at which water boils, between affliction itself and all the sorrows that, even though they may be very violent, very deep and very lasting, are not affliction in the strict sense. There is a limit; on the far side of it we have affliction but not on the near side. This limit is not purely objective; all sorts of personal factors have to be taken into account. The same event may plunge one human being into affliction and not another....
    — Simone Weil

To invoke an analogy, consider a movie: it consists of thousands upon thousands of individual pictures, and each of them makes sense and carries a meaning, yet the meaning of the whole film cannot be seen before its last sequence is shown. However, we cannot understand the whole film without having first understood each of its components, each of the individual pictures. Isn't it the same with life?
    — Viktor Frankl

Foreword

March 2005

Everyone wants to know if I've come to terms with what happened. *Come to terms* — what a strange phrase for "acceptance." Terms are words. Terms are time. Terms are the agreed-upon parameters of a relationship.

I didn't agree to this.

Right now I have only the fact of James's death, and facts alone won't help me. Before there are terms, any terms, to come to, I need to know what happened out in the woods, when he died. I don't mean whether or not it was an accident, or not only that; either way, my husband decided on danger that day. What I need to understand is *why*. What pushed him there? I thought we'd both recovered from the toll of my surgery, that James was finally moving forward. Did I miss something in the months leading up to James's retirement? I *must* have missed something, the first time through. Something big. Something telling.

But figuring out what happened to James, to us...this will not be easy. I don't expect to stumble across the truth and recognize it in a flash, or hear a voice yell "This is it!" the way your gut does, when you fall in love. No, that's not the way this story will end. If it ends. Clearly, I don't know how to get there. Or how to begin. I am in shambles. Aghast. Afflicted, a mute. "I" stands for "Imposter" now. Because that woman, James's wife? She's vanished. Banished, gone underground; absconded with the goods. What happened to James happened to her, too, in a way. The person I was, with James, died when he did.

The weekend it happened, I'd not gone to the farm. I've often wondered if that had been part of James's plan. Not that he was upset with me for not being there, come Saturday (though there might have been that, too), but that the opportunity should not be wasted. If it happened that way, that is — if it wasn't an accident.

What if I could watch our life together unfold again, if I could unreel it, exhume it, observe it scene by random scene? Not only that one day or week, or even the months before, but the years before that: the *whole* of our life. Would that do it? Would that be enough to get me there, to the truth about what happened to James? To us?

Somehow I don't think so. Somehow, I think there is something deeper I need to get at, to dig out from my life *before* I met James. I'm the only one left who might be able to tell me the truth about myself. If I could see my *entire* life from one step back, watch it but at the same time remove myself from it, then maybe the true story about James and me would reveal itself. It might emerge like an apparition, oozing out of the spaces between the scrambled episodes.

There wasn't a lot of time between the end of my relationship with Ted and the start of life with James. There could be something there, back then — something about me, or in me, in the person I'd become with Ted that festered, and festers still. What happened to her, to the woman I'd been during the years I shared with him, once he cut ties — where did she go? James didn't meet her; I didn't take her with me when I moved into my life with James, my life after Ted. And the girl before her, before Ted and I fell in love — what about her, that girl who carried a burnished, buried love for Josh, from her teens into her twenties? I left her behind when Ted came along; is she, too, part of this fray, this knotted tangle that came to strangle and estrange us, James and me?

Time itself seems broken, it sits in frozen pieces that need to melt and merge to form a solution. Time needs to flow again, so I can bring back the messy necessities of mind and heart for the reckoning: the false and the true, the subconscious glue that has kept my sclerotic life together. Because every bit of me has to be dissected, laid bare, exposed to the elements. There is no other way to move forward, no restart button or blueprint to follow, no script to tell me what to say or how to be.

My doctor suggested that I start keeping a journal. Writing my thoughts out every day, he thinks, might help me sort through the indecipherable mess of my mind. I said I'd prefer another prescription for Ativan, thank you very much. The discord between all those blank pages and the disarray in my head is too much to overcome. Besides, you don't just *keep* a diary, you are supposed to keep it *alive*, like a pet. I can barely keep myself alive right now. And memories do not add up to a life, anyway, not even when strung together day by day or week by week. There is so much more that falls between the cracks, unremembered or deliberately forgotten. And if I can't remember everything, how do I go on then? Because I'm afraid I might not be able to. Remember everything, I mean.

"Go on now, Maslen. Remember. Make yourself remember." Jesus, I said that out loud. And referring to myself in the second person, to boot. Isn't that a sign of madness? To be beside oneself, outside of oneself? Well. Maybe that's good; maybe that's exactly the step back I need, to make this work. To make something of nothing.

Okay, you — get on with it, then. "Make yourself remember. Go on."

Make. Your. Self.

Remember.

Go on.

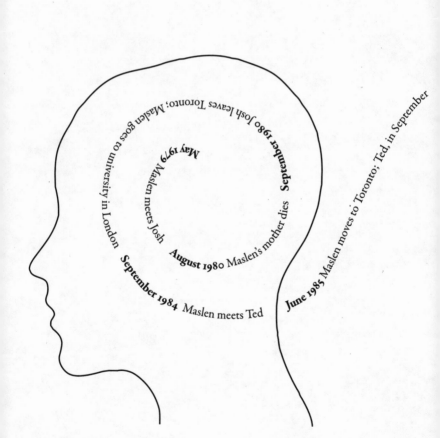

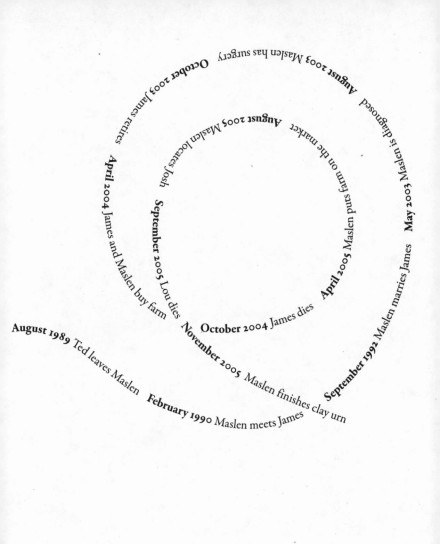

I. *Begin*

one

Sometimes, when James and I still shared a bed, I'd lie on my back, eyes closed, and listen to my husband breathing. James had never snored; his respiration had always been regular, slow and subdued — so much so that I'd turn, periodically throughout the night, to watch for the rising and falling of his chest, for the movement of the sheet that covered us, to make sure he was still with me. Later, when he began to have nightmares, he'd wake up panting, out of breath, as if he'd been trying to run away or run after something, or someone.

In the beginning I would not have believed we'd come to be so physically separate, James and I, that one day we'd lie side by side not touching, not entwined like a caduceus as we fell asleep.

Our story was simple. James and I met in February, a few months after Ted ended our engagement and moved out of the city. I was taking a ceramics class at the Y where James and his best friend Tony worked out with weights. I'd become sick of myself after spending a stir-crazy holiday alone, my first without Ted in five years. My sister, Gina, had given me a Continuing Ed. course coupon for Christmas, to get me out of my apartment. "You spend too much time in your head," she liked to say about me.

I wanted to take the Art History course, so I could sit in the dark looking at slides of masterpieces without having to talk to anyone, but it was full. I already knew How to Use Computers and How to Write for Business, so that left Pottery for Beginners. It was held in an airless studio with a clear-glass viewing pane in the interior wall, facing the hallway.

As I kneaded some clay during the first class, I sensed a gaze on my face, so I glanced up and saw a man smiling at me. I smiled back, shrugged, and looked down again. The next week he hung about in the hallway like a teenager. I finished washing up and approached him as I walked toward the exit. "Hello," I said in a tone that could have let either of us walk away without losing face, but he wasn't going anywhere. "The name's 'James,' actually," he said, his Sean Connery dead on. "As in 'Bond, James Bond.'" That broke me up and I laughed more than James had expected me to. "She was a pushover," he joked whenever he told the story. "I wooed her with a silly impression."

Every time one of us recounted how we met, our relationship seemed to gain ground. By telling it over and over in our first few weeks together, we gave our union a *gravitas* that had seemed absent, I thought, at first.

It's quiet, too quiet, in here. The snowfall has hushed the houses on our street this morning. *My* street, not ours. It's just my street now.

When we met, James had his own condo uptown, though he all but moved into my tiny apartment soon after. We bought this place a couple of years later, just before we married, and it suited us. A two-bedroom bungalow seemed to be all the space we'd ever need. We didn't fill it with a lot of furniture, but the house did start to feel confining to James, once he retired and spent seven days a week here. I guess it felt constraining to me, too, when James stopped engaging with the world, and the atmosphere at home became laden with tension I didn't know how to break. Sleep came as relief to both of us at night.

lu

I'd attracted James with aloofness, I suppose. Some men are drawn to that quality in women, consider it a test, even. James admitted later that getting me to go out with him had been an irresistible challenge. I looked so intent on triumphing over that lump of clay, he said, and yet when I looked up and smiled at him, my face radiated a potential for joy he wouldn't have guessed was there, behind the screen of seriousness. "I knew you would be interesting when I saw you in a lab coat instead of an apron, like the other women wore. I had to find out what was going through that mind of yours."

James mentioned that scene again when he proposed to me. "When I saw you smile the first time, I wanted to make you feel that happy all the time. I wanted to be the one who could do that." When I said yes, he looked as if he'd won a contest. I knew James had been telling Tony everything about our relationship from the get-go, and I wondered if he'd made a bet with his friend about how long it might take to win me over.

I won, too, finding James. But in the early days I was highly swayable, and seeing James was a pleasant distraction while I waited for Ted to come to his senses and back to me, to what I thought of as my real life, our life together. The two men crossed paths just once, disturbing my sense of time and place and what I was doing, with whom. James had let himself into my apartment after work, as he often did — he was a teacher, so his day ended earlier than mine — and when I got home he was browning onions for a tomato sauce in my ill-equipped kitchen. He said the phone had been ringing every few minutes, but no one had left a message. This irritated me. The next time it rang, I was brusque and abrupt with my "Hello?" Blood-bubbling anxiety rippled through me at the sound of Ted's voice asking, "Maslen, is that *you*?"

Ted was in town for the weekend and had tickets to the Jays; that's why he called, to invite me to go to the playoff game with him. "Come on, it'll be like old times," he said with a slight pout in his voice, as if I would hurt his feelings if I didn't accept. My instinct was to do just that, to run out the door and leave James — living, breathing, fucking James — in my apartment to eat spaghetti alone and lock up behind him when he left; but I took a deep breath and said, "No, I can't," which Ted hadn't expected. "Oh." Long pause. "Well, then..." he said, and we both stayed on the line for a few more moments, as if one of us was about to figure out what to do or say to the other. With James five feet away from me, I couldn't ask Ted where he was living, or how I could get in touch with him later — not unless I was willing to tell James everything, to put that morass of my recent past on the table between us. So all I said to James after I hung up was, "A ghost." James nodded. His trust in me and confidence in himself precluded the need for any further explanation, it seemed. We never spoke of the call or that ghost again.

ello

Confidence, at least in terms of sex appeal — that was all I'd say James and Ted had in common. Ted's body language exuded availability and interest, and he drew women to him with a smile that promised a pleasant surprise, as though he had a secret to share or a gift to give; when he used it on me, my usual defences against such put-on charm waned despite myself. James's allure worked differently; he didn't think twice about whether or not I would be attracted to him, so he didn't need to play that game. He knew himself, he was comfortable and content with who he was and what he had to offer. That quality, that solid self-assurance without the self-centred show, was partly why I found him physically irresistible. After our first night together, the pull to be with him was intense and instinctive; it was as if, whenever I saw him, my inner organs and intuition started issuing orders that I mate, that I copulate and populate, that I give myself over to this desire no matter where it might lead. So I did, and I was surprised when it quickly led me to happiness, and, two years later, to a comfortable marriage that worked. Until it didn't.

ello

James surprised me one Monday morning a couple of years ago by running into the bedroom wearing only a scuba diving mask and flippers, shouting, "Beach day! Maslen, wake up, it's beach day!" I should have been dressed at least half an hour before but I'd been silencing my alarm clock with the snooze button every few minutes, unable to rouse myself. I had been down about work for a few weeks at that point — the language school where I was an administrator had been sold, and the new owners were making aesthetic and policy changes, "to give the operation a more corporate look and feel," we were told. I felt less and less like I belonged there, and getting up and going each morning was becoming harder, so James was trying his best to cheer me up. "We're going to play hooky today, Maslen. I've called in sick." When I protested, he cut me off. "Honey, it's not really a lie. We both need a mental health day." He handed me the phone. "Your turn."

James took on my emotions, not as his own, exactly, but as his responsibility. He didn't dwell or delve, as I did, but he believed it was his job to make me happy, to *keep* me happy. On days when I turned inward more than usual, when I veered, even slightly, toward sadness, he didn't absorb my downturned mood or worry that he might have had a role to play in bringing it about. To harbour concern about his place in my heart wouldn't have occurred to him. James's approach, always, was to pull me out of myself with laughter.

Our sick day, the day James pulled me off of the mattress and into his embrace, might have been the last time he was himself, completely himself. It was mid-May and too cool for bathing suits, so after we made love and showered we took the subway down to Queen, and an eastbound streetcar to the Beaches. We walked to the Fox and considered taking in a matinee, but the day was too beautiful to sit in a dark theatre. After perusing the goods in second-hand bookstores and funky consignment shops filled with antiques painted turquoise and purple, we had sweet-and-sour chicken balls and wonton soup at the diner known as the Goof, and then we strolled, arm in arm, along the windy boardwalk, which — other than a few dog walkers — we had to ourselves.

James kissed my forehead or my cheek every few yards, and once, when he dipped me a little as if we were in a ballroom, we lingered in the kiss like a couple captured in a still from a black-and-white movie. Before we went home that day, James stood on a promontory and shouted part of Hamlet's "to be" soliloquy at the seagulls. It was the only speech he remembered from high school, and he called it out like a celebratory song. As I watched and listened, and remembered how much I'd loved that play from the first time I read it, I became filled with joy. James, for years, had always seemed to know how to show me where the joy was.

It was only a few days later that I had to tell him the news my doctor called me about: this time, the lump in my breast was malignant. When James didn't say anything, I added, "It's fine, hon. I'll just have it removed." James, eyes narrowed, said, "Why? Why you?" and I said, "Why *not* me?"

I'm lucky, that was my first thought. It was a small, contained tumour that could be completely excised; I'd not been randomly hit with something worse, like ovarian or pancreatic cancer. Some of our friends and acquaintances had faced brain tumours and coronary disease, others had children with frightening problems like juvenile diabetes and debilitating developmental abnormalities. My mother died of acute leukemia before she was fifty, and all I had to deal with at forty-three was a little lump! "Things happen to people," I told James, "horrible things that can ruin your life, even if you don't die right away. That's not me. I'm going to be fine!" But *he* wasn't fine, and I didn't get it. "James, come on. It's not like I'm losing an arm or a leg."

"I'd love you even then," he said, but that wasn't my point. I just couldn't get him to see my point, and he couldn't get me to see his — I still don't know what his was. My diagnosis, it seemed, had shunted us to parallax positions, as if suddenly we saw our future, our coupledom, through very different lenses.

ell

"To Maslen and James, and to your future!" Tony toasted for the third or fourth time, holding up his refilled goblet, and we all clinked glasses again. We were at a restaurant, celebrating our marriage with Tony and my best friend, Nancy, who had stood for me; Tony was James's best man. They had been friends since they were kids; they travelled to Europe after teachers' college, and then spent a semester teaching Business English to employees of a large corporation in Kyoto before taking permanent positions at the school where they still taught, in the north end of the city.

Tony was my competition, in a way, so I was relieved, when James introduced us, that we hit it off. Tony was as important to James as a brother; dislike on either of our parts would have stirred up an untenable tension that I knew James and I wouldn't be able to surmount or survive. But we did survive; we thrived, even, our little group. It was just the three of us for years and years, because while Tony was always dating, he made sure it never lasted long.

One night he and his date were over for dinner, and James served a risotto with baked yams and Cuban chicken, simmered in orange juice with pan-fried onions and cumin seeds. The garlic was the coup. Using a scalpel he brought home from the lab at the high school where he taught Biology, James had made several incisions in each breast, dissecting the skin from the flesh. Then he'd inserted whole garlic cloves into these pockets, clamping the edges of the skin together with those tiny-toothed clips that come with Tensor bandages, before adding the chicken to the pot.

I don't remember Tony's girl's name; she barely said a word all night. As we ate, Tony thought up medically related titles for cookbooks that James could make a killing on. *Cooking with Needles*; *Flavour Emergencies; Kitchen Operations.* The three of us were drinking the bottles of red Tony had brought, getting louder and trying to outdo one another, while the girlfriend sipped at sparkling water so she could drive Tony home. I know it wasn't fair of us, and it wasn't like me to be so inconsiderate, but it was fun to exclude her. I know the need to be part of a group is normal, and I've always been aberrant that way; but after that night I thought I understood why those in a circle can be cruel to those outside of it: it's not the thrill of power, primarily, but the fear of a shake-up, of instability, of loss. I liked being the sole female, playing that role in our trio. You can trust the structure of a triad, I thought then, the way you are supposed to be able to trust a family.

ﻉﻉﻉ

Not being a part of Ted's crowd was fine with me. By the time Ted graduated from medical school, he'd spent a lot more time with people I didn't know than he spent with me. Maybe that was my first mistake, not wanting to hang out with them more often. No, not mistake — it was probably the first significant difference between us that I should have paid attention to. The person Ted became in the end wasn't drastically different from the man I'd fallen in love with five years before, but different he was.

In the beginning, Ted and I talked as if we had to get caught up after some grievous separation during which time we'd done our growing up. One day when we were still silly with new love for each other, Ted jumped into a grocery cart that was abandoned outside of my building, and I pushed it back to the store across the street. A woman heading to her car in the parking lot smiled at us and said, "It must be love!" After that day, we'd go to the store at night, grab a cart, and I'd push Ted through the empty parking lot while we took turns making up "if" questions: *Would you love me if I was bald? If I was a midget? Would you love me if I was a quadriplegic? If I had no arms?* We always said, "Yes! Yes! Yes!" — which was so easy to do, because at that age you never expect disaster will strike, do you? You think you're immortal when you're in your twenties; you think you're *both* immortal when you're in love. And you think that that love is permanent, too — and that you have all the time in the world to keep it alive.

Our first picture together was taken in the curtained booth at the mall. Ted liked posing for photographs. He was always seeking the admiring lens; being camera-ready was part of his persona. We crammed ourselves in to get a strip of four black-and-white snaps of our pressed-together faces. There was a blinding flash with each click, so we forced our eyes to stay wide open as if we had toothpicks between the lids. It made us look both amazed and afraid at the same time.

ee

When I started sleeping with Ted, who thought condoms were *so* high school, I asked a student-clinic doctor who looked to be about seventy-five years old for an IUD. I couldn't go on the pill because it would make my debilitating migraines more frequent, and because I was prone to breast cysts — a double whammy for side effects; but the doctor I saw wouldn't abide my request. He said young women my age tended to have many partners, and that there were many bugs out there that cling to the device's wires "and lead to god-knows-what down the road," meaning infertility. I didn't particularly like the idea of having an object embedded inside of me, the way a working desert camel has stones shoved through its cervix, so I didn't argue with him, but Ted was ticked. He insisted I get a diaphragm.

Ted came with me to the campus clinic for "the fitting." We joked that it sounded like I was buying a wedding dress or a custom-made bra. I filled in a form in the waiting room, and Ted asked me if he had to sign anything, to declare that it was his dick that was involved. "Not unless I'm going to have to prove paternity down the road," I said; he laughed and turned my face to him, cupping my chin, and we kissed.

Ted and I had planned out the next decade of our lives, the first year we were together. He'd finish medical school while I worked, doing "something interesting," and then we'd go wherever his career took him, and we'd travel as much as we could until we settled somewhere to raise our children. He had all kinds of ideas about what he wanted to accomplish in the world, from making cancer-research discoveries at the Mayo Clinic to going on space missions as an astronaut to building a clinic for the poor in South America while living in a yurt. Grandiose? Sure. But Ted's excitement was contagious, and I had no trouble imagining us living any one of those lives. I would have gone anywhere with him.

Falling for Ted, falling with him, was so tender. We fell, but it felt like we were rising. I expected to stay up there, well above the line between sadness and happiness, forever — I'd just stay where I'd landed that first day. And I did. For five years, I barely looked down.

lu

A year after we met in university, at Western in London, I moved back to Toronto, and Ted followed a few months later. I'd started working as an international recruitment officer for an ESL school, a job that took me to countries I might otherwise not get to, and I loved it — the travel, the bonds I developed with students and their families. For the next couple of years, Ted would pout for a few days before each of my trips, and he'd be upset if I didn't have time to call him from a pay phone before I boarded the plane for wherever I was headed. Later, though, he'd grow impatient during the calls I did make, and we didn't have much to say to each other. I thought that was normal; we'd been together for over four years by then, long enough, it seemed, for the novelty to have worn off a little. Surely that happens, I thought, even if you are very much in love. When I'd ask him if he'd miss me, he'd say he wouldn't have time for that, he had clinical rotations to get through.

On some of those long flights, though, I worried that Ted was flirting with nurses or spending too much time studying with a certain female classmate he occasionally talked about. At those times I tried to remember what it was about me that Ted had fallen in love with. Who was I when our being together felt, for both of us, like being alive in a completely new way? I'd forgotten who I'd been, at the beginning of us.

Toward the end, I'd started to ask Ted only if he'd be thinking of me while I was away. Not missing, per se, just thinking about. "Yeah, sure," he'd mumble. Finally, I stopped asking; I just told him to think of me. "Think *hard,*" I once added, but either he didn't get it or he wasn't listening.

two

"Maslen, you are everything to me." James had written this on the last anniversary card he gave to me, the September before he died. It had upset me, this confession from James — James, who'd needed no one, when we met; self-sufficient and wholly satisfied James, who'd seduced me into a comfortable zone we inhabited — cohabited, I thought. Ours was a plateau of contentedness that had been difficult to reach, for me. Years in the making, in fact. And then, suddenly, he'd shifted ground on me. How had we come to this?

I couldn't lift my face to look at James after I read his message. Some of the words he'd penned in ink began to dissolve, blue streaks trailing behind the drops that splashed and spread across the paper. James must have thought he'd touched me then, reached me, broken through the calm he'd loved, at first, but gradually came to resent. It was my strength that he resented, I think, after I was diagnosed and did not collapse. And then, weeks later, he became despondent. I didn't know why, but he was despondent for a few months, at least until we hit upon the hobby farm as an answer to his needs.

We'd been married for thirteen years, that September. He died in October.

ee

I waited until after Christmas to go back to work. But when I walked through the doors each morning of that first week, I was unsteady on my feet and shaky in my limbs, and I had the urge to keep going around the revolving door until it deposited me out to the sidewalk again. It seemed to me that I wasn't supposed to be there. The decision to end my career early was easy to make.

Some months before my diagnosis, I'd been thinking about retiring anyway. James encouraged it; I hadn't enjoyed my job very much since the corporate takeover, and we had paid off our house, so we'd be able to live comfortably on James's salary as long as he kept his teaching position. His pension would be decent enough to live on for a while, too, and money from the sale of our house later on would carry us through old age.

As it turned out, James retired before I did. I hoped the country property we'd found — a farmhouse with some acreage — would be a distraction for him after he left teaching. I was fairly certain that it would reconnect him with the outdoors, with the physicality he used to enjoy when he jogged and lifted weights — when he cared about keeping his body conditioned, when he was proud of being more fit than I was, almost twelve years his junior.

James immediately took to the field behind the farmhouse, to the shaggy wildness that ran all the way back to the woods at the edge of our land. He grew up in a rural area outside of Barrie, just south of the farm, so the area was familiar to him; but I've always been a city girl, and the vastness of the view behind the house unnerved me. I didn't want to deprive James of the peace it seemed to give him, though, so we adjusted to my being in the city while James stayed on the farm, and I visited on weekends. "Conjugals," we called them, before our marriage began to suffer. How odd that sounds — the marriage suffering, I mean, as if it were a person.

$\ell\ell\ell$

We bought this house a few months before we got married. It has a certain ease; the yard is low-maintenance, which suits me, though James would have preferred greenery to the rocks and pebbles in our small patch of front yard. It was probably a typical-size house for a small family when it was built in the late forties or early fifties, with one bathroom for two adults and two or even three children, who'd share the second bedroom. We kept the retro feel — the pelmet above the picture window, the checkerboard black and white tiles on the kitchen floor, the rounded arches between the living and dining rooms. These days they call tiny homes like ours "tear-downs," because most of them get replaced by two-storey mausoleum-like structures, with footprints stretching to the lot lines. For years, realtors have been putting letters in our mailbox, asking if we'd like to put our home on the market, but we were never tempted. Neither of us needed or wanted any more than what we already had.

At the farm, we had four bedrooms upstairs, a living room, a room with a woodstove, a dining room, and a sunroom; James joked that we needed walkie-talkies so we didn't lose each other. We furnished two bedrooms and bought some second-hand furniture at an auction in a town nearby. The kitchen came with a harvest table that could have seated a family of ten. I imagined a tired, plump, practical woman who spent hours making bread and serving meat and potato midday meals to her brood — a husband, several brawny boys and, if she was lucky, a girl or two to help with housework. A woman with little choice in her life. Her home had become a "hobby" property for us, city people I'm sure she would have disliked.

I didn't like being there. With all that land and open sky, I couldn't relax enough to fall sleep until the wee hours. It was too dark, too quiet.

lll

When James's health got worse, when he'd gasp himself awake three or four times each night, I moved to the guest room across the hall. James was exhausted all the time, so we saw our family doctor.

"It could be sleep apnea," he said. "It's a disorder where you stop breathing, for no reason at all. Your body becomes oxygen-deprived and wakes you up. To make sure you inhale." James wouldn't see a sleep specialist, though. He refused to spend the night away from me in a lab, hooked up to equipment and watched over by strangers. I didn't blame him for that; there was something humiliating about the procedure, the relinquishing of control. I didn't think that apnea was the problem, anyway. James wouldn't tell the doctor about his nightmares, at least not in front of me.

lll

After I'd been with James for about a year but was still living in my own apartment, Ted called one night at two a.m. I was still awake because James had left only a few minutes before; he had an early-morning squash game and had forgotten his racquet at home, so he wasn't sleeping over that night. I assumed it was him calling to say goodnight one more time.

Ted was surprised I didn't sound sleepy, so I told him my boyfriend had kept me up. How good it felt to say that. But Ted didn't react at all; the call was all about him, about my failure to acknowledge something important. "This is the first time you didn't wish me a happy birthday," he said. "No card, no mesh— no message." He wouldn't remember talking to me the next day, that much was clear. I reminded him I didn't have his address or phone number. There was a long pause and I could hear him breathing. I knew that laboured sound well; after Ted spent a night out drinking, he'd breathe through his mouth when he fell asleep, drawing in gulps of air as if the alcohol hadn't left enough room in his blood for oxygen. I said, "What is it, Ted, what do you want?" and finally he said something that sounded like, "Why aren't you here with me Mazz I'm here do you hear me?"

လာ

I left James alone at the farm for longer and longer periods of time, skipping one or two weekend visits in a row. But I didn't *leave* him. Our marriage had not derailed. We were still together, moving in the same direction, but we were no longer sitting together on the train; we'd each moved to the window seats on opposite sides of the car. I couldn't tell James this, but I didn't want to go to him — over there, to the worried side he favoured, where he wanted me to join him. I hadn't become despondent over my own medical crisis, and I wasn't going to overreact to his invented one. Surely he knew me well enough to understand that?

The distance between us gradually lengthened as the days and nights came and went, came and went. The gap grew wider without my noticing.

ㅤㅤㅤㅤㅤㅤㅤ℘

My double mastectomy was two years ago, come August. I recuperated quickly, but James didn't seem able to accept that. At the time I wondered if he had hoped to take a few weeks' leave from the classroom to nurse me, if he'd imagined I'd need him in that way. When I watched him put lesson plans into his knapsack and go out the door, I had the strange feeling that he was disappointed in me for recovering so well.

Some weeks later, James became convinced there was something wrong with him, with his lungs. He'd never been a hypochondriac, so our doctor took his complaints seriously, but all of his test results were negative. The CT scan, MRI, chest x-ray, stress test, blood work: all normal. Still, in the evenings at home he'd choke up suddenly, gasping for air and clutching at his neck; and then it started happening in the middle of the day, more and more often. Eventually the doctor concluded that James must be burned out from teaching. His father's deterioration and my illness could have been triggers that pushed James over the limit. The doctor encouraged him to take it easy, recommended early retirement, and put him on Valium.

A doctor put me on Valium the day after Ted left me shattered. That's exactly how it felt, too — I was in a million pieces, worse than Humpty Dumpty; I was paralyzed, catatonic. My boss, Nancy, arranged an emergency house call from my family doctor; before she returned to the school, she picked up my prescription and came back to put the first dose at the back of my tongue. "Maslen, come on, please," she said, after I gagged on the sourness and spit the tablet out. "It's easier to get my cat to swallow a pill! Open up, okay? You'll feel better, I promise." She took the bottle with her and left me two days' worth at a time. I was too numb to understand I was on a suicide watch.

After a month I was able to accomplish one or two things each day, like washing my hair or buying peanut butter; but I was still fairly doped up and not ready to go back to work. During one of Nancy's daily calls, she reminded me about an education fair that I was supposed to attend; I told her it would be impossible.

"Maslen, my girl, you have to get over him. You're an independent woman with a job to do, right? A job you *need* to do." I didn't say anything. "This isn't the nineteenth century, you know — you can't sue Ted for breach of promise, like some Jane Austen character!" I didn't answer. "That was supposed to make you laugh." Nancy had been married to Oscar for two decades by then. Oscar was a friend of the cousin who sponsored Nancy to emigrate from Egypt; she wasn't in love, that would come later, but she knew the marriage would help her application to stay in Canada. "Maslen. No man is worth what you are doing to yourself."

That was over thirteen years ago. No, fifteen.

lee

Semi-conscious in the recovery room after surgery, I was kept so sedated that I began to hallucinate and, I was told, to talk out loud. I imagined I was speaking to Ted. I told him that this time, it wasn't benign, and this time, I really did lose body parts — two of them! I heard him say, "I still love you, Mazzie! I'd love you even if you were just a head!" But that wasn't true; Ted did stop loving me, though exactly when that happened I'm still not sure. And long before that day when I embarrassed myself with drug-induced antics, I'd lost track of him.

That's not true, either — Ted disappeared, that's what happened. He left the city for his internship without telling me where he was going. Without thinking about what that would do to me. The impact it would have.

How did "impact" become a *verb*? It doesn't even make sense, to claim something's "impacted" you — unless you need a dentist. Or an enema. James always laughed when I said things like this, at least until I had the surgery.

Making James laugh had been so easy. And Tony, too; it was easy for me to be relaxed with the two of them. After James and I had been dating for a month or two, I realized I had my sense of humour back. Laughing felt so good. Ted had been so moody and unresponsive in our last year together that I'd stopped attempting to joke with him; after he left me, I came to doubt that I'd ever been funny at all. With James, all we did when we weren't in bed together was laugh. Sometimes we laughed in bed, too. There were no early lovers' spats; in fact we never argued, not even after we'd been married for years.

So it was strange when James became irritable. It started sometime before my operation. He'd be annoyed at me for not putting the lid on the jam jar properly, for instance, or for leaving the light on in the basement. But I wasn't concerned. He annoyed me, too, when he put the lids on jars so tightly that I had to ask him to open them, or when he turned the light off while I was still in the basement laundry room, and I'd have to climb the stairs blind. I noticed the change in him, yes, but I thought it was probably about time we got on each other's nerves, now and then.

I didn't argue with Ted, either, but for different reasons. If we'd stayed together, though — if I'd had the nerve to push back — I imagine there would have been some serious, nail-scratches-down-his-back kind of fighting. I remember thinking shortly before marrying James that if I were to see Ted somewhere — on the subway, say, or in a lineup at the LCBO — I might need to be physically restrained from pounding my fists on his chest and shrieking like a cat in heat.

I often did go back to Ted, in my mind — to the scenes I replayed like movie clips — until I married James, and vowed to forget. I had to, to give James a fighting chance. And me, too. To give me a chance to love James as I should. Did. As I did.

three

Early in our relationship, when our bodies were new to each other, James was keen to find out what I liked best in bed. And out. He was an explorer, and his discoveries delighted him, while some even surprised me. I liked walking down the street holding his hand, wearing no panties under my dress, wondering if a breeze might lift it, if I'd let that happen; I liked his fingers probing my vagina in the dark at the movies, even when someone was seated on my other side; and I liked standing in front of my kitchen window facing the parking lot, holding a vibrating dildo against James's glans, then putting it, sperm-covered, inside of me until I came.

We sometimes imagined Tony was back there in the parking lot, astride one of his motorbikes, watching us. James would whisper in my ear, "Of course, you'll need to do something for him, too..." and I'd say yes and we'd come at the same time. After a few months, to prolong the pleasure before I answered James's question, I whispered, "When? When are we going have Tony out there, for real?" and we exploded: our orgasms were so powerful, the lingering so persistent that we couldn't separate from each other for half an hour afterward.

I'm not sure if James ever told Tony we'd included him in that sex scenario, but I liked to think he had. He probably did. After divorcing their first wives, James and Tony competed over women, and one way they did this was to tell each other what their dates had said during and after sex. Tony won first prize with this classic, according to James: "Some people have greatness thrust upon them; others have greatness thrust *into* them." I don't remember what I might have said along those lines for James to report, but whatever it was, it added a buzz to seeing Tony socially. For a while he'd smile and look askance at me on greeting; and if we happened to sit next to each other on a sofa or in a bar booth, his left thigh touching my right, neither of us would budge.

Toward the end of the intimate life I shared with James, I played a game he didn't know about. I would lightly guide his hand, slide it across my face, from my cheekbone to my jaw and the tip of my chin, then slide his fingers down my left side, over ribs he called speed bumps, teasing us both by slowing him down on the way to my hip bone. Then I'd put the pad of his middle finger at the top of my clit and slide it down to my cunt, and start tapping, slapping his finger against it until two of his fingers plunged in and out and continued to pleasure me there.

I'd close my eyes and remember lying with Ted, both of us so slender our hips would bruise each other's flesh. I'd think of the day he skipped an Obstetrics lecture and found me reading in the campus medical library, where I was waiting for him, and took me home to his apartment — and what I liked to remember was the moment I realized, with Ted inside of me, that his roommate was standing in the dim doorway, barely visible, watching. James, without knowing it, would take me all the way to that exact moment when the warming wave started, and it would course through my body and move up and out through my arms, my legs, my ebullient toes.

      eee

I met Ted in the final year of my BA, when I took a required Introduction to Modern Literature course. Ted, thinking it would be an easy A, was taking it to raise his grade point average. When he walked into the classroom, he immediately stood out from those pale, puffy, sexless boys who found solace in books. What would Ted need solace for? He wore his hair side-parted in a classic cut, short at the sides and longer on top, and he had a craggy, working-class profile with smile-lines by his eyes that gave him a look of permanent happiness. He wore beat-up cowboy boots and an old, beltless black trench coat. Tucked into Levi's, his button-down shirt was as white as a new lab coat.

Most university students still carried knapsacks in those days, though a few sad souls carted around hard-shell briefcases they probably received as high-school graduation gifts. My carpet-bag purse suited the low-couture, vintage style I cultivated, and it was large enough to hold my course books and notepads, while Ted carried a World War II–era case I later learned was a Gladstone. He'd bought it at a pawn shop because it reminded him of an oversized doctor's bag. It was hard not to notice Ted, but after he'd walk by I wouldn't look over to see where he sat, or with whom. That might have been why he noticed me — because I didn't pay much attention to him.

Partway through September, he walked straight toward me and slid his bag under my desk, bumping my feet, interrupting a conversation I was having with the person beside me. Then he leaned his elbows on the desk, facing me, and asked me to help him with the course. "We can be study buddies," he said, smiling. "You can tell me what it all means." His deep-set dark-brown eyes seemed to sparkle, but really, they were devouring black holes, sucking everything in.

We were having a dripping-hot Indian summer that fall. I knew Ted had a girlfriend, a blond Business major named Barb, but I also knew that they were seeing other people — at least that was what Ted told me. He was quick to flirt and just as quick to walk away, and I could pretend to be like that, too, when I wanted to. So I called him — maybe I even called his bluff. The ruse I used was that we could talk about our first assignment, an analysis of the last stanza of Robert Lowell's "Skunk Hour." But when Ted arrived, I was wearing a black one-piece bathing suit with denim cut-offs over it, to hide my skinny thighs. "I'm going out to sit in the sun," I said. "You coming?"

We were both olive-skinned and tanned quickly. I had taped aluminum foil over one of my Springsteen double-album covers to intensify the rays of the sun, and though I faithfully used sunscreen as Josh insisted I do, I could feel my skin cells sizzling. The redness was a welcome camouflage for the nervous blushing I was prone to. Ted asked me if I ever went topless, and when I said, "Only in France," he seemed to believe that I'd been there.

We talked non-stop, about music, friends and family, religion, our ambitions; I behaved as though I knew myself through and through. I told Ted I'd taken a left turn away from a life of science and was more interested in pursuing a life of the mind. I said this so confidently that he didn't dare ask me what that meant, which was a relief because I had no idea. On the way inside to get a cold drink, we passed the mirror in the lobby of my building; he put his hand on my shoulder to stop me, and held it there. "We look really good together," he said, "don't you think?" I took his wrist, led him down the corridor to the door of my apartment.

In the bathroom I threw a man-sized blue-and-white striped shirt over my bathing suit, then pushed its straps off my shoulders. "Oh, you got dressed," Ted said when he saw me, but he cheered up when I asked him for one of his famous back rubs; Tanis, my roommate, had heard from her Biology classmates that Ted bragged about his skill to entice girls to undress. Face down on the sofa, I rested my chin on my folded arms and said, "Knead me, you fool," so Ted slid his hands up under the shirt-tail. I let him massage my muscles for a while before I slowly rotated onto my back. His feather-light fingertips brushed my skin, glided along my turning torso and onto my breasts; his surprise at this windfall turned to a smile of pleasure when he felt my nipples pushing against his hands.

Nearly a year later, I graduated from Western and moved back to Toronto to work. I took a lease on a small studio apartment, because Ted was supposed to stay on in London, to study for yet another year and then try again to gain admission to medical school. He blamed me for the last round of rejections. It was because he'd fallen in love with me, he said, that he didn't work hard enough. He fell and he failed. No — I'd *pulled him down*, that was how he put it; I'd felled him, as if he were a tree.

Using a diaphragm for birth control was awkward. I could never time it right or get used to the interruption, so I wore it every day. When I became itchy and uncomfortable, I had to stop using the spermicide for a few months. By the time Ted started medical school in Toronto (he got an offer of late admission, in late September), I'd missed a period and was sick to my stomach most mornings. The stick in the kit from the drug store turned blue.

I was both panicked and excited: the timing was not what Ted and I had planned, but we were going to have children someday anyway, so why not start our family now? I called my sister first, to talk — to hear her say that it was okay, that it was great if I had my first baby while I was still living close to her, so that the child would become her kids' favourite cousin before Ted and I moved away.

But Gina was annoyed. She said times were different now, that "it" could be taken care of. "You have no idea, Mazz, how much work kids are. Think about it, you know how Anna drains me! And sex? Forget about it. For a long time after, it ain't going to happen. Besides, Ted just started medical school. You can't do this now. Don't be stupid, just call that clinic on Harbord. Okay?" A couple of days went by, and I hadn't yet told Ted about the test. I planned to call him when I got home from work the next night.

The cramping began before my stop, and I could barely squeeze through the doors of the subway car as they closed. When I reached street level I doubled over, clinging to the turnstile, breathing hard until the pain subsided. People pushed against me, cursing that I was in their way.

It was early October and unusually cold, and a little bit of light snow like goose-down floated in the air, melting on my skin. I inhaled and blew my breath out slowly through my lips, the way I'd seen actresses do on TV when their pregnant characters went into labour. Once home, I found that a thick fluid the colour of beets had flooded my panties; my body was flushing it out of me with wave after wave of pain. Later, the globular clots that fell into the toilet were deep, deep garnet, almost black, and it seemed a long time passed before it was over. I called Ted, not right away, and I told him only that I'd had some stomach cramps.

When I told him the truth the next time I saw him, I expected he'd embrace me, tell me not to worry, we had lots of time — cry with me, even. I knew it was better to prepare and plan for children, but to me the miscarriage was still a loss. I thought Ted would understand this, when I confessed what had happened, but he barely blinked. "Why should I be upset about something that I didn't even know had happened?"

lu

After many months of thinking, of wondering what really happened to James and why, I am not any wiser. But I have decided this: if James caused it, if he had hidden himself in the woods and waited for the right moment to move, to rustle dry leaves underfoot so the gun's sight would swing toward him, then I'd forgive him.

I know what it's like to think the day might come — is near, even — when there'll be no other option. I did. At fifteen, midway through grade nine — my last year of junior high — my closest girlfriends made new friends and began spending time with boys I didn't want to know. I felt abandoned, no longer *known*, and a strange shame settled itself deep inside me. It infiltrated and spread itself through me like a controlling parasite, pulling us both down below the lowest depths where, welded together, we hovered, holding each other tight in the dark. My core had otherwise emptied out. I knew there was something missing in me, and I awoke each day feeling that my shell, my carapace, was hollow, hollow and echoic, and that I was only a partial person. Some dark beast had become my master. My own cold heart hated me.

I half lived, hidden in a black cavern with slippery sides and an aperture so narrow it curtailed my breath. I carried a large container emptied of Cover Girl loose face powder and filled with a bottle of extra-strength Aspirin. The pills were insurance, assurance that I'd be ready for the moment to come — and I was certain it would come — when the emptiness swelled and eclipsed the slim possibility that I could emerge and be a whole person again.

Getting out of those depths was like an exercise in climbing for novices. Learning to find a foothold, uncertain that the rock-face would hold me as I moved up, ledge by ledge, was far harder to do during the week at school than achieving high grades had ever been. In time, the core of shame turned grey, like a shadow, light enough to provide a porthole glimpse of the air that awaited, and I kept going. I don't know why, but I did. I pulled myself up as if I were harnessed to a future, successful me. Once I surfaced that summer, I knew that, come September, I couldn't go to the high school in our neighbourhood, because my despair, the extent of which was known by friends and classmates who were headed there, would have — through them — followed me.

As I recovered that summer, I imagined a loosely woven fabric with prickly filaments, like burlap, growing across the opening in the burrow I'd inhabited. It would remain a friable cover, I was sure, because once aware that you have that particular strength — the ability to choose *non*life, not being — then falling back in one day, any day, becomes a permanent possibility.

ℓℓ

I used to listen to an "oldies" radio station that took me back to my youth. My parents played a lot of Frank Sinatra, Sarah Vaughan, Johnnie Ray, Nat King Cole — I grew up on their flat-note melodies and lyrics. I'd come to see that all songs were love songs: no one seemed to write any other kind, no matter what the generation. James liked jazz with no vocals, upbeat tunes that lifted him, made him want to move, and I liked those too — Charlie Parker, Dave Brubeck, Thelonious Monk, Artie Shaw. He kept a stash of his favourites in my apartment.

One night, when James was over at my place and I had the radio on, we heard Nat singing "A Blossom Fell." I smiled slightly but must have looked forlorn, because James asked why I liked to listen to music that made me feel sad. "Well... it gives me pleasure, too," I tried to explain, but when I saw the puzzled look on James's face, I couldn't find the right words.

"My taste is not all doom and gloom," I reminded him. I pulled a few records from my collection. "Look: Led Zeppelin, Peter Gabriel, Kate Bush — okay, she's introspective, forget her. But here's Boz Scaggs, the Police, Springsteen, of course...and here's Roxy Music." We spent the evening playing one song from each album and then made love to *Time Out*.

I thought about James's question a lot after that, and I played the radio less and less often. He was right, many of songs on that station were about lovers who had gone away. When Ted twisted and torqued my heart, I came to know the music viscerally; it was both torture and company of sorts, the kind you reach for when you're sure the damage is irreparable. The despair of others can feel like commiseration, at times like that. Listening to those songs then made me feel vaguely human again.

I first heard those tunes as a child, when they made sad promises that I didn't understand. Then I met Josh, my fierce, first love, and the lyrics befriended me, threaded their way into my being. I began to understand that sadness and love were a natural pair. I thought of my friendship with Josh as a piece of jewellery made from a precious metal. I kept it close, and I polished it, and I wore it like a medal.

The first winter after Josh left Toronto for Europe to model for Versace, Patsy Cline's "Crazy" became my favourite. When I found the record in my parents' collection of LPs, I made a tape for my Walkman so I could listen to it alone, luxuriating in my longing for that boy.

I kept Patsy a secret. In the neighbourhood where I grew up, country music, even if Willie Nelson did write it, wasn't so much uncool as unheard of. We lived in Denlow Estates, a Jewish subdivision uptown, north of Forest Hill, but we weren't Jewish. We didn't go to church, either; Gina and I had to beg our father to put up outside lights at Christmas; even then, all he'd do was replace the clear floodlights that normally shone on the house with blue or green bulbs. I didn't know what "Protestant" and "Catholic" meant until my friends asked me what kind of Christian I was, and my mother had to explain the various factions to me. So yes, we were different; but our neighbours and friends went to synagogue only on high holidays, so it wasn't religion that separated my family from theirs.

When I went to my friends' houses after school, the atmosphere was relaxed and casual; we watched TV in the family room, where there were newspapers spread out on an L-shaped sofa, and heavy art books on ottomans or large coffee tables. The clutter, like the furniture, was comfortable. (At our house, my mother had begun to cover surfaces with dried flowers and covered dishes and Royal Doulton figurines.) We could help ourselves to snacks in the kitchen — apples and pears or oranges in a bowl on the counter, plain yogurt with toasted granola kept in glass jars on a shelf, matzo or bagels with cream cheese, slices of challah with jam. I'd often not want dinner —roast beef or brown-sugared broiled pork chops with boiled frozen vegetables was typical fare — when I got home.

I loved those houses, and I loved being with my friends and their families. I wanted parents like Shelley's parents, who would take me to Mel Brooks movies and to the Pickle Barrel for dinner. I wanted to go to *shul* on Saturdays so I could complain about it with everyone else. And when I was older, I wanted to be part of a community that stood together because they had to, had always had to; where everyone knew everyone else's family and valued each other because of who they were, and because they were here. Because they were *here:* they were alive and loved and that was what mattered most.

ℓℓ

My sister, Gina, is four years older than me and began dating when she was in grade nine. She had a crush on a popular boy named Michael, and she bragged to me that they'd gone to "third base" in his car one night. Our mother overheard us and she gave my sister a talking-to, not because Gina had gone too far but because Michael was Jewish. "There's no point," she said, "because you'll never be accepted into a family like his anyway. You aren't one of the *chosen* people." I didn't understand what she meant by that. I was about eleven, and I didn't know anything about anti-Semitism or the diasporas or the Holocaust, or how Israel came to be, or why; but what my mother said, in that tone, sounded wrong to me.

Once Gina met Ben, whose family background was Welsh, that was that: her future had been decided at sixteen. When I was sixteen, I was attending an alternative high school where students learned independently, with few rules and lots of flexibility. We called our teachers by their first names. We smoked in class — and classes were small, with five or ten kids at most, held just once or twice a week in each subject. The school attracted kids with serious outside interests that consumed great chunks of their time, like playing sports on provincial or national teams, studying piano at the Conservatory, training in ballet, publishing poetry, or acting in commercials; but it also drew studious types who wanted to work through the high-school curriculum quickly and get to university ahead of schedule. I finished high school a year early.

Students could enrol from all over the city, but most had transferred from York Mills or Forest Hill Collegiate, so my new friends, too, were Jewish. Jennifer was a competitive figure skater; Rob, my first boyfriend, was ambitious and aiming for Western's business program; others were guitar players, writers, comedians. We hung out in the Common Room, a large open space with scratched-up hardwood floors; second-hand, stained, saggy sofas and chairs; and lots of ashtrays.

The majority of boys were older than me, and some were Gina's former classmates, including Michael. Grade ten that year was a small cohort, and Jennifer and I quickly bonded. We became known as the "hot" girls to the group of guys we considered the coolest; they paid us innocent attention, for the most part, as if Jennifer and I were mascots or pets or younger sisters. We smoked up with Michael, in the back of his tiny Honda Civic, at a drive-in showing *E.T.*; we bummed cigarettes from Joe, Rob, and Daniel, who drove us whenever we asked to Baskin-Robbins up on Sheppard Ave. for milkshakes (or, on fewer occasions, to the public library on Yonge). We learned how to flirt and toy and tease those eighteen-year-olds, who called us jailbait until we weren't.

Michael asked me to go out to dinner with him. Gina wouldn't believe me when I told her; I said no, anyway, because I couldn't get the image of Michael's fingers inside my sister's panties out of my head. His buddy Rob intrigued me, though; he reminded me of Al Pacino, and the depth I suspected he hid beneath his soft-voiced, monosyllabic conversation attracted me more than his looks. I was startled when I was walking to the subway one afternoon and he stopped his dad's car — an Audi, I think — to ask if he could drive me home.

In the spring there were sightings of Rob's car in our driveway, which went on for some weeks and well into the summer. Josh started to park his Datsun in front of the house that fall, after Rob left for university. Gina's friends wondered at first if she was seeing Rob and then Josh without telling them. Gina told me that I'd gained a reputation at York Mills, that people were calling me the shiksa sister.

ले

Josh said that at our school, everyone other than us seemed like a "Charlie in the Box" — a line he took from the Christmas cartoon about Rudolph, who went to the Island of Misfit Toys. Josh's impression of Charlie's strained, sad prepubescent voice was hilarious. I was fast-tracking my studies to get into the medical-school stream early — that was what I told Josh when he asked why I didn't go to York Mills; that was where his girlfriend, who lived near my neighbourhood, went. I didn't ask Josh why he transferred from Forest Hill in the first place, though. I knew he'd been on a Junior A hockey team when he was younger, but he only played for fun now, so that didn't seem to explain the switch in schools. And he didn't become a model until his second year of grade thirteen, after he won a contest that awarded prizes to the best-looking male and female photographed by the newspaper that year.

Josh's attendance was sporadic, and when he did pull into the parking lot in his Datsun 240Z, the girls who knew him from Forest Hill rushed out to greet him. Before I knew Josh, I'd roll my eyes along with Jennifer whenever we saw this happen. Jennifer thought he must be completely conceited, having all of those Jewish-American Princesses after him (it was okay for her to call those girls JAPs, Jennifer said, because she was Jewish herself). Those in the clique wore designer jeans, Ralph Lauren button-down blouses, and diamond earrings; they carried the latest Roots bags and styled their hair Farrah Fawcett style, flipped and highlighted. Josh's girlfriend, Gina said, was the most popular girl at York Mills. "What can he see in her?" I wondered, when Jennifer and I talked about it. "She's so superficial." "They're all spoiled brats," Jennifer said, "but she is the queen of the JAPs. She is the Princess of all Princesses." I thought Josh and his girlfriend were like characters in a fairy tale, so the nickname that Jennifer came up with for her — the Princess — took on that connotation for me, and stuck.

ℓℓℓ

Jennifer spent hours at her skating club, training with her coach. ("She's world-famous," Jennifer told me, "but if anyone here knew she's Jewish, they'd probably drop her.") After she finished her lesson, we'd order lunch and charge it to her account. Sometimes Jennifer would order french fries, which were taboo while she was in training, but she'd pay cash so her mother wouldn't find out. We sat at our own table, apart from the other skaters. "They're so prissy," Jennifer said. "Their mothers look at me, like, 'How did *she* get in here?' It's okay for their daughters to be around gay skaters, but Jewish ones? That's another story."

ee

When we sat at the breakfast table after I slept over at Jennifer's house, her mother nagged her for putting too much sour cream on her latkes or not enough sliced melon on her plate. "Ma, enough already!" Jennifer would say, and we'd all laugh. This was a new concept for me, relaxing with your family as if you were friends. In our house, the basic rule for communication was, "If you can't say anything nice, say nothing at all." My favourite was the "no singing at the table" rule. It was one of my father's; he had a few. He'd leave notes around the house with orders, too. He taped one to the handle of the door to the rec room: "Turn the lights OFF when you come back upstairs! — The Management."

Jennifer began skipping some of her skating-practice sessions since she and I'd become friends; she had also fallen behind in her course work. Her father blamed me — her first goyim friend — for the changes in his daughter's behaviour. He rarely addressed me, except indirectly through Jennifer: "So sweetheart, tell me what you two are going to do with your day?" Jennifer played it perfectly: "Believe me, dad," she'd say, "you don't *want* to know!" She'd kiss him on his cheek as we left the table.

On Sunday afternoons, we usually went to one of our favourite bakeries or cafés for brownies or carrot cake. We'd drink cups and cups of coffee and smoke half a package of Belmont Milds each, using vintage cigarette holders that Jennifer stole from an aunt in Florida. We'd go home in the evening shaking from caffeine and nicotine and sugar, wound up about what we might say to Josh if we saw him at school the next day.

ℓℓℓ

Josh and I got to know each other before I finished grade ten. By this time, he'd started to arrive later in the day, when Jennifer was gone for skating practice and the older girls were at home watching soaps like *General Hospital* and *The Young and the Restless*. I usually stayed in the quiet, emptied study room to work through trigonometry and calculus problems. Josh sometimes visited his favourite teacher, Abe; through the wall I'd hear them talking, the low rumble of Josh's voice mesmerizing me. Then I'd hear Abe's door close, and I'd see Josh in the doorway, peripherally, but I wouldn't look up until he'd walk into the room and sit down across from me. "Are you saving this seat?" he asked, because Rob, who was not a friend of his, often sat there. Then Josh would open his textbook and start doodling on a notepad, humming, until I raised my eyes to him and smiled.

Did I look interesting to Josh then, the way I looked to James when he saw me that night at the pottery studio? I wonder. I'd not thought of that before, of how I came across to Josh before he knew me. I've forgotten so much about Josh, and that surprises me. When I think of him now — I am letting myself, I am forcing myself to think of Josh, now — I am aware that what I let surface when I knew him, even to myself, was but a titch of what I felt. For a long time. A long time ago.

Josh called me his "goy toy" or his "gentile gal," which sounded as wimpy to me as "WASP" sounded sour. "I may be a gentile," I said to him on the phone the first time he called me, "but I wouldn't be *gentle*. In case you were wondering." He was probably smiling when he said, "I don't doubt it, Mazz, 'You Sexy Thing,'" a song we both liked. "I bet you go down on a dime, too." I didn't know what that meant. I displayed a consistent lack of need and a fake confidence with Josh, and it was working.

I called Jennifer right away, after Josh and I spoke on the phone that night. She'd wanted to hear about my exchanges with him at school on days she spent at the rink, and I thought she'd want to hear about the phone call, too. But Jennifer was neither pleased nor pleasant. She said if Josh was being crude when he spoke to me ("going down on a dime," she said, meant you were a slut), then he didn't see me as having any *real* potential, partner-wise, and that — since he was always polite and respectful to her — his choice between us was becoming clear. In the beginning, I'd not expected Josh to take either one of us seriously; yet it seemed that we'd become competitors, Jennifer and I.

My friendship with Jennifer ended in flames in November of the next school year, when she switched back to Forest Hill Collegiate. In December she called to tell me that, according to her brother Barry, Rob was dating the Princess. We both knew that Josh had broken up with her the summer before she left for Western, and I was happy if she'd moved on; I hadn't loved Rob anyway. When I said, "So what?" Jennifer added this: "Rob is telling everyone Josh is gay, and *that's* the real reason he broke up with the Princess. So you didn't really win anything after all, Maslen. *That's* what."

Soon Josh would tell me this: "I like you a lot more now, Mazz, without Jennifer being around all the time. You're more grown-up than she is." He told me about the time Jennifer and her brother had gone to one of his hockey games the year before. I knew about it, because Jennifer had told me Barry had tickets, and I remembered what she said to me on the phone after the game that night: "Mazz, he is so sexy in his gear, with his hair all sweaty. I thought I'd die — Josh, the best-looking guy in Toronto, skating right in front of me. I swear he was looking at me!" I'd fretted about that, at the time, but Josh told me Jennifer had looked like a little kid at a parade.

lee

When Josh was five, his father and mother divorced and his dad got full custody; Josh hardly saw his mom after that, and his grandmother moved in to help raise him. This was all Josh said, the first time he joined us for Sunday dinner, when my mother asked questions about his family. I frowned at her, to dissuade her from pressing him further, because Josh had only recently told me about his mom's hospital stays and psychiatric problems. "Interview's over, Mom," I said. Josh smiled and my father smiled, too, when I said that.

"I like your dad," Josh told me after that meal. "He's a cool guy." I didn't think of my father as cool, not in the way Josh meant.

Josh kept a photo of his father on the table next to his bed. I knew his dad had died when Josh was fifteen, but I didn't know how or when, so when I saw the photo the first time, I asked Josh what happened. "Heart attack. He was on the tennis court. It was instant. There wasn't anything anyone could do." When I said I was sorry, Josh turned away. It wasn't like him to stop talking, to withdraw, and I sensed that he didn't want to, really; that talking about his dad was hard, but important to him. So, very quietly, I said, "You don't look like your dad, Josh." In the picture, his dad appeared to be blond, on the short side, and stern. "I know," Josh said, turning back to face me. "I take after my mother. Good looking, great smile — but crazy." He was smiling, and I laughed as if *that* was the crazy part — as if Josh, with those legions of leggy beauties lusting for him, would ever be on the fringe, unhinged, alone.

lu

Josh spent part of a winter semester going to college in the States before he decided to model full time, but school didn't pan out, so he left for Italy in the fall. Then, after more than a year of taking assignments all over Europe, he'd grown tired of modelling; so he moved to New York to take acting lessons and audition for films. He phoned me often, usually when he was either really happy or somewhat bored.

During one of our calls, he said he was stalled in class and running out of cash. "Can't you model part time again?" I asked, but he said he couldn't do it anymore, he hated the superficiality of that life. "Put the Gucci on, pose, pose again, take it off. Put Armani on, pout, turn, take it off. I'll have nothing to show for myself when I'm forty."

I wasn't sure where he was going with that. "You think you'll stop getting work, because your looks will be gone?" "No, it's not that. It's...it's like, what am I going to tell my kids about what I've done with my life? Hold up eight-by-ten glossies and magazine covers and say, 'Just *look* at that hair'?"

~~~

Josh and I went to a lot of movies before he left Toronto the first time. *Being There, Airplane!, The Big Red One.* He always bought my ticket, and I was disappointed in myself because of it, both for letting him follow the sexist convention and for liking it. I usually took the subway to meet Josh at the theatre and went home the same way. But one night after the movie — we'd seen *Young Frankenstein*, I think — Josh drove me home. Gina and Ben were sitting in the den, watching *Saturday Night Live* on TV. Ben was usually outgoing, but after Josh and I sat down, he became subdued. Gina was her usual silly self, playing with her hair and giggling at everything Josh said. Josh *was* funny, very funny, but I never giggled the way girls at school did, swarming him with smiles and touches on the arm at every word. It bothered me that Josh seemed to be enjoying Gina's company, and I was quiet, too. When my father came in to say good night — an insomniac, he delayed going up as long as he could — Josh stood up and shook Dad's hand. I thought that was so sweet that I couldn't help but smile.

When I walked Josh to the door, he said goodbye and we kissed for the first time. Behind me I heard Ben say to Gina, "It'll never last." I didn't know if Ben meant Josh was too good-looking for me or if he thought I was too smart for Josh, but I wasn't upset either way, because to Ben, Josh and I were a pair. An "it." We had been named into existence. It was an unexpected compliment from Ben, and it changed how I saw myself.

I never thought I was pretty — my nose is a little too wide, my forehead too high — but my mother used to say I was *interesting*-looking. I have sculpted cheekbones, big brown eyes that are almost black, and a heart-shaped face. I'd noticed that my eyes looked larger with mascara smudged under them in the morning; kohl eyeliner was not in style at the time, but when I found *kajal* pencils in an old-style pharmacy run by an Indian family near the Bloor subway, I started to rim both lash lines in black.

My hair, which Jennifer envied, was dead-straight and the colour of dark chocolate, and I wore it side-parted, bobbed, a little longer at the front and shorter at the nape. This was in the late seventies, when girls wore their hair long and loose. Josh liked my cut, the angle of it, he said, when I told him I was bored with my look. "Why not cut bangs across your forehead and dye your hair jet black, then, and wear white kabuki face powder? Oh, and pluck out your eyebrows and draw thick black lines in their place, while you're at it." I'd hit a nerve. Did I sound vain, to him? Did I remind him of the other girls, the giggling gaggle?

With Ted I felt beautiful, because he told me I was, over and over, right to the end. James rarely spoke of beauty or commented on anyone's features, but when we started out, before I knew how deeply he cared for me, I still looked at myself through Ted's eyes; I waited for James to tell me that he, too, thought I was lovely, but he *showed* me, instead. And eventually, though it took years, I was able to look in the mirror without focusing on flaws or wondering what others noticed about my appearance. Now I simply see my face, and I have James to thank for that.

მ

I missed Josh when he wasn't around, but I didn't disintegrate. We hadn't become a couple, for one thing, though our friendship made me feel protected; just thinking about him soothed. But Ted — well, that was different. We'd become completely entwined. I'd let that happen, I'd allowed it and wanted it so much that after he disappeared from my life, I felt I didn't exist anymore. We'd been so close, for so long, that without him — solo — who was I? Who was left *of* me, after Ted left me? I wasn't sure I could stand up on my own anymore, and for a time, bedridden, I didn't try. The ligaments in my legs might as well have been severed.

When I was no longer floored by abandonment, I considered moving as far away as possible. Perhaps I wouldn't miss Ted as much, I thought, if I went somewhere we'd never been together. In Toronto, every step I took was in *our* city, the subway ride downtown was the route to his place, the ringing phone was sure to be Ted calling.

So when I saw an ad for a job similar to mine at an ESL school in Vancouver, I applied. This was in the day when employers were still allowed to ask women about their plans for having babies. During the telephone interview, when I answered that I didn't think I wanted any children, the mother of two I was speaking with said, "That's selfish, don't you think?" When I told Gina, who had Anna by then, she said she was glad I didn't get the job, and she was glad that I didn't have kids yet, too. "When Anna is driving me insane, who else could I get to take her off my hands for a few hours?"

James didn't want children. "I've been teaching for over twenty years, so believe me — I've had enough of kids." He said this soon after we met. I believed him, and I was grateful, too. I told James that same night that I'd never wanted children, and I let him think that until the end. But it wasn't entirely true.

When I was with Ted, I did want to have a baby — two, really, to make up our eventual family. With James, though, our twosome was enough; we met, we were together, and that was enough. I wasn't waiting to go somewhere else with James; we were there, where we wanted to be, already. Here, I mean. At least that's what I thought I felt back then, about the children issue. About not wanting to have any children with James.

Our friends were childless and, other than Tony, they had settled, too. Nancy, at my office, had been married to Oscar for almost as long as James had been teaching. They'd tried to have kids for years, but Nancy said Oscar's sperm count was too low, and he refused to adopt because the child would be a constant reminder that he wasn't man enough to sire his own. Most of the others we knew were teachers who either chose not to have children (James's crowd) or were too unstable to think about it (mine). At the language school where I worked, high teacher turnover was the norm; the industry attracted risk takers, I noticed, the kind of people who were desperate

to find a way out of their lives. "They *want* to be uprooted,"
I told James once, when we were getting to know each other.
"I've watched teacher after teacher take off to unfamiliar places
where they can reinvent themselves."

James asked me during that conversation if I'd liked my job for
the same reason. "All that travel you did, before you took your
new position — was it a chance for you to lose yourself? To get
away from your life?" I was instantly stymied. Not only was I
surprised at James's ease in getting right to the point, but I was
shaken by it. James, a near stranger, was asking me to confront
the possibility that had I been using the busyness of work to
evade some deep truth about myself.

Gina dropped over for coffee a few days later, and I told her
about my dates with James. "I bet this guy will be good for
you," she said. "*And* I think he's romantic. I mean, bringing you
flowers each time he comes over to your apartment?" There was
a rose in a bud vase, on the window ledge, and a mixed bouquet
on the coffee table. "He seems to see inside my head sometimes.
I didn't expect that from him." "Well," she said, "maybe you've
met your match. But promise me this: you'll get rid of those
flowers once they die, okay?"

ﻟﻠﻟ

We stopped giving Mom flowers on her birthday and
Mother's Day, because she'd only add them to her collection
of desiccated blooms. She'd treat entire bouquets with a sealant
spray and dry them in silica beads sold in craft stores, back
when people didn't worry about carcinogens floating around in
the air they breathed. There'd been vases of preserved red roses,

yellow lilies, and gentian irises covering every visible surface in the house. Even the walls were peppered with small ceramic versions of potted blooms, pieces that sat on a smattering of shelves she'd hammered in place herself.

When we were teenagers, we begged Mom to toss the dried-out displays, which made the living room look like some ancient, abandoned funeral parlour. "But why should their beauty be so brief?" she'd reply, as if her question explained the meaning of life itself. When she died, Gina and I carried armloads of the best-kept bunches, thickened with dust, to the cemetery, and we set them in heavy brass containers on her grave. We knew the flowers would disintegrate in time, exposed to the weather, but we were glad to get them out of the house, and they did make the plot look less desolate. "I guess the groundskeeper will be putting sod down, soon," Gina said. "It will look better then." "And maybe later we can plant something that stays green year-round," I said. "Like a patch of periwinkle. That's a perennial, right?" But neither of us visited her plot in the winter, and by spring we both had forgotten about my idea.

I'm no gardener, but I have been able to keep a collection of easy-to-grow plants alive: two large-leafed avocados (grown from the pit), a pot of wandering Jew (do people still call them that?), and trails of pothos which, supported by thumbtacks, soon vined their way across the archway between our living and dining rooms.

Pothos is Greek for "longing." When new leaves unfurl, droplets of water splash onto the floor, like rain.

Three weeks after my mother died, I left for my first year at university. I didn't talk about her very much to the new people I was meeting. I'm not sure whether it was because I watched her deteriorate or because I knew that there wasn't a true filial relationship between us, but letting my mother go had left me with a formal, quartz-like contentment. But I dreamed of her often in the months that followed. My dreams usually had something to do with death (hers) and guilt (mine).

I didn't go back home very often, and when I did, I had difficulty remembering what her presence in the house had felt like. We'd erased it: the day after Mom died, Gina, Dad, and I began the process of removing the dust-caked tchotchkes, the reams of ribbons and pillows and other paraphernalia of the decorating hobby that consumed her for most of her life. It was satisfying, accomplishing this, and we didn't feel sad as we worked. With window after window cleared, we were amazed by the light that began to pour into the room.

Then we tackled her closets. The piles of rumpled garments, the tangles of wire hangers, and the heap of shoes that blanketed the floor of her walk-in were astounding. Mom didn't buy expensive clothes or items in fashion; she bought secondhand, mostly, but she tried to update old pieces — sewing colourful ribbon onto a plain ski jacket, for example, when colour-block styles were in, or adding rhinestones to clutches with glue during the glitter craze.

My dreams about Mom became more frequent; it was as if my mind were worrying a stone, a stubborn one that held secrets about my mother and me. On a whim I bought a bonsai to tend. It was tiny, like Mom's pottery miniatures, and I thought it might give me some insight into my mother's lifelong need for constrained, managed beauty — the dried flowers, the fully made-up face at the breakfast table, the girdles beneath those nineteen-seventies coordinated pant suits she donned each day to do her errands at the mall. But my experiment failed. I didn't glean any new understanding of her by clipping back the small, feather-like branches of my wee evergreen. I knew that she'd been afraid to let go of things, that she'd used her collections to build a barricade of sorts, one that wrapped around her like a shawl to keep her from feeling too much, to keep other people, especially her children, at a remove. But I still don't know why.

After I stopped trimming my tree, it didn't get much larger. I figured it had given up on growing long before I brought it home with me.

lee

Josh said during one of our calls that he wanted to give up modelling. He couldn't stand the people he had to deal with in the world of high fashion. "You mean you're ill-suited?" I said, but he wasn't in a mood for laughs. I didn't see his point, at the time. Modelling was glamorous, wasn't it? And easy money — that's what he'd told me before he left Toronto for Italy. He'd abandoned his attempt at college after a single, strained semester the previous winter, just as he had given up after a year and a half of taking grade thirteen courses at our school.

I visited Josh in New York once. I'd decided to go there in the early spring with Linda, Lise, and Phil, visual-arts majors who'd invited me to join them on an art crawl before they launched into their year-end studio projects. Josh said he was excited that I was coming to see him, but I was nervous. He was a model in New York City, for god's sake; who was I? By then I'd decided I wasn't going to be a doctor, but I had no career plan. I wasn't anything yet.

My friends and I shared a double room in a one-star hotel in Times Square that had cockroaches the size of small mice and scratchy towels with huge, ragged holes in them. I arranged to meet Josh at the café where my friends and I planned to have lunch after spending our first morning at the Met. We were on the patio when Linda saw Josh striding toward us, and she froze. Lise and Phil turned their heads to see what she was looking at, and they, too, were riveted. "Holy shit, Mazz — he's stunning!" Lise whispered in my ear. "He looks like a young Paul Newman!" The zipper of his grey leather jacket, which was open, glinted in the sun as Josh approached our table. The viridian cashmere sweater he wore over a white shirt matched his eyes, I noted, when he leaned down to hug me. "You still smell like Mazz," he said before he let me go. After introductions and handshakes, I arranged to meet my friends back at "the hotel," which I didn't name, out of shame.

Josh put his arm around my shoulder and pulled me toward the street. He wanted to know what I thought of the Met, which paintings in which rooms I'd seen that morning. "It's so massive, isn't it, Mazz? We could get lost in there! We'll go together next time you visit, okay?" He squeezed me against his hip. Men and women on the sidewalk glanced at Josh and held their gaze on his face, their lips slightly parted, slowing their steps and swivelling on the balls of their feet as we passed.

We walked and walked and I didn't know where we were, but Josh had taken a specific route and we arrived at one of his favourite Japanese tea houses. We kept talking over shared pots of a tea that had popped rice grains in it. It was called *genmaicha*, and it was delicious — like a nourishing broth, I thought. The place also sold packages of tea, and before we left, Josh bought one for me to take home. It was very expensive and I protested, but Josh insisted. "This stuff will get you through your all-nighters," he said. "It's called 'Fuck You Jew' tea. No, really!" He took the small, sealed pouch out of the bag and showed me the label. "See? *Fukujyu Sencha*. Jew haters, the Japanese, but they do make great sushi. Do you like sushi? I'll take you out for dinner when you come back to see me." He was a bit manic, excited to be showing me around his city. "I'll have my own place then, and you can stay with me. Maybe I'll be on Broadway by then. Or on off-off-Broadway, at least."

It was late in the day when we arrived at the loft he shared with another model in the Village. Renting a small space in New York City in the eighties was four times what it cost in Toronto, and since Josh had cut back on modelling to make time for acting classes, he couldn't afford to live alone. There was a folding screen that divided the space in two, but couldn't have provided any privacy for either of them. "Make yourself at home — but only on *this* side of the room," he lisped, mocking his roommate, I supposed. "It's psychological, for him," Josh explained. "He says it suggests there are two rooms in here. Lucky for me, he travels a lot. But he's doing a shoot in town right now. He'll be here soon."

Josh picked up a matchbook and lit a stick of incense and a few votive candles he'd placed on the windowsill and on the tiny kitchen counter. I was standing by the door, watching him move around the room, when he walked over to me and took both of my hands in his. "Here is an exercise we do in class, Mazz. We're supposed to get in touch with our feelings, keeping our minds on the moment. And then we tell everyone what we're feeling. So now, Mazz? I'm feeling really happy that you're here with me." We were both smiling, squeezing each other's fingers, and then we embraced. "To be here, right now, with you. Really, really happy." I said, "Me too, Josh," worried that my eyeliner would rub off and stain his cashmere.

He walked me to the bus stop and gave me a token. We kissed and Josh said, "Love you," so I said, "Me too," and let go of his hand. As I climbed the stairs, Josh called out, "Thanks for coming to see me Mazzie!" He stood there looking up at me with his hands in his pockets, until the bus pulled away.

"Of course I've thought, *Why not? Why shouldn't we?*" Josh said. "You *know* how much you mean to me."

Josh had called early, before I left for class, to talk about my latest letter — the Letter, the one I mailed after my visit to his loft, the honest one I couldn't *not* send any longer. His reaction was straightforward. The conversation could have gone much, much worse: he could have been patronizing, or kind — and that would have killed me. What he said was this: "The easiest thing in the world would be to get inside you, and make you pregnant." (*Pregnant?*) "But I'd be a schmuck if I did that to you. I don't want to be a schmuck, for once." Then he told me he'd messed up his friendship with Rachel that way. (*Rachel? Really?*) "I don't want to do that to us, Mazz." He said a lot of other things that I don't remember because my ears were ringing with the realization that this was the end — not of our friendship, not yet anyway, but of my suspension of disbelief that it was possible for us to be together.

My roommate, Tanis, had encouraged me to write that letter to Josh, after I got back from New York and told her about the afternoon we spent in his loft. She knew more about my feelings for Josh than my other friends did, so when I told her about his early-morning call she was amazed that I wasn't rolling on the floor, smashing my head against walls, howling into pillows. Strangely, though, all that day and during most of that semester, I was fine. I felt relieved.

In the immediate aftermath, it was as if I were watching another Maslen tame her raging, rampant longing. I admired her for handling it so well, and I convinced myself that I was finally ready to judge potential romances on their own merit, instead of measuring them against the potential partnership I imagined having with Josh. I went out with lots of people — classmates, friends of friends, professors — until I met Ted. Between these brief pairings, I pondered why I'd felt good, even high, after Josh rejected my reach for romance, and I decided it was because I was free. My passion had been deflected, but I was also relieved of the anxiety, its constant, crushing companion. It had been my best, false self that Josh grew to love. The fear of not being good enough for him went away, for good. I wouldn't be caught wanting him again.

And for a time, when my impossible longing seemed to cease, I landed in the pure, clear waters of friendship with Josh. His honest refusal of me had left smooth edges on both sides, somehow, like a clean break in a bone; the state of our relationship was suddenly uncomplicated and thus, I thought, entirely reparable.

લુ

We did make each other happy, Josh and I, when we spent time together. There were all those afternoons we'd leave school in his car. Josh would pull out of the parking lot with a screech of tires, trying to impress me with his stick-shift swagger, no doubt; we'd take the Allen expressway down to Forest Hill to hang out in the apartment-like set-up he had in the basement of his house, to listen to records; or we'd go to the Art Gallery of Ontario, usually on Wednesdays, when admission was free. Once, we splurged and bought tickets to a special exhibit of abstract expressionism, but neither of us got it. I couldn't stop laughing when Josh started to parody a tour guide narrating what a Franz Kline painting seemed to be saying: "The black swaths here, you see, clearly indicate that the artist is conflicted about his childhood. He is imitating a four-year-old's kindergarten artwork in this marvelous piece, which is about the crisis of identity in the twentieth century..." The docents asked us to keep our voices down, but as always when strangers spoke to Josh, they looked more pleased than angry.

We saw a lot of sculpture at the AGO, too, all the famous pieces — monoliths by Henry Moore, bronzes by Rodin, Giacometti's elongated figures, Picasso's heads, mixed-media pieces by Schwitters. The Netherlandish portraits drew Josh the most, which surprised me: awkward, angular faces with highly detailed, extremely pale profiles against pitch-black backgrounds were beautiful, he thought. With their high foreheads — bared and exaggerated by tightly pulled-back hair on women, but covered with thick, dark bangs, on men — and their large, fleshy noses, the subjects were anything but attractive to my eye. After considering a Hans Memling for some time, Josh turned to me and said, "You feel like you *know* these people, don't you?" And suddenly, I thought I knew what he meant. Despite the heavy gilt frames around their portraits, the sitters were not fancy folk. The skin on their faces was marred by moles, blemishes, thin red spidery broken blood vessels; their eyes were often vivid blue and gleamed as if wet, and capable of seeing you. They were faces of people who knew hardship, for whom staying alive was serious business. The models were proud to be sitting for the artist, to be portrayed as themselves. Not vain, but proud.

As we wandered through the gallery, women would follow Josh with their eyes, and I knew they must be wondering what he was doing with me. I too expected that Josh would end up with a beauty like Catherine Oxenberg, a blond of semi-royal stock I'd seen in *Vogue*: her princess lifestyle and her oval face, with its pale, perfect skin and clear green eyes, made her a perfect mate for Josh. I distinctly remember thinking when I put down the magazine and glanced in the mirror that I was a defective specimen indeed.

My insecurities were reinforced almost daily by Gina's barbs. "God, Maslen, would you just give up already?" I'd be drying my hair in the bathroom we shared, or putting on my eyeliner, and she'd start banging on the locked door. "You're so ugly, it won't make any difference! I've got to get ready now, to go out with Ben. Unlike you, I have a boyfriend." Even Josh showing up at the house to see me didn't stop her. "You think Josh would ever want you? *Beauty and the Beast* — that's you." I think she was shocked (I know I was) when I said, "Oh, you finally learned how to read?" The confidence I'd been practising was beginning to come more easily, it seemed. "Wait until you discover the Nancy Drew series, you'll love it."

I found an old philosophy anthology of mine when James and I were unpacking boxes in our new living room. Before I placed it with others on the built-in shelving unit, I flipped through the underlined, asterisked, arrowed, and otherwise marked-up pages, and I paused at this passage in a piece by Simone Weil:

> Preference for a human being can be of two kinds. Either we are seeking some particular good in him, or we need him. In a general way, all possible attachments come under one of these heads. We are drawn toward a thing, either because there is some good we are seeking from it, or because we cannot do without it. Sometimes the two motives coincide.

My attraction to James was of the first kind, the "seeking something good" kind, I thought that day, and I still think it was. James had never been one for analyses of the heart or philosophical discussions, so I didn't ask him how he would categorize his attraction to me. But I was fairly certain that need was not an issue for either of us.

I had discussed this passage with Josh during his bookish phase, well before I sent the Letter. He was bettering himself, reading his way through the great thinkers, he said, as part of his training to be an actor. We'd call each other and read out an excerpt from a book we both had picked up, and talk about what it meant. We'd had lengthy, open discussions about Camus and Sartre before, but with Weil, I held back. I couldn't tell Josh I could not do without him.

So I lied. I told Josh I thought we were friends because we'd found something good in each other, some unusual quality that we hadn't found in other people. He agreed, but then he said this: "Sometimes we seek the not-good in others, too. Maybe you like the *not*-good in me, Mazz." At the time I thought he meant his fear of commitment to one person — after all, he'd broken off with his girlfriend of three years to free himself, he said, from a predictable future, a life with no leaps. We didn't talk much longer that night, and we didn't talk about Weil again.

≈

I went back to the AGO earlier this spring. James was never interested in art; I went alone once in a while, after work, but I hadn't been there in a few years. When I found the Canadian room, I looked for a long time at Tom Thomson's work, with its trowelled, clay-like paint in pigments that crashed into each other. I could feel vivid orange dapple through me, I could hear scumbled textures singing. The dark bark of his trees seemed to hum with deep, dry notes pulled from the thick daubs of paint that rose from the flat surface in peaks. I stared, up close, at individual stabs of oil paint, at the slathered colours pushing up and across at angles that seemed to make streaks move across the canvas as I stood there. I could *see* the past there, I could almost see the act of painting *happening*. Those lines of paint smears seemed, to me, a means of measuring time, and looking at them was like seeing it cycle, over and over again. If I stood there long enough, I wondered, might I go back there, too, to the past? I felt slightly dizzy then, as if my blood sugar were getting low or I'd stood up too fast after lying prone for too long. And I sensed, for a second or two, that Josh was there with me.

How odd, the mind.

four

Lately I've been dreaming about making things out of clay. Last night I dreamed I was making a pinch pot, but as I worked at it I was daydreaming within the dream, and before I noticed how much time had passed the clay had sucked the moisture out of my fingers. The surface of my skin had tightened, and fissures crept across my hands. I can't stand the sensation of desiccation; I used to dip my hand frequently into the water-filled margarine containers during my pottery classes, but in my reverie, there was no dish, no relief. I reached for a dirty, soaked sponge and squeezed drops into my mouth. It wasn't enough, so I poured the thick, fetid slip at the bottom of an abandoned bowl down my throat. I coughed myself awake and opened my eyes and called out "James!" as if he would hear me and rush in with a glass of cool, clear water.

lu

I stayed over at James's condo one night, for a change, and when I woke up with cramps, I asked to use his hot water bottle. He told me he didn't have one; then he disappeared into the bathroom, and I heard the tap running for a few minutes. When he came back to the bedroom, James was carrying a wrung-out, steaming hand towel, which he held out toward me like an offering. I lifted my T-shirt, and he gently laid the towel across my belly. When it cooled, he repeated the process, and after the third round I fell back asleep.

In the morning, when I told him he was the sweetest man I'd ever met, James said it was nothing, just a trick he'd learned from his mother when he was little and had growing pains in his legs. "My shin bones would ache and ache, and I'd be moaning in the night," he said. "The warm towels she wrapped around my calves kept me quiet enough that my father didn't wake up. I think that was the main reason she came up with the idea, to keep my dad from hearing me cry." After James told me his father was the kind of man who would say to a kid, "I'll give you something to cry about!" he started to imitate Ralph Kramden in *The Honeymooners*: he made a fist and punched the air, saying, "To the moon, Alice, to the moon!" When we stopped laughing, James sighed and said, "Some men shouldn't have children."

$\approx$

In the spring after I met Ted, he became a Big Brother. He joined the program to beef up the "service to society" section on his application to medical school. Ted knew exactly how to play it, how to get people to think he was not only wonderful but sincere. And maybe he was, in the case of Charlie, the seven-year-old he was matched with. Charlie loved Ted — and so, as it turned out, did Charlie's mother. Ted could charm the pants off anyone, as he put it. He told me not to worry about Charlie's mom, because he wasn't interested in older women. I don't know about the mother, but Charlie had his heart smashed when Ted accepted an offer of late admission the following September and moved to Toronto to attend medical school.

I found a lump in my breast that summer, while Ted was still in London. We were both terrified. This was a few years before AIDS was everywhere, and cancer, the Big C, was still the worst thing that could happen to you. Ted came to Toronto to be with me for the biopsy, then called me twice a day to ask if the pathology had come back yet. When I got the news from my doctor's office that I was clear, I called Ted right away. He wanted a copy of the report. "I'm going to frame it like a diploma, Mazz. I'm going to hang it on the wall."

llu

James's body is gone. So is our marriage, the entity that the two of us created, and shared. I didn't merge with James, not the way I did with Ted. We didn't lose ourselves, James and me; we didn't pour ourselves into a single vessel. This perhaps is what gives me an edge, now. I am still me, not half of a whole. Two out of three leaves me.

Relationships. We talk about them as if they're separate entities: there is you, me, and "our relationship." When James died, I lost my husband *and* our relationship. The corporation of "us" dissolved.

"Corporation" is from the Latin *corpus* (body). A corporation has the legal status of a person, yet the adjective "corporate" implies "impersonal." The adjective "corporeal" makes me think of swollen private parts, of sexual pleasuring.

I imagine James's voice doing an impersonation of W.C. Fields: "Corporeal. Ah yes, a veritable cornucopia of carnality." But this sounds sad to me, instead of funny; my James did impressions all the time, but he wouldn't have put those words together.

How I miss him. His kindness. His companionship. His body: James's warm body, his skin and his musculature, his touch.

I didn't know what I wanted sexually until I met James and we spent most of our time together in bed. Sex with Ted was always the same: he focused on himself, never thinking that I might want or need some finessing. Until James, I had no idea what I'd been missing. Or that I could be so loud — that was a new side of myself that surfaced. (Josh asked me, out of the blue, when we were sitting next to each other in a study room at school, "Do you make a lot of noise when you do it, Mazzie?" I usually rolled my eyes at his sexual non sequiturs, but I went along with him and said, "There's only one way to find out...")

I would never have asked Ted to do what James did with me, to me. Ted was too conservative for anything beyond the ordinary. I'd tried to interest him in phone sex once, when we were apart and I was missing him — missing the way we used to live together, staying for days at a time at one of our apartments, in London, until a roommate complained; but he hung up on me. Casanova and all that, sure, but Ted was not attentive, not in that way.

He definitely improved in bed, though, toward what became the end of our relationship. Funny, I'd almost forgotten about that. One night, he bent and pushed back on my left knee for a better angle, and when he entered me, I said, "Oooh, seems like you've been practising." I hadn't meant "with someone else," but Ted paused for a split second after my comment; I might have seen a glimmer of guilt on his face, but if so, it was too fleeting to catch.

The first time James saw me, I probably had muddy streaks of clay on my forehead from tucking strands of hair behind my ears, to keep it out of my eyes. But he didn't seem to notice. Later, his not noticing visual clues about a person became one of those annoying qualities that one gets used to in a partner, just as James must have gotten used to my paying attention to what other people look like, how they present themselves to the world.

My smock was smeared that night with reddish-brown slashes of drying clay that I'd wiped from my hands. I'd centred the body properly, but when the surface began spinning, the clay started to slide, and it went over the edge before I could stop it. The results of my attempts to throw a bowl on the wheel that night looked like the slop bucket from a gallbladder operation.

So I started hand-building pots. And I discovered that I liked the feel of the dense, wet clay between my thumb and forefinger. It seemed sexual, this way of working with the material; slip-slathered, the folds of clay that I pressed back into the centre of the pot, to solidify the curves for its wall, were like flattened wings or labia. And I was proud of the way I could smooth the entire surface of a small bowl with a single drop of water, if I worked quickly enough. My fingertips were permanently stained terra-cotta in those days, and my palms looked like drought-baked earth at the height of summer.

Sometimes when I worked with clay and got its texture as smooth as cream cheese, I had the urge to bite it, to taste the dirt in it. Gina craved dirt when she was carrying Anna; she wanted to scoop handfuls of mud into her mouth, for months, the whole summer of her pregnancy. I hadn't understood that urge then and wondered if the compulsion I resisted was similar to hers, to what she'd been unable to satisfy.

Finding One's Way with Clay, the textbook for my course was called. The cover had been glued on upside down, and a well-preserved moth fell out of the middle the first time I turned the book right side up. It reminded me of the flower I'd come across not long before in a Webster dictionary that had belonged to my mother. My sister and I suspected that Mom read the dictionary, a fixture in our kitchen, all day while we were at school. She drove us crazy using words we didn't understand — "inchoate," "conflagration," "dirigible" — showing off her vocabulary, refusing to be easy with us.

eee

That dead moth in my book was luminescent green with transparent wings. When it dropped onto my lap, I put it in my left palm and looked at it under the light. I wondered what the chances were for this little guy to have ended up here, pressed between pages filled with words and pictures of earthenware. He must have been going about his business, flying above the printing press to reach a window on the other side, perhaps, when pages 58 and 59 rolled off, slamming him down to pages 60 and 61, lying in wait below. Each sheet of paper weighed nothing, but the next and the next and the next would have kept coming, one after the other, as unstoppable as the days passing.

I flipped through the pages of the text recently, to see those pictures of professionally finished pieces again. Most images were black and white, but those of glazed pots were in colour, and in these I could see that the clay surfaces were not perfectly smooth. The clay had many blemishes that the sheer glaze covered, but did not hide.

eee

Josh gave me copies of every photograph he had taken for his portfolio, which were touched up to ensure not a single pore was visible. Whenever he came back to Toronto for a break from an assignment he'd finished somewhere in the world, I asked if he'd had any new headshots done. He pretended I'd said "hand jobs" and said, "No, but you can give me one if you like." It was part of our shtick. Whenever we were in a theatre, waiting for the movie to start, he'd say, "You can play with it in the dark, if you want," and I'd push on his arm in pretend disgust. The cerebral sidekick — that's who I'd turned into, with Josh. And I didn't know how to get out of character, once I'd become her.

I'd learned how to beat off a boy before Josh and I became friends. Rob, like Josh, transferred to the alternative high school from Forest Hill. We hung out in the Common Room together, smoking and talking while Mark or Stuart strummed Dylan on their guitars, or listening to visiting poets who still dressed like hippies nearly a decade after the sixties ended — Susan Musgrave and Gwendolyn MacEwen both gave readings, though I didn't know who they were, at the time. Rob had intense brown eyes like mine, and sometimes we'd just sit and look at each other across a coffee table. I was compelled to hold his stare when I caught him looking at me, studying my face. Josh couldn't stand him.

In August Rob dealt blackjack at the Canadian National Exhibition, known as the CNE or the Ex. He was made to wear a silly Styrofoam flat-top with a narrow, flat brim and red-striped hatband; he looked foolish, but the pay was good. I took the streetcar there most nights and waited for him to finish working, and he'd drive me home. It was always after midnight by then; we'd go downstairs to the rec room, which smelled like cigarette smoke, and I'd lie on top of him on the sofa.

The first time, he held me while we kissed; Rob smoked, too, and I liked the taste of it in his mouth. The last few times he came over, after he rubbed my clit and fingered me, Rob unzipped his jeans and pulled out his erection, putting his hand on top of mine, moving it up and down until I found and kept the right rhythm. My head was on his abdomen, and his moist cock smelled like stale bread. It wasn't unpleasant, the smell, but it wasn't exactly tantalizing, either. When he came, his semen squirted onto my face, just missing my eye. I wiped it away with the hem of my broomstick skirt and was careful to wash off the white residue, before tossing my outfit into the laundry hamper. I saw no need to alert my mother to these late-night basement activities. Talking about sex had never been easy for Mom; when I asked if she'd tell me about the facts of life a second time, a week after we'd had the talk, she winced a little, though she did retell the story. (I was eight, and I'd not forgotten the details — I just wanted to hear them again.)

In grade eight, when I hit puberty, my body's chemistry changed in an odd way: I had to stop wearing my grandmother's sterling chain-link necklace because an hour after I polished it with toothpaste, it would blacken again, leaving a charcoal garland around my neck. Gina said this proved there was an invisible toxic field around me that boys instinctively stayed away from. And they did, until I decided to go to the other school.

Rob noticed me right away, he said, the day I arrived to register. In the first week of school, when he saw me walking out to Yonge Street, he slowed down his car and offered me a ride home. I was wearing a pleated, plaid skirt from the fifties in shades of teal and rust to my ankles, and a Chinese silk blouse in a lighter shade of teal, clothes I felt good in; but I was flustered by Rob's attention. I knew about his social ranking at Forest Hill, and it was disconcerting to be standing on the sidewalk, talking to him through the rolled-down window of his Audi. When I said, "No thanks, I like to walk," he shrugged his shoulders and drove away. I hadn't meant to be coy, but later he said he liked me for reacting that way.

When I told my sister that Rob had offered to drive me home, she stared at me in disbelief. "*Rob* stopped for you? In *that* outfit?" Her eyes scanned my skirt; she looked at my boots, which were flat-heeled with pointed toes, as if they were a special affront. My sister was ashamed of my emerging fashion sense — sourced from Kensington Market retro shops, Chinatown, and Little India — which I called "vinternational." Gina's term for it was rather less eloquent.

Gina favoured the ridiculous uniform of rich kids in our neighbourhood: Lee jeans or overalls and clunky Grebs, or Kodiaks, those steel-toed boot that construction workers wore. She knew I hated them, but she'd convinced our mother to give me a pair for my fifteenth birthday. Their existence depressed me every time I saw them in my closet, so I dropped them into a Goodwill donation box. When I told Rob that story, a few months after we'd met, he started calling me his little rebel.

Before Rob left for university, we took a walk to the park near my parents' house. I wore a pair of cotton harem pants, a semi-sheer, crinkled beige blouse (but no bra) from India, and well-worn huarache sandals. We talked as we walked along the trail that led from the community centre into the valley. Then we climbed a hill and lay on our backs side by side. He'd already told me he didn't want to be my first, because it was too much of a responsibility. "Besides," he said that day, "you're smart and pretty and sweet, but between us there's nothing to hold on to." Later, when I confided this to Josh, he told me I should have pointed to Rob's crotch and said, "I know what you mean."

ℓℓℓ

Ralph Lauren cologne — that was what I smelled, whenever Josh hugged me. His entire body seemed to exude the essence of Polo, which was one of the birthday gifts I gave him every year. He loved my lilac scent, too (I wore Diorissimo). "You still smell like Mazzie," he said before we kissed hello or goodbye, after not seeing each other for a while.

At university I shared an apartment with Tanis, the daughter of my father's colleague. Josh called a lot from New York in those days. If Tanis answered, Josh would say, "Me again. Tell Mazz it's her boyfriend." After a few weeks Tanis would tell me to get the phone whenever it rang. "It's probably for you again."

I'd known Josh for almost three years, but the timbre of his voice still made me feel like molten metal. I made shorthand lists of things to tell him on the phone. In person, I wouldn't have needed a prop to think of things to say; but on the phone, after we'd been apart for a while, I could freeze and be too quiet, which made Josh think I was mad at him, or pretending to be mad at him. (I did that, too, sometimes.) I kept my notes at the ready, tucked behind the last page of the pad Tanis and I used for phone messages.

Sometimes Josh was energetic on these calls and talked non-stop. He told me stories about his life in New York: which celebrities he'd seen at Studio 54 on the weekend; where he'd met the girl he was now dating; what modelling assignments he had picked up. He was going for auditions, socializing with Blythe Danner, hanging out with Todd Rundgren. He was up, optimistic; he wanted to see me soon.

Sometimes the calls came in clusters, one each night for a few days in a row, and had a pattern. The first call was filled with chat; when he called the second or third time, he might say, "Can't help it. I had the Mazzie urge again today." But by the fourth call, his voice sounded different. "Yeah, it's just me. Say something funny, Mazz. I need a boost." I could always pull him out of the dumps, he said. "You are one of the few people in the world I can be myself with." It puzzled me that the higher Josh rose, the lower he seemed to feel.

ееи

I didn't scissor the photographs of Josh out of the publications he appeared in, because I preferred to keep the magazines intact. I liked to flip through the glossy pages randomly, as if for the first time, and to come across his face without knowing exactly where I'd find him. That way, it was like one of his surprise visits; he'd often show up at my house without calling ahead, and if I wasn't home, he'd tell my mother it was okay, he just had an urge to see me, that's all.

I held on to them for years, those magazines. I moved them with me from apartment to apartment, even though they were as heavy as bricks. At some point, while I was still with Ted, I accepted the fact that Josh had moved on, and in a massive closet cleanup, I got rid of them. I even tossed out his letters and all of those postcards he'd sent from Milan, St. Moritz, Paris, New York, Oslo — wherever there was an assignment for him. "Miss you, Mazz," he'd say. "Love you, Mazzie. Write soon." Ted hadn't felt threatened, since he knew Josh and I had lost touch, but he was happy when I told him I'd cleared out some of the ephemera from my past nonetheless. When James came into my life, I didn't talk about Josh at all. I suppose I thought I had nothing to say about him, by then.

ееи

Ted's classmates thought he had it made, with me: I was into baseball, I could talk about art, golf, hockey, and medicine, and I drove a manual car. They were especially impressed by the manual car, for some reason. Most of the medical students were male, and I didn't get on well with their girlfriends, who were interested in shopping, decorating their future houses, and eyeing engagement rings. So Ted and I didn't socialize with them all that much. Besides, I travelled so much with my job that we wanted to spend time alone with each other, when I was home.

I also worked for years to get into medical school. That was who I was supposed to become, a doctor — I had my father, Josh, Gina, and everyone else convinced. But doubt percolated and persisted in second year, when I took a lab course in Cellular Physiology, and all of the slides looked identical to me. How would I learn to diagnose a sickness if I couldn't differentiate one cell from another? One night at three a.m. I sat up in bed and thought, *I don't have to do this.* The relief made me euphoric; my lungs expanded and I palpitated with pleasure all over. *This must be the way you'd feel,* I thought, *breaking up with someone you didn't love, at least not in the way you wanted to.* I shared this with Ted when I told him why I'd changed my mind about Medicine, but I didn't include it in the story I told James, when we met, about abandoning my Biology degree.

ℓℓℓ

Ted's father had studied Medicine at the University of Toronto in the fifties. He knew that a few of his colleagues' kids were in medical school now, so he asked Ted to bring his class list with him when we visited on Thanksgiving weekend. I recognized some of his classmates' names, which didn't surprise me; a lot of people I grew up with had talked about going to medical school.

"Wow, there are a lot of Jewish names here," Ted's dad said. "We only had five Jews in a class of one-fifty." I asked him why he'd counted them in the first place. "Because the medical school did. There was a quota system back then, limiting the number of Jews who could be accepted into the program," he said. "The university, the hospitals — they all worked that way." Then he smiled, as if he couldn't wait for the punchline of the joke he was about to tell. "I guess the chosen people weren't often chosen to study medicine!" He expected me to laugh with him, and when I didn't he kept talking, as if he could win me over. Still, I said nothing. "You know, Maslen, poor Ted here would have made it in much earlier, if the system had stayed in place."

Ted and I were getting into the car later that night, on our way to meet some friends for drinks. "I didn't know your dad is anti-Semitic," I said as casually as I could, but Ted defended him. "That's just how it was in those days, Mazz." He started backing out of the driveway. "He didn't make the rules. He didn't know any better. No one did." I stared at Ted, who was working himself into a near-rage — not against his father, but against me. "Don't forget, Mazz, my dad started with *nothing*. He had to work hard to get where he is. He was a paper boy when he was a kid, and he gave every penny to his mother. He put himself through school." Then he waved his arm at the two-storey, three-car-garage Tudor house we were about to drive away from. "He *made* all this happen. For us, for his family. That was all he could think about — making it. He made himself into something."

I married James more than a year after Ted last contacted me, because I was thirty-one years old and couldn't think of a reason not to. Besides, James wouldn't take no for an answer. That was what I liked most about him, I said, when I spoke about James at our wedding dinner — his knowing what he wanted, and going after it, and taking it.

Tony made several toasts. He welcomed me to the child-free tribe. If he ever got married again, he'd follow our lead: keep it simple, keep it small. Tony liked me from the first time he met me, he said; he was glad James found his Tonto, even though he, Tony, was now the Lone Bachelor, having to fend for himself in the wilds of single life. I promised I would let James out to play, once in a while.

The year before James died, we moved his father, Lou, into an old-age home. Each resident's room was identified by a removable bronze nameplate on the door; an empty slot indicated an absence of the ultimate kind. Whenever this happened, the few personal belongings of the deceased were put into clear plastic bags and left on top of the stripped, plasticized mattress for a day or two in case any family members showed up to claim photographs in broken frames, hand mirrors smeared with fingermarks, jars of Vaseline, or pastel-coloured velour tops that were standard Christmas gifts for men and women alike. I'd see dentures lying loose in the detritus like discarded smiles.

Lou had been tough for me to get to know, mostly because James was very clear from the beginning about the fixed limits he placed on his own relationship with his father. For the first few years, whenever we visited Lou at his house, I reminded myself of two stories that James had shared with me:

1. Lou did not attend James's graduation because he held strict ideas about what men should do for a living, and teaching was not one of them; and

2. Lou wanted James to learn how to hunt, to fish, to shoot at squirrels like boys did in his day, but James refused all of it; he couldn't even stand putting a worm on the hook. James liked to feed the birds, to watch butterflies emerge from cocoons underneath the eaves, to play catch with their dog, Blackie. One day Blackie was hit by a car and was dying in the road. Lou approached, handed James a rifle, and walked away.

Yet Lou had become a lonely old man with a spry sense of humour and a lingering, charming zest, and I grew to love him the way I would a grandfather. The father my husband grew up with was not the same person who'd become my father-in-law. I don't think James understood how I could behave with Lou as if I didn't know what James had lived through. I didn't understand that unforgiving streak in James — though if I had, I doubt I would have been able to behave any differently.

five

After university, before I found my job at the language school, I took an aptitude test that included 3-D problems. Afterward I was told by the career counsellor that I should avoid carpentry, which was hardly a surprise. James wasn't much for manual work, either; to this day, the unmitred baseboards in our kitchen lean loose against the wall. When he started to build a massive rock wall behind the farmhouse, I wondered where this stone-smith had come from.

I was looking out the kitchen window once when I saw him remove one of the stones he'd fitted into place and then throw it, hard, to the ground. James was going on sixty, though he looked older to me, just then, almost as old as Lou. But then he picked up another rock and I watched him ease it into the gap, standing back to gauge the size or the colour — I wasn't sure which — and the anger and frustration was gone from his face. I wish I'd asked him more questions about his project, and what it meant to him; I think I was so grateful that he was interested in it that I didn't really worry about why. Anyway, at that moment, my husband suddenly looked very young. I relaxed and decided I'd tell him this later, when he came inside needing food more than solitude. I'd put my arms around him and tell him he looked like a little boy, building a fort out there.

When I was a child, there was a song our whole school knew by heart. Groups of kids would start singing it in the yard at recess, their voices escalating to a frantic level as they competed to out-shout each other:

> *Oh, they built the ship* Titanic, *to sail the ocean blue.*
> *And they thought they had a ship that the water*
>   *wouldn't go through.*
> *But the good Lord raised his hand, said the ship*
>   *would never land.*
> *It was sad when the great ship went down.*

> *Oh it was sad, so sad! Yes it was sad, so sad!*
> *It was sad when the great ship went down (to the*
>   *bottom of the —).*
> *Husbands and wives, little children lost their lives.*
> *It was sad when the great ship went down.*

> *It sunk. Kerplunk. What a hunk of junk. P.U.*
>   *It stunk!*

We didn't know what the lyrics were about. Children laughing at dead children? God deciding to kill everyone on board? None of us knew what "Ring around the Rosie" was about, either, though the girls often sang it exuberantly in the spring. We'd walk in a circle, holding hands and smiling right up to the end, when we'd swing our arms — "Hush-a! Hush-a!" — and then scream, "We all fall DOWN!" as we dropped to the ground.

You can lose everything, absolutely everything, at less than a moment's notice. I suppose that's what those songs were teaching us: to make play out of fear and sorrow. Death happens; we might as well sing about it, to keep going. To keep going.

ℓℓℓ

My niece was sitting on the kitchen floor, playing with the plastic farm set that I'd brought with me to Gina's. Not quite one, Anna picked up a horse and said, "Neigh," and I rewarded her by clapping. Anna grabbed a cow, and said, "Moo!" and we both laughed. Then she dropped the toy and pointed at me, smiling at her own cleverness, and said, "Muzz!" It was shocking, not because Anna knew my name (more or less), but because of the deep tug within me the instant she said it. It was like a magnetic force, pulling us together; a physical attraction, almost. I thought that what I felt when she called me Muzz must be something close to maternal love.

No one, other than James and my mother, called me Maslen. Josh favoured Mazzie, which I liked too, because it reminded me of a name out of *As I Lay Dying*; James thought Mazzie was too close to Bessie, like a nickname for a car. Mazz was also out of the question for James, because it sounded like an insect, to him. I think my husband took me far too seriously sometimes.

ℓℓℓ

As Ted became ever more serious about his studies, I missed seeing his silly side. And I missed seeing him. When he was accepted at U of T and moved to Toronto a few months after I did, he said he couldn't live at my place — not because it was too small (which it was), but because he needed to be near classmates, study groups, hospitals. I didn't pretend that I wasn't disappointed, and he told me I was being selfish. "I finally get into med school, and you want me to flunk out, Mazz? Is *that* what you want?"

There were other clues I might have picked up earlier. We'd stopped telling each other everything after our second year together, but he wasn't secretive, and when we did spend time together — to the last day — I didn't doubt that we were still in love. I didn't want — no, I *refused* — to doubt. By then I'd become so good at managing my reactions to Ted that I could have rationalized anything.

℮℮

Something inside me shifted, when I met James. I felt a twinge of optimism at the glimpse of possibility, a slight lessening of the suffocating load of loneliness I'd been carrying for the six months since Ted left. A tiny bright beam let me see, briefly, another way to be, and a quiet, gentle voice said just one word: *perhaps*.

That voice had been right. I heard it again, the day James and I offered on the farm and we talked about what he might do with the land. I hoped James could hear it, too, and that it would keep talking to him. I suppose I was counting on that happening, because I didn't seem to have any sway of my own with James by then.

℮℮

A woman from the accounting department at work, someone I didn't like very much, told a story in the lunch room that I couldn't shake for a long time. It was about an accident she'd come across on Highway 400. She might have made some of it up, this woman. She didn't like me much, either — she was heavy-set and mannish, and was sarcastic about my coordinated outfits and earrings ("Oh, aren't we matchy-matchy today!"); she knew that James and I were the new owners of a property up that way, that soon we'd be driving that road all the time.

This woman was driving north to a friend's cottage the afternoon she saw the crash scene. There were no flashing lights, since no police or ambulance had arrived yet, so she thought she should do something. She pulled over and walked toward the vehicles, a car and a transport hauling tires, and as she approached the truck she saw the driver sitting in his cab, trembling and sweaty. He'd hit the compact car that was lying in the ditch, pointing in the wrong direction. Half the windshield was gone, she said, and the other half was a shattered haze, so she couldn't see the person at the wheel until she got closer. The body, which was still strapped in, was missing its head.

I thought of this headless driver from then on, whenever James and I were on the highway going to the farm. I drove on these trips; though James had been retired for a few months by then, he was still having anxiety attacks, debilitating episodes that would have put us in danger if he'd had control of the car. I didn't tell him the story, for both of our sakes.

ℓℓ

Gina, at fifteen, took our dad's car out on Sunday nights after he was asleep, and drove her friends around. One Monday morning, Dad went out to the garage as usual but came back into the house before he'd started the engine. "Who moved the mirror and the driver's seat? Motormouth, get down here!" Motormouth — that's what our father used to call Gina when he was angry at her. But it had become an endearment, really, because he knew that Gina found it funny, so he kept on saying it.

Gina and I were in the bathroom upstairs, getting ready for school. "Learn from the master," she whispered to me, before leaning over the banister to answer. "It was me, Dad! I wanted to find out what it felt like to sit behind the wheel. I can't wait for our driving lessons this summer, that's all. Sorry." Her little finger, indeed. When Dad left, Gina told me that if I said anything to either parent, I'd live to regret it. She grabbed onto my skinny upper arm as she spoke, to make her point, and it took days for the pinch-marks to fade.

The action you perform with your fingers on a clay body when making a pot by hand is called a "pinch-bite." The vocabulary for a potter's material is anatomical. Chunks of it are called *clay bodies*. You take a clay *body*, my book said, and you make a *vessel* out of it: a pot with a *belly,* or a vase with a *neck*. Slip is the *blood*, which is just a watered-down bit of the clay it is taken from. Slip joins parts together by drying out, pulling a cup and a *hand*le, or a *foot*ing and a bowl toward each other until they are one. The piece is glazed, with or without colour, and this coating is the *skin*. Out of the kiln, twice baked into final form, it has *bones*. The vessel is something new made from something old, which itself came from nothing, if you go back far enough.

I paid close attention to the pages on pinch potting in *Finding One's Way*. I learned what clay is made of — it comes from minerals and decaying animals and plants in the earth, the silt settling by accretion into beds next to or below the surface of water — and how its elements interact and are transformed. Moulding clay, for me, was like meditating without a mantra. I couldn't help but ponder time and being and physical presence while I worked with it. Perhaps it had something to do with James, with meeting James at that time, or with a need to find some new meaning, or to become a new person.

ℓℓℓ

Why Josh wanted to become someone new, I couldn't say. But he used to talk about a Transcendental Meditation class he enrolled in, when he moved to New York City, to help him find his way. He hesitated to sign up, he said, because of his mother: she was enmeshed in the Far East meditation movement in the sixties and was on a manic bender when she fled to India, four-year-old son in hand. Josh watched her give birth to her guru's child, down on the mat she and Josh shared in their cell at the ashram. He said his half-sister — what was her name? — was the ugliest wriggling little thing he'd ever seen, when she emerged from between his mother's legs. He was five, by then.

But she was a pretty child, with a light Kashmiri complexion and black curly hair. By the time his father went to India to take the kids home, Josh's hair had grown past his shoulders and his dad told him he looked like the baby's older sister. The girl went to live in New York with an aunt, spending some time each summer with Josh, his grandmother, and his dad in Toronto.

lll

I remember Josh liked to play the big brother when his sister visited, driving her wherever she needed to go, buying clothes for her and taking her to concerts. I met her once, when the three of us went to hear Genesis at the CNE grounds, the year that "Follow You Follow Me" was a hit. As we sat on the ground with Josh in the middle, I remember worrying that the sun would liquefy my makeup before the set was over. I hadn't wanted Josh's sister to come with us, but I was glad that she was there to distract Josh, so he wouldn't be looking at my face the whole time.

lll

When I was in university, I always put on my "face," my full makeup, before I dialed Josh's number. I didn't realize how strange that was, until now.

When we spoke Josh told me what he was reading—Isherwood, Baldwin—and I told him what I was writing for class. My assignments were "representations of female consciousness" in Woolf, "birthing imagery in *Surfacing*"—that kind of thing. It was the heyday of feminist literary theory, and my professors told me I had nailed the critical approach, that I should do graduate work on women writers. "If you do, you'll be studying the same thing as Rachel," Josh said in passing. I knew Rachel was at U of T doing a Ph.D., but Josh hadn't spoken of her for a couple of years. "What a couple of mensches."

Between calls, I wrote to Josh — long, well-scripted letters about my thoughts and memories and impressions. I turned nearly every experience I had into a story for him. Sometimes I was writing letters in my head about the things I was doing at the same time I was doing them — pouring solvents into beakers in the chemistry lab, when I was still in the Biology program; eating campus-cafeteria broccoli covered with melted Cheez Whiz; or seeing an exhibit at the gallery in downtown London with Aldo, a guy I dated for a while. My present life was *over there*, at a remove from myself, lived as it was for the purpose of entertaining Josh, of drawing him to me, of forcing him to think about me — at least for the time it took him to read the handwritten missives from the smart girl back home.

*

With James, there was no posing. Our being together felt natural; that was how I described our fledgling relationship, when I called Gina to talk about it. James had arrived, and our connection simply existed, on its own terms, without any need to draw him closer or to imagine what might happen in the future. I suspected, in the beginning, that if we continued as a couple, if our pairing lasted, I might eventually understand what contentment felt like. Perhaps, I thought, I could learn how to be. Just be.

*

Early on, when I was at Ted's apartment in London for the first time, I heard the kettle boiling in his galley kitchen. He was going to make instant coffee, all he ever had, but he didn't get up to pour the water when I nudged him. Instead he looked me in the eyes and said, "I'm falling, Mazz. And I don't mean off the couch." I smiled and kissed him, or tried to, because we both were smiling. When I pulled back, I said, "Bear? I'm already down on the ground." Later in the evening, he gave me an exquisite piece of glazed pottery he shouldn't have splurged on. It was a tall, slim coffee pot, pale blue with yellow lines that swirled in an abstract pattern, made in Turkey. He'd bought it at the international craft fair in the student centre, he said. "It's for us, but I want you to hang on to it. As a symbol." Of domesticity, I assumed, or perhaps of adventure. Either way, it was a start.

೭ಀಀ

It took James many visits to the pottery studio where he'd first seen me before I would agree to have a coffee with him. Then, one night, I let James walk me home. I asked him in for a drink, and that was it — we became a couple.

೭ಀಀ

I've always liked older men, and I was surprisingly confident talking with male professors. I spent time chatting with them during office hours, which led to on-campus lunches with a couple, and off-campus dinners with one in particular. It was mostly innocent. The married biblical scholar with silver-speckled hair swept back from his forehead reminded me of an actor I couldn't place; in class he spoke directly to me, as if no one else were in the room, and after my art trip to New York City we had several extended conversations about the Cloisters while the forty other students waited for his lecture to begin. I changed my mind about the political scientist after a few conversations that took too much effort to keep going, which made it awkward when he asked if I'd be his date at the department's reception for a visiting diplomat. I said I had to study for an exam early the next morning and was relieved when he ignored me for the rest of the semester.

I was most interested in Prof. L., who was Jewish, and who'd given me permission to take his advanced literature course without having the prerequisite. We shared an addiction to Woody Allen films and Indian food, neither of which were easy to find in London in the eighties. He'd been a business major headed for law school before he'd discovered he could apply his analytical bent to literature, and teach.

I liked Professor L.'s voice, its intonations. If he called before going to get takeout, he'd ask, "Do you want to come with?" — the phrase Jennifer used to ask me, for example, to her skating club; Josh used it, too, when he'd invite me to run errands for his grandmother with him.

I told Josh about Prof. L. on the phone one night, and after a long pause he said, "I always knew you'd end up with a professor, Mazzie." Even though this happened after the Letter, Josh sounded sad to me, so I told him I hadn't ended up with anyone, not yet. "I'm only twenty-four. Everything is still ahead!"

I was still new to literary studies then — I really didn't know much at all — but I was trying to *look* intelligent — in a vintage sort of way, like Virginia Woolf or Simone de Beauvoir — by wearing my now-longer hair pinned in a loose topknot. Gina said I looked like a light bulb, with my hair piled up on my head that way, but Prof. L. said it was classic, and he liked it on me. (He put this and a few other complimentary observations in a note tucked into a graded paper he was returning to me, a few weeks into the term. Reading it in my apartment that night, I thought, *Wow, you really shouldn't have put that in writing.*)

Prof. L. didn't act like a world-renowned scholar or show off his knowledge the way some of my other professors did. He thought we should keep our relationship platonic (I remember trying to make a joke out of that, saying something stupid about Aristotle) until his course was over; he didn't want anyone to accuse him of unethical behaviour at that stage of his career. He made sure that couldn't happen: when I received my results for the year, my mark in Prof. L.'s course had gone down by two percentage points.

ℓℓℓ

Soon after Ted graduated with his MD — on a day that was already hazy and grimy, the worst kind of weather for migrainous me — he woke me up and said he had something to tell me.

The first time he said that, we'd been together only a few weeks, and I'd said I had something to tell him, too. We were celebrating the end of mid-terms with a night in at his place. We splurged on Chinese takeout and, because it was cheap, a bottle of the only Canadian white wine you could get in the eighties — not Baby Duck, but close. We'd spread a blanket out on the living-room floor as if we were on a picnic, and Ted pulled a single rose out from behind his back. I kept it for the rest of that year, despite my aversion to dried flowers.

What he said that night on the blanket was this: "You're *so* beautiful. And it's natural to love beautiful things. Maybe that's why I love you." I said that was *exactly* what I was going to tell him. "That I'm beautiful?" "No, that I love you." "Phew!" he said, "I thought you were going to tell me you were pregnant!" We rolled around on the floor in each other's arms, laughing.

What Ted needed to tell me on that hot, sticky Toronto morning five years later was this: he wanted a break. He wasn't ready for the next step. He needed another few years, he said, before he'd be ready for the future we'd been talking about since the day we met.

I was on my side and Ted was lying behind me, one arm flung over my waist as he spoke. I didn't say anything and the minutes went by. I gripped his wrist, hard, to prove to myself that he was still there. But he wasn't, not really. He'd already let me go.

fit

There was no big bang when I met James, no magic, no map to each other. Our life was built of layer after layer of time, the two of us standing next to each other. It was a matter of collusion instead of collision, decisions instead of chances, deliberate satisfaction instead of unattainable desire. It was a good life, one that I'd expected would end in our old age, James going first only because he had an nearly twelve-year head start on living.

⇚

I needed to make room for some of James's things in my tiny apartment. I threw away some items I'd stashed in the linen cupboard, including a failed plate I'd made in my beginners' pottery class — a heavy slab, thick with glazes that bled into each other and produced unnameable, ugly colours. But James rescued it from the trash. "It reminds me of our first conversation, and how we met." I thought I heard a slight whine in his voice; it was the first inkling I had that James might be more sentimental than he let on, and I wasn't sure I liked it. But I'd kept the Turkish coffee pot from Ted for all those years, after all.

The next year, when James helped me pack up for our move into this bungalow, I put the pottery plate in a box destined for the Salvation Army. Again James found it, and said he wanted to keep it. "James," I said, "we can't hang on to every object we've ever owned for the rest of our lives." But he insisted. "I don't want to keep *every* object, Maslen. I just want to keep the plate, okay?"

I don't know where that plate ended up. I don't remember throwing it away, but I can't recall seeing it again, either, after I moved out of my apartment.

I'd taken that place six years before, when I moved back to Toronto to start my job. I took the Yonge subway from Lawrence Station to the ESL school south of Dundas every morning. From the first day en route, I thought of Josh when the train stopped at Eglinton Station, where I used to catch the bus to go to his house. It had been well over a year since I'd heard from Josh by then, and I hadn't been thinking much about him — not since I met Ted, in fact. But for a while, twice a day at that stop, I'd feel a weight settle in my chest, and I'd sink momentarily beneath a little bit of sadness. Sometimes I'd forget to inhale for a few seconds and then suddenly suck in a lot of air, as if surfacing after being underwater for too long. I was embarrassed at making a noise like that in public, so I'd fake a cough and wonder where I'd ever gotten the gall, back then, to spend afternoons with that beautiful boy.

The last address I had for Josh was in Oslo, where his then-girlfriend, Ingrid, was from. They'd met on a shoot for *Vogue* and stayed with her family between assignments — I knew that much; he told me about her in his last two letters. I assumed it wouldn't last, that he wouldn't stay overseas permanently, because of her. "No attachments, Mazz, you know me," he'd say, and I was always relieved to hear it. He'd always had lots of women, stunningly beautiful women, in his life, but none of his affairs lasted very long.

ఎఎ

Gina was always the beautiful one. We never did look like sisters, even before her plastic surgery last summer. Gina always had big, round green eyes, thick chestnut hair, and a curvy build, which she sometimes hated. She would pound on her hips and ask why she ended up with the big butt instead of me, though she knew that with my flat chest, I would have traded bodies with her in a flash. Most of the time she'd tell me I was ugly, that I'd never find a boyfriend, I'd never get married. At twelve, when I was reading my father's copy of *Great Expectations*, I immediately understood what Pip meant about his sister's contempt for him: "[it] was so strong that it became infectious, and I caught it."

By the time I started university, the fall after my mother died, Gina had softened toward me. She'd been married to Ben for a few months and was hosting her first Thanksgiving dinner at their house, in Ajax. At the table, Ben offered to say grace, but none of us wanted him to. I suggested we each make a statement about gratitude, instead, and I offered to go first. "Gina, thank you for having Dad and me over today. I am grateful that you and I have become friends, now that we're both adults. Also," I added, half joking, "I forgive you for your general nastiness toward me when we were growing up."

Ben laughed, but Gina said she didn't know what I was talking about. I don't think she'd simply forgotten what she'd been like, and I don't think she was attempting to manipulate me or make me doubt myself, either. I think she believed that her version, her memory of her own behaviour, was the truth. Dad chose not to comment, other than to say he was grateful for the food before us. Then he asked me to pass the mashed potatoes. They were made from flakes that came in a box, so I knew he wouldn't like them. Mom wouldn't have served such fare to a dog (I could actually hear her saying this — "I wouldn't serve that mush to a dog, Gina!"). Neither Dad nor I wanted to set Gina off, so we each ate as much as we could and hid the rest under half slices of bread.

⁂

I didn't see Gina very often after James and I married. There was no falling-out between us, but she was busy with her kids and her house in Ajax, and James and I liked to spend our Saturdays walking along the Danforth, or through Little India, or, in good weather, on the boardwalk in the Beaches. We saw more of Gina when her children got older, and James liked to impress her by cooking dinners at our place, when Ben was away on business. Her favourite meal of James's was spaghetti with brown sugar, chili pepper flakes, and red wine in the tomato sauce; she also copied out his easy chicken-and-crab-soup recipe, with fresh tarragon, cream, and sherry stirred into the packaged mix, but I'm sure she never made either dish for herself.

Gina drove out to the farm to visit us once, when Ben was away and the kids were at day camp. I made tuna sandwiches for lunch and used James's trick of stirring a little white sugar into the mayonnaise to cut the fishy taste. I put a couple in the fridge for James to eat later.

That day in the kitchen, Gina said, "Too bad James doesn't cook anymore. Maybe retirement isn't good for him. Maybe he should sign up for substitute teaching or something." Everyone, including Gina, thought James had taken early retirement because of my "journey," as the oncologists liked to call it. James did not want his private medical information shared with anyone, and I didn't betray his trust.

"He's had enough of teaching," I told her. James didn't retire as much as recuse himself from regular life. Buying the farm was a gamble, but we were running out of options. "We bought this place for him. He's earned the right to play a little, at this point in his life." What I said to Gina was true; but whatever was bothering James, and whatever the wall meant to him, I knew that he wasn't playing a game.

లల

With Ted, I played my hand, and won. Making choices, I thought, was one of the easiest things in the world to do. I felt so powerful when Ted and I were together, when he was responsive and giving, and wanted to be with me forever.

We spent every evening and every weekend together, for nearly a year, in London. We alternated between apartments based on our roommates' schedules. I kept clean underwear and an extra set of my makeup and toiletries at his place, instead of putting them into an overnight bag when I planned to stay over.

When we were at my place — at the apartment I shared with Tanis — Ted did his best to change my roommate's opinion of him, but she wasn't having any of his charm. "Let me put it this way," she said when I asked why she didn't like him. "If he becomes a doctor, I bet he'll specialize in gynecology. Face it, he's a flirt and a jerk."

But he wasn't those things with me. He brought me gifts — a hardcover edition of *Mrs Dalloway*, when I told him it was my favourite novel, inscribed in his hand: "To Mazzie, the love of my life, for all time — T." He wouldn't let me get out of bed in the morning because he didn't like to say goodbye. When I eventually got dressed, if we'd spent the night in his room, he would hide my keys and wallet from me. At the pub on campus, where we'd meet after his evening biochemistry lab, he'd hold my hand and ask what I'd eaten during the day, who I'd spoken to, what I'd been reading while I waited for him. We wanted every moment of each other. We were children who wanted what we wanted, now and now and now.

I used to think back to my early days with Ted to remind myself what it felt like to fall in love. This was before I met James, and for a few months after, too. When I thought about falling for Ted, it was not with nostalgia; it was almost a re-enactment, a reactivation. In an instant, I'd become the person I was with him in that place, at that time. I was in *that* mood, wearing *those* clothes and hearing *his* voice say *those* words. Feeling his skin against mine, the temperature of his hands. For a long time, it was a relief to find those scenes were still there, to have my inner life waiting for me to peek into, like an enveloped indulgence. But as James and I became stronger, I had to stop going back, for James's sake and for mine.

lee

In an essay for my Modern Lit professor, I argued that Virginia Woolf challenged her day's gendered understanding of the inner life via her character, Peter Walsh: "First, she renders Peter's mind in the act of remembering decades-old scenes with Clarissa, revivifying emotional experiences in the present — a ruminating tendency not usually ascribed to men, in literature; second, she feminizes the rhythm and language of Peter's haunted thoughts using long, run-on sentences, multiple clauses separated by commas, heightened descriptions of the senses," etc. etc. It was a game of sorts, I knew it was, but it earned an A+. Ted thought I was some kind of magician, creating convincing sentences that he could barely understand. I'd put a spell on him, he'd say, in the months leading up to our first summer together.

I don't want to think about Ted. I wouldn't be thinking of him now, if this hadn't happened to James — if I'd not been forced to look back, to look inside, to weigh the invisible and the absent. And I am ashamed by some of my thoughts: even now, I can't imagine Ted dying without feeling as though there is a small, hard lump burning in my chest, a pain that sears much more than it should for the relatively short time he'd spent in my life. I know it's wrong to feel this way about Ted. Especially now, after having had James in my life for so long. And after losing him so soon.

Every day, for most of the day, James drove the beat-up Volvo station wagon we'd found abandoned in the barn to retrieve rocks — field stones, pushed out of the way when settlers cleared the land for farming. He harvested hundreds and hundreds of them from the end of our long, narrow property. He'd fill up large plastic buckets by hand and drive them back toward the house, to add them to his quarry. He unloaded them slowly, assessing their general size and shape and sorting them into piles: this one for the interior of section two, that for the exterior of the top row of section seven, and so on.

I watched from the window as he worked, because if I went outside, he'd stop. He didn't talk to me about his project, and I worried that asking why he was obsessed with it might make him feel judged or questioned, which would not be helpful. And after a few months, his symptoms began to wane — at least, he no longer talked about them, so I assumed they had.

That was the beginning, I thought, when I tried to piece the recent past together for the insurance company: it was during James's final few months teaching that a crushing anxiety would come out of nowhere and grab at his throat. When it happened, he'd call me at work and I'd have to take the subway up to Finch Station; Tony would pick me up and drive back to the school where he and James both taught. James was always waiting for me in the parking lot, sitting on the passenger side of his car, looking ashamed.

That was where I always started it off, the story of James's disappearance; for months after he died, I still believed that those panic attacks were the beginning of the end.

    lee

James's first marriage ended after four years. He married Andrea because he thought he could help her become "who she was meant to be," he said. She had so much potential! The way he talked about the marriage made it sound like an extracurricular project, and I thought James was something of a condescending ass for talking about it that way. From the pictures he showed me after we moved into our bungalow, Andrea seemed attractive in a natural sort of way: no makeup, ivory complexion, blond hair pulled back into a ponytail. But she was needy and negative, James said, and she wrapped herself in a cloak of melancholy. Then she told him she changed her mind, she wanted children after all; she wanted them so badly that she had a hysterical pregnancy. When James wouldn't capitulate, Andrea turned para-spiritual on him. Accusations came with her new belief in reincarnation: James had tried to kill her in a former life, one in which they were, bizarrely, also married to each other. They didn't grow apart, James said, they *broke* apart. "'Irreconcilable differences' didn't even *begin* to explain what happened with us."

    lee

"No wonder people start wars, when two sisters in the same family can't even get along," my mother would say, walking away in disgust whenever Gina and I fought. So she didn't see what happened when Gina pushed me out of a chair onto the hardwood floor and I broke my tibia, at age four; or when, at seven, my left radius cracked after Gina stuck her foot out to trip me; or when two of my toes were fractured, at ten, because Gina's textbook-filled knapsack "slipped off" the kitchen counter. I was brittle-boned (I hated the taste of milk), I was often preoccupied, and I was very clumsy; my mother was sure that these traits explained my injuries.

Eventually it was my father who stepped in when he couldn't stand listening to our yelling matches anymore. This was after I'd found my favourite turtleneck with its arms ripped off and my new midi-skirt cut into a mini on the floor of Gina's closet. Dad put a lock on my bedroom door to keep Gina out, and I added the key to the string necklace I wore with my bicycle-lock key, until I left junior high and took the bus to high school. My clothes were safe by then, since my unusual wardrobe was of no interest to Gina, other than as fodder for insults. "Maslen," my father advised, when I still reacted to my sister's taunts, "you can't wear your heart on your sleeve all the time. You'll have to toughen up."

ᘓᘓ

One Saturday the spring before we found the farm, James and Tony went for a hike north of the city, and I visited my father. I didn't see him often; we'd never been close, and it was fine with me that he apportioned his late-found interest in maintaining family ties among Gina and her kids.

We didn't know how to talk to each other, Dad and I, so we spoke of Gina's children, our only mutual interest. He thought Gina and Ben were raising them without enough discipline; whenever he went to their house, he said, meals were completely chaotic. Then he surprised me and said he remembered my friend Josh coming to our family dinners, which made me smile, though I was also sad; I hadn't thought about Josh for such a long time. I had an urge to reach out, to try once more to track him down. When Dad turned the television on to watch the golf game, I called Josh's grandmother's number, which I thought I'd fixed in my brain. But I must have forgotten it after all, I thought, because the line was out of service.

On my way home I decided to drive over to Josh's house, to say hello to his grandmother in person. As soon as I got there I became anxious, just as I used to when I was getting to know Josh, spinning myself into a state of terrible anticipation, certain that everything I'd planned was about to go wrong. This anxiety was not entirely without basis: our first try to see a movie together was derailed when his neighbour, Rachel, showed up at his place (she needed to talk); another time, I waited at school for two hours, certain that he regretted saying he'd meet me for lunch (he'd gotten the days mixed up).

I was getting out of my car when a man and woman opened the front door of the house and led their two children to the minivan I was blocking in the driveway. I apologized for intruding, and said I was looking for the family of a friend who had grown up in this house. The wife told me they'd bought the place years before, in an estate sale. And with that my mood — which had risen gently when Dad talked about Josh, half an hour before — dropped into a crevasse. I was so stupid! Of course she'd be dead by now, Josh's grandmother! How had so much time passed? And where could Josh be now?

After Josh called in response to the Letter, that potent piece of paper, I remembered one of his calls to me from a year or two before. His model-girlfriend-of-the-month (he didn't give a name) wanted him to move in with her; his grandmother wanted him to come back home, to help out (he didn't say with what); and his modelling agency wanted him to fly all over the world (anywhere, anytime). He didn't know what he wanted. At the end of the call, he said he was grateful to me for listening. What he loved about both me and Rachel was we accepted him without question, moods and all.

During his final year of medical school, it was Ted who became moody. He expressed this through anger, which I attributed to overwork: like all of the senior students, he did thirty-six-hour shifts in hospital rotations while preparing for the national Board exams. His class's hockey team suspended its games for the interim, which meant he couldn't skate and play-fight his stress away. I tried not to put any of my needs at his feet for those final months of his program. He had always been my confidant, and I'd shared everything with him about work, friends, family — you name it; but I reminded myself that keeping emotional distance from Ted would be necessary only for the short term. That made it easier to get through the episode of melancholy I'd begun to slide into.

All through the summer of that year I'd been thinking about my mother. It was almost the anniversary of her death, and though he'd never met my mom, Ted had always come with me to put flowers on her grave in August. When he forgot about it, I didn't mention it to him, and I went alone. That night when I got home, Ted said he wasn't going to stay over, and I broke down. He gathered up his things and told me to pull myself together. It wasn't fair to let my mood barometer go up or down based on where he happened to be. If I couldn't help it, then that was my tough luck. People were always telling me I had to be tougher, harder than I was, it seemed.

eu

I knew that being annoyed at James for his moods and anxiety attacks was not fair, so I tried not to show it. I compared it to his fear of flying, which hadn't lasted. "Remember when you had tremors and shortness of breath on takeoff? We never think of that anymore!" I expected that he'd snap out of it soon, because he was still James, and that was what James would do.

I let James think I'd always been on an even keel, but the truth is, it was James who grounded me. Without him, without his emerging, persistent presence in my life all those years ago, I think I'd have remained stagnant, locked in a vacuum of absence, mulling myself to sleep at night thinking of the past. Which is where I seem to be, by necessity, now.

Hannah Arendt said that thinking is a fight against time, because the activity of reflection brings that which is absent — the past — into the mind's present. You would think it might console, this resurrection, but it hasn't yet, for me. Because it's not reflection, what I'm in the midst of, now: it's an attempt to forget, it's a peeling away, it's a lifting off. It's an attempt to see James, and our marriage, anew.

lee

I have to admit that whenever I left James alone on the farm, I didn't miss him. Not in the way I knew I should. And what I did feel, instead, was relief. Going home was a reprieve from not understanding what was wrong with him, with us.

lee

Things James stopped doing after my diagnosis:

> – lifting weights
> – going for his daily jogs
> – cooking meals
> – scouting for organic produce at the St. Lawrence
>   Market
> – reminding me to take yogurt and fruit to work
> – wanting sex
> – making lists

But the stones, their weight and their waiting to be found, soothed James somehow. He worked for hours at a time, for days on end, with those stones, the spring after my surgery. This pleased me, even though he seemed farther away. Some kind of equilibrium was establishing itself, I thought, both in James's mind and in our marriage.

When I was there with him on the weekends, we ate silent meals of eggs, salads, fresh bread from the market, things that I could manage. It didn't disturb me that we had so little to talk about in those days; we'd been together for too many years by then to be worried about that. James seemed calmer, to me, and that was enough. It seemed like enough to me then.

Unless I was travelling for work, Ted and I mostly saw each other on the weekends from September to April for the four years he spent in medical school. Every time he left my apartment to go back to his shared one, I'd stand at the window, half-hidden behind the curtain, and watch him walk down the sidewalk until he disappeared. I'd have the urge to run after him and felt a push within myself to remember, to cement the details of how we spent the previous two days together: shopping in Kensington Market for vintage purses (for me) and fedoras (for him, but I wore them), eating lunch in subterranean Chinatown restaurants, or listening to a set at the Rex on Queen West. Over a beer or two, we'd talk about moving somewhere like Belize, where we could live on next to nothing; Ted imagined opening a clinic, and I thought about starting a small English school. "I don't want to be like my dad," he said, "and stay around here running a family practice for my whole life. He thinks taking a cruise with continuing education for doctors is travelling. A *cruise*!"

When the weekend was over and Ted put on his well-worn cowboy boots — "I'm going to be buried in these," he used to say — it seemed as if I'd imagined much of it, so I worked at remembering our time together. It was an instinct I had from the beginning, to lock in moments, to record my encounters with Ted deeply and clearly. I'd commit to mind the physical details: the feel of my jeans sliding down my legs, the colour of Ted's shirt and socks, the smell of his deodorant, the taste of the food we'd shared, the feel of the sheets tangled around my ankles.

I can summon such episodes still. They can tease or cause distress, but more than anything, they make me curious about where they come from. They are not permanent, but they are not fleeting, either. They are outside of time, neither here nor there and yet both here and there, when I want them to be.

~~

After my surgery I wasn't in pain, but I was uncomfortable, and the incisions were itchy. James was still on summer vacation that first week of August, when a nurse from Community Care came every day to measure the fluids, check the sutures, change the dressings. Two tubes had been force-fed into my chest, in and out of deep incisions, and they formed symmetrical half hearts just under my skin that I could trace with my fingers. Seeing the tubes' contours in the bathroom mirror, I had the urge to outline a Valentine on top of them by running a tube of lipstick along my bulged-out flesh. "I've prettied myself up!" I imagined saying to James, but he was still too distraught to risk it.

I looked like a chemistry experiment. Bottles collecting draining liquid dangled where the tube ends surfaced at either side of my chest. I was supposed to be exercising so my pectorals wouldn't become rigid or limit the range of my arm movements, but stretching with those tubes inside of me felt dangerous and unnatural, so I instinctively held off doing them for fear of tearing the sutures open. "I'll get in shape later," I told the nurse.

I had hoped James might turn the huge, century-old barn, long empty of livestock and plows, into a home gym where he could lift weights and even run on a track during the winter months. When we bought the place, we talked about renting out the back field to a couple who'd posted a sign at the grocery mart: "Will pay for growing hay on your land." But James hadn't followed up. He'd decided instead that the long stretch we owned behind the house was perfect for building his mammoth rock structure — something taller than he was, and thicker than an overgrown hedge. He'd use mud for mortar if he had to, and fit the stones by close study and intuition. He etched the partial U-shape of the wall in the ground first, with a shovel. The line he drew undulated for forty feet along the west lotline, crossing over and curving back up to the house for about twenty feet in the shape of a partial U. It was an exaggerated fence, an open corral, and it made a statement; but exactly what James wanted to say, I wasn't sure. I knew that the finished work, come September, would be strange, and beautiful, and that building his stone wall that summer was exactly what James needed to do.

Throughout my teens, I volunteered at the North York General Hospital during the summer, to familiarize myself with the atmosphere of sickness and disease. One of the patients was a woman dying of cervical cancer, whose children were five and seven. Their artwork was pinned to a bulletin board next to her bed; crayoned suns shone down on blue stick people representing her family. The head nurse, who knew I wanted to become a doctor, saw me wiping my eyes after leaving the room one afternoon. "You can't let cases get to you," she said. "You won't survive a single shift."

Candystripers, we girls were called, because we wore pink pinstriped cotton dresses with short sleeves and a zipper closure at the front, from hem to collar bone. Mine was closer-fitting than any other clothes I wore, and it made me uncomfortable to feel the male patients' eyes on my body. A bedridden Italian man with a bad back spent all of July on my ward, and every day he asked me in halting English if I'd marry him. Josh laughed when I relayed the story and said he wasn't surprised — he thought those uniforms were sexy. Later, when I told Ted that he wasn't the first man who'd wanted to marry me, he tried for some time to find out who that smitten fellow had been.

lu

When Ted got back to his place after we slept together the first time, at mine, he called every few minutes. He called and he called, and each time I picked up, he said, "I can't stop thinking about you, Mazz!" We'd talk for an hour then hang up, and five minutes later, the phone would ring again. "Teddy, stop!" I said, laughing. "I can't study either, but *I'm* not trying to get into medical school." My roommate *was* trying, though; Ted's phone calls were aggravating Tanis. After a few weeks it became simpler to take my *Norton Anthology of English Literature* and go to Ted's place to read while he studied for his science midterms. While he *tried* to study.

Tanis left for the summer and we gave up our apartment, so at the end of the school year I moved into Ted's. My job didn't start for a few weeks, and Ted had paid his summer-school tuition, so we were running low on money. Ted made peanut butter sandwiches, fried bacon, and scrambled eggs, and my culinary repertoire was even more limited. I'd avoided learning how to cook on principle — I told my mother I would not play that role just because I was born female. ("You'll only be burning your bra to spite your stomach," she warned, and I suppose she had a point.)

Ted lit candles most nights, and I set the card table using paper towels for serviettes. We thought we had everything, as long as we had each other — until the rejection letters arrived. I wanted him to fail, he said. I wanted him to sit around and read books with me and talk about art and make plans to travel to Turkey and Egypt together. Now he had to take courses over again, thanks to me. I'd turned his mind to mush. He hoped I was happy.

From then on, I woke every morning feeling clammy, cold, and anxious. I wanted to stop July and the continuation of my life alone in Toronto from happening. I lay in bed, tensing my legs and bending my ankles, toes pointing up, imagining that my heels pressing into the mattress were digging into the earth, slowing down time. Ted would ask me to stop it, to get up if I was going to squirm around and bother him.

⁓

James was explaining to Tony what had intrigued him when he saw me at the Y the first time. "Aside from those big eyes of hers, I thought, *She must be an interesting person, since she's taking a pottery course.*" I added that I'd failed the wheel-throwing tests, and laughed, but James wouldn't let me put myself down. "She's double-jointed," he said, and winked at Tony. I loved to see the deep crow's feet at the outer corners of James's eyes.

If my attention drifted on weekends when James stayed over, he'd ask what was wrong. I was still going to Ted in my mind then, because it was comforting to know the depth and power and certainty of feeling I'd had for him was still there. But I couldn't tell James. I didn't know how to explain the sad joy I indulged in when my thoughts went back to Ted, or the lost and solemn mood a return from one of these vignettes instilled in me, or the lovely weight of the melancholy lingering in that place people call the heart.

Eventually my heart began to call me back, back to James, pounding its message into me — "here-now, here-now, here-now" — the ache from its living beat crashing into my reverie. Forcing me to face the fact that whoever I'd been when Ted's love first razed me — and whoever *he'd* been, then, as well— well, those people didn't exist anymore. I managed to stop fighting time, to stop recalling what I'd lost, and I thought I'd left the past and Ted behind.

II. Beguiled

seven

The admitting nurse in pre-op frowned when she opened my file. "Cheryl" was written on her name tag beside a pink heart with a happy face drawn inside of it. "Oh, I see you're having a bilateral mastectomy today," she said. "I'm so sorry." "It's okay, Cheryl, really," I said. I wanted to push her pity right back at her, shove it across the desk into her lap, but I also needed to be cautious about what I said in front of James, who was still distressed about my diagnosis. "This surgery is a very good thing." I touched my breasts. "They're just double trouble, at the moment." James's right hand felt damp when I took it in my left. I leaned toward him for some privacy. "Come on, James," I whispered, "laugh with me a little," but even his smile trembled.

Cheryl hurried through her spiel, telling me what to expect once I'd been rolled into the operating room and what would happen to me in recovery, after it was over. I had no interest in the brochure she gave me about the local support group for cancer survivors, who met for monthly coffee and cookies in a church hall downtown, and Cheryl seemed offended as she put it back down on her desk. "Good luck, Maslen." She stood and shook my hand. "I've never heard that name before. Where does it come from?"

"It was my grandmother's family name, before she married," I said. "My older sister was named after our maternal grandmother, and I was supposed to be named after our *father's* mother. But she had an ugly, old-fashioned first name, so my mom kept her promise by calling me Maslen." James and I turned toward the door to the patient-preparation room. "Can you imagine?" I said over my shoulder. "I could have ended up with no breasts *and* been named Gertrude!"

Areola is a pretty name.

When I rolled onto one side, my body would press on the drainage bottle just enough that, by morning, dark-red streaks stained the bedsheet. The sight of blood upset James — not just any blood, but *my* blood, blood that was bright as a rose in the clear plastic containers, or brown as mud where it had spilled and dried. He slept in the guest room after the first night I was home, and he stayed away for a long while, well after the drains were gone.

I didn't expect James to initiate sex for a while after the surgery, but months later we still hadn't made love more than a few times. I always wore a camisole so he could choose to remove it when he was ready to face the scars. He never did take it off, though. He was gentle with me, as if he was afraid I might break if he pressed too hard, or that more of me would disappear if he wasn't careful. He was no longer gluttonous — no longer wanting to revel in my body, to consume, not just consummate — and I missed that. A few times, I tied his hands with a scarf to the headboard and I'd say *harder, slam it harder*, the way he used to like me to, but he wasn't into it. When one of us said, "Let's go to bed," we meant it was time for sleep. I think I decided then that it was simply a matter of aging. We were entering a new stage of life as a couple. Surely not all men want to screw until the day they die?

Once I began to sleep alone, I began to dream about *living* alone again; I dreamed about the weeks I spent in my apartment in Toronto before Ted got into medical school, and then about the first few months he lived in the city, but not with me. I awoke from these dreams with a vague, transient sense that I'd just seen Ted the day before, and I missed him in a way I hadn't for a long, long time. I see now that I was letting Ted back in.

ееи

When Ted ended up at U of T in the fall, I suggested that I register for graduate studies in English; the department was practically next door to the Faculty of Medicine, so we could meet for lunch every day. He was discouraging. "What is graduate work in literature, anyway? You walk around the stacks, blowing dust off of old books, hoping to discover one that no one's ever read? Or maybe you sit in an armchair reading stories and discussing them. Oh, wait — that's a book club." He was joking, sort of, and I laughed, a little, then changed the subject.

That was an odd moment for me; it was as if I'd watched a slice of Ted slide away — the person who, when we'd met, had been keen on talking about so many subjects and ideas. It left a new, sharp edge to him that I hadn't noticed before. I suppose that was why I began to tell Prof. L. about my personal interests and relationship-related matters in my letters.

I don't know if I thought of Prof. L. as a father figure, a psychoanalyst, a lost opportunity, or a close friend. The self I revealed to him was entirely different than any other version of me, completely unlike the writer of missives to Josh. When I sent an envelope off to Prof. L., it was thick with pages of what Ted would call self-indulgence.

In one of his letters, Prof. L. asked if I'd reconsidered my plans for graduate school. I hadn't; I still thought I might do a master's after Ted and I had our adventures, once he was in practice — or maybe even after we had a kid or two. While Ted was in medical school, I was happy to travel on my own, recruiting students. My job suited me; I couldn't have worked in an office, day after day, without going crazy from boredom. Ted was pleased with my decision, too. Neither one of us wanted to live an ordinary life. We didn't know what ours was going to look like, not yet, and that was exciting. We were "keeping our options open," Ted said whenever his parents asked about our plans.

Between my trips, I browsed second-hand stores on Harbord Street for better editions of my favourites — *A Portrait of the Artist as a Young Man* and *The Waves* and *The Waste Land* — and I picked up novels that hadn't been on my BA curriculum. I also found a copy of Sontag's *On Photography*, and as I read it, I could feel my brain opening up. Then I read *Illness as Metaphor,* twice in one sitting.

I wanted Ted to read it, too. I had some ideas percolating about the connections between writing and medicine, about language and belief, science and art — all of which would have excited Josh — and I thought it would be something for Ted and me to explore together. I bought him his own copy, brand new, as a present. "No thanks," he said when I handed it to him. He didn't have time to read for fun. Besides, he said, *Illness* sounded like it was full of fancy philosophical footwork, and nothing useful. "Thinking about language *is* useful," I wanted to say. "This book could make you a better doctor, even." But I took the gift back and tucked it away. I'd bring it up again later, when Ted's workload wasn't so heavy.

℮℮

I asked the secretary in the Graduate English Department for syllabi from the previous year so I could stay up on trends in literary criticism, in case I changed my mind about graduate school. The pressed-board bookshelves with cheap copies of the undergraduate canon that lined my living-dining-sleeping space soon warped from the weight of hardcover editions by the heavyweights: Barthes, Kristeva, Derrida, Lacan, Foucault. Since I had a salary and didn't spend much going out, I could afford those expensive books.

I don't have them anymore. None made the cut when James and I moved to the bungalow. Putting them in a box for the library, I remembered what Ted had thought about the program I'd toyed with taking. He said it would have been a waste of time because none of it went anywhere. I guess he could have been talking about us, too.

It is important, when gambling, to keep a poker face. A face of stone. It prevents you from revealing any sign, any emotion or other indication of what you hold in your hand, of what move you will make next.

One muggy summer night a month or so before Ted moved away for good, neither of us could sleep, so I asked for a massage. His hands felt half-hearted in the effort, and he was silent, so I asked what he was thinking about. When he said, "I don't have to tell you everything," I pretended I hadn't noticed the irritation in his voice. "Okay, don't tell me," I said rising, pushing him back-first onto the mattress and climbing on top of him. "I'll just look at you, then. I can read your face, you know." I kissed his chin. "Every quiver." I kissed his mouth, closed my eyes, and sucked a little on his lower lip. "Every look, every blink." I kissed his closed eyelids, one at a time. "Love you, Teddy Bear." He usually smiled when I called him that, but my tongue couldn't feel any laugh lines deepening at the corner of his eye, so I opened both of mine. A thin bar of street light streamed through the gap between the curtains and shone on his face; his expression was serious, almost accusatory. Before he rolled himself out of bed, he said this: "You don't know me nearly as well as you think you do."

A snapshot moment, that scene was a spot of time that produced a physical sensation I couldn't name, but it had something to do with capture, with freeze-framing. Many years later, I read a *Scientific American* article about researchers using MRIs to investigate the brain's activity during memory activation, and

I understood what was going on when I mentally fixed a scene with Ted: the neurons connecting, the synapses sizzling. I could almost hear the sounds they made, too, like sped-up camera shutters snapping, slamming each detail into place.

ℓℓℓ

Lately I've been dreaming of Josh again. It's as if memories are being pulled out of the limbic limbo of my brain, fibre by fibre, to form a filigree pattern resembling the shape of those feelings that belonged to Josh. There must be hundreds of well-inscribed scenes from our times together, lying in wait. Now that I'm alone, letting my mind roam, I am starting to recall details about our friendship that I'd left alone for ages.

Sleeping with him was something I often had dreams about when I knew him, too, but they embarrassed me when I woke up and remembered that he could have any woman he wanted in the city of Toronto. Or New York. Anywhere in the world, really. For a long time I stayed afraid that no one else would measure up to him. But Ted came close.

ℓℓℓ

Ted wasn't a doctor, or even in medical school, when I had that first cyst removed from my right breast. That scar faded to pink but didn't disappear completely; after Ted studied surgery in his third-year rotation, he touched it one night and said the doctor who'd operated on me was obviously old-school, his technique primitive. I was young enough then to think that my body's scar would be unique, that I'd have it always, and that the scare of cancer taking me would be as close as we'd ever come to the possibility of being apart.

For the double mastectomy, my doctor insisted that I book six weeks off work to convalesce, but I knew I wouldn't need that much time. James knew that, too, or should have known: I'd recovered quickly when, a few years after we married, I had an operation on a Thursday to remove an ovarian tumour, and was back to work by Monday. It had been a large dermoid, the kind that wraps itself around a core of hair and teeth and bits of bone that grow in the wrong place at the wrong time. Benign, so it could have been left, but to avoid the potential agony of a future torsion, my gynecologist took the whole organ out.

She assured me that I could conceive with one ovary; she didn't know that James and I didn't want the life we'd made disrupted.

ell

Ted wanted a little girl first, he said, and I wanted a little boy. He asked me what age limit I'd set for having kids. "About thirty-two," I said off the top of my head, and that seemed to satisfy him. I wasn't worried about it; women were having babies well into their thirties in those days.

I was twenty-four when I met Ted, and he was twenty-six. I was almost thirty when he left.

ell

While I was still on extended bereavement leave from work, Gina's kids, Anna and David, both sent me requests to be their "Friend" on a website called Facebook. Gina said she'd tried to learn how to use it, but she's as hopeless with computers as James was. Neither he nor Tony joined, because teachers had to protect their reputations, they said. Being online Friends with students was not exactly kosher.

Going public with my life didn't feel right to me at first, either. How could I create a consistent online persona, when I am someone different with every person I know? Slightly different, anyway. An extrovert might think I am shy, while someone less outgoing than I am would see me as warm and easy to talk to. Then again, maybe a smattering of selves in cyberspace is a fair approximation of a person.

In the months after I quit my job I was feeling more and more isolated, so in the spring, on a particularly bad day when I thought Facebook might at least be a source of entertainment, I made a scant profile, and searched for a few friends from university. I found Tanis right away. She became a dermatologist, and she lives in Windsor with her lawyer husband; they have the two children she always said she wanted. Drifting from people who had children was natural, and most of my close friends from university had followed that predictable path. I didn't need to reconnect with them to feel that I knew them. The problem was me, with the difference between who I'd been then and who I'd become.

I'm still not comfortable with Facebook. I feel exposed, found out, guilty of not being the person I am publicly claiming to be. Of constructing a person who does not exist. Ted once complained that I wasn't socially stable, that my personality was too fluid. He wanted me to present myself a certain way to his friends, to be the same strong person I was with him, in the beginning.

ee

From day one, Ted and I both felt as if we had known each other for years. I didn't have that instant closeness with James, though. I never pretended that I did, or probed for details about his past, or other relationships. And James didn't wonder about whom I'd been with or who I'd been before I met him, either. Who we were now, with each other, was what mattered to us. Just not for the same reasons.

If I were to bump into Ted somewhere now — at a walk-in clinic, say, or an emergency room — I'd probably revert, instantly, to my former, needy self, an anxious version of me that James never met. James never wanted me to be sensitive, clingy, or needy; my independent nature was one of the things he said he loved about me. Why did he want me to be bowled over by my diagnosis? The tumour was caught early, I reminded him. I was taking care of it; I'd be fine. I thought James would be fine, too, once the malignancy was cut from my body, but the wait was hard on him. He called in sick so many times in May and June that his colleagues must have thought he was acting the cancer patient.

James's anxiety hasn't gone away. Or maybe it's come back, and I've picked it up, like a virus. It's certainly not dead, his distress; it is nudging me, making itself known again, inside of me this time.

ee

The radio-oncologist I was referred to said if I followed his recommendation — three months of daily radiation — the chance of recurrence and death was statistically insignificant.

"Attitude makes a big impact on outcomes for cancer patients, Maslen. Your chances are very good without a mastectomy," he chided when I told him I was taking the surgical route. I wasn't going to become one of those radiated women who worry for the rest of their lives that they'll personify that so-called insignificant statistic labelled PMR, for "Percentage with Metastasized Recurrence." I didn't care that this doctor saw me as an alarmist. All I wanted was to be alive in five years' time.

After the surgery I discovered I'd also been referred to a plastic surgeon; reconstruction could be done as a separate procedure, so the surgeon who visited me post-op in the hospital was taking another crack at convincing me. He said it was selfish not to reconstruct, that I should think of my husband. He'd caught me off guard, so I didn't know what to say. I accepted his print-out with diagrams of silicone implants lined up in a row, from small to large. I was to decide on the bust size I wanted, then call his office when I was ready to proceed.

I would have liked to talk to a doctor I knew personally, someone who would understand my perspective, when I was thrust into the world of ultrasounds, biopsies, mammograms, and treatment plans. I needed to talk to someone who would support my refusal of the three Rs: removal of the lump and surrounding tissue; radiation; reconstruction. Not Tanis, who was a doctor by then; we'd not been in touch since I left London.

Ted was practising somewhere, I knew. What would Ted think? Allowing myself to envision him standing before me in a white coat, reviewing my medical record through glasses perched on his nose, produced a familiar desperation in me. It was panic, the same kind I'd felt when Ted told me there'd been an "administrative glitch" regarding his upcoming internship, which of course wasn't true. My body was signalling danger, whether I admitted it to myself or not.

I didn't make any effort to find Ted, then; but I did start to think about him once in a while. And as James and I drifted, in the months after my surgery and into his retirement, I thought about him a little more often.

eight

When I got the call at the office, I listened, thanked my family doctor for letting me know, and hung up the phone. On my way to talk to Nancy, who'd become my closest friend as well as my boss, I stepped into the stationery room. I didn't think about what I was doing as I grabbed a Hilroy exercise book, which looked exactly the same as it did in primary school; I stuck a white mailing label on its cover, found a Sharpie, and wrote "The Boob Diaries" in permanent, black ink.

The Boob Diaries

May 3rd
Gina, James, even Nancy will be extremely upset when I talk about this, so I'm going to minimize those conversations. I'll use this book to record what is happening to me, to document considerations and conversations with doctors, and to record my decisions, in case I need reminding later on. It will have to substitute for talking with someone who understands me.

So here we go...

Dr. R. called me at work today, to say the pathology has come back. Not good — a second opinion was sought and the diagnosis confirmed. High-grade malignant cells, though seemingly contained. He has referred me to Dr. A., a general surgeon. I asked him if a mastectomy will be an option but he didn't want to presume. Dr. A. will explain all the options, he said.

Okay, then.

I went home at lunch to talk to J. He was on his laptop in the living room, and he looked up when I opened the door. I never come home midday, so he was frowning at my appearance.

"I have something to tell you," I say. He smiles, expecting good news, because I'm smiling. Then I tell him what Dr. R. said.

I watch confusion scuttle across his face before pain reaches his brain, as if he's reacting in slow motion to a stab in his back from the blade of some phantom enemy. He stands up, staggers the few steps to where I am, and embraces me.

"It's okay, hon," I say, patting him on the back. "I'll be fine. It's early, very early. It could be much worse."

I don't feel anything. I know I should be scared, or sorrowful, or *something* — and that I should be moved by James's reaction, by his fear of my mortality, if nothing else. But I'm not.

May 4th

This is so ironic. I wasn't worried about the cyst, which had grown larger since the previous ultrasound, but my family doctor was. In April he insisted I see a surgeon, who would order a biopsy to rule out cancer. That's when the fun began. The radiologist who did the procedure missed the lump entirely, but when I questioned him about it he said it just *felt* that way to me — the needle goes in on an angle, etc. etc. Dr. A. wouldn't say her colleague had missed the lump, only that the results were inconclusive, but she ordered a repeat biopsy, this time under a needle-guided procedure using the mammogram machine.

The second biopsy was done by the same radiologist who did the first one, but he acted as if he'd never met me before. While my breast was pressed between the mammogram plates, he looked at the projected image and inserted needles to locate the lesion precisely. I knew the samples he cut out hit the mark by how it felt compared to the first time. He wished me luck when he left the room, and I wondered if that was an appropriate remark to make, considering.

May 5th

It was 3 a.m. and we were both awake. J. held me. We said nothing.

May 21st

I make jokes in my head that I can't tell J., but they make me laugh anyway:

– That's it, no more wet T-shirt competitions for me!
– At least I won't have to line up for the ladies' room at the theatre anymore.
– Paint my toenails, doll, and take me to the Mardi Gras!

May 24th
I imagine telling Gina funny titles for a movie about what I'm going through. *Boobless in Boston. Titless in Toronto. Jugless in Jerusalem.*

May 30th
Consultation with Dr. A. this morning. When we walked in, the secretary said hello in a subdued tone, probably thinking I didn't know the results of the biopsy yet and that I would be getting a shock shortly.

Dr. A. suggested a lumpectomy and radiation, with mammograms every six months for a couple of years, and wanted to refer me to another specialist. I told her I want a mastectomy, to be done with it. No reconstruction, either, no fiddling around with the tissue. I'd heard of people who went through the process of expansion with the pain and the infections that typically complicate things, and then the cancer came back — so no, thank you. She asked James what he thought, which annoyed me. They're my breasts! He said he just wants me alive, which is what I knew he would say.

James insisted she order a mammogram of the other side, too, because he thinks he can feel another small lump there, though I am not convinced.

June 12th

I picked up the mammogram results at the Records Department this afternoon. James was right. The left breast also has "suspicious calcifications." I booked another appointment to discuss with Dr. A. for June 27th.

I haven't told J. about my appointment next week with the radio-oncologist, partly because he is still so upset, and partly because I don't want to have to argue with another doctor and try to keep James's mood up at the same time.

June 16th

Consultation today with radio-onc., who wants me to come every day for 12 weeks to have beams shot through the tumour. I repeated what I'd said to Dr. A. — that I don't want a lumpectomy followed by radiation, I want the full surgery. Bilateral. I told him the mammogram showed suspicious calcifications in the other breast, too, and I may as well have them both off.

His nurse says that what I want is overkill. "It's like putting on huge galoshes for a little spring shower!"

The cancer clinic has had a cancellation, apparently, and I can begin treatments next week. "I'll put your name down while you think about it some more," said the nurse. She booked me in for a measurement and fitting of the body cast, which will hold me in place so the beam hits the exact spot, every time. "There's a limit on what the tissue can take, and we don't want any misfires."

June 17th
I cancelled the measurement booking by leaving a phone message on the nurse's answering service last night.

June 27th
Dr. A. is nervous. Removing healthy tissue is against the standard of care. One breast, the diagnosed one, will be removed, but she isn't comfortable taking off the other one, since it might be fine. Only a biopsy or lumpectomy — which I refuse to waste time with — will be determinative. James spoke up and said that it is prophylactic and also cosmetic, to make me balanced — surely she can understand that? She went away to call a surgical colleague who has more experience. She'll call when she hears back.

July 13th
Dr. A. agreed to do the full surgery. She realized that a lumpectomy, her preference, would have to be so large to capture the suspicious tissue that she'd take half the breast off anyway. It is booked for August 24th. I

worked it out with Nancy: I'll take my vacation days to avoid going on short-term disability, which HR has suggested I do. Don't see why a lack of breasts would be considered a disability. I mean, really.

It dawned on me today that after I have this surgery, I'll be down two breasts and one ovary. Uterus aside, that leaves me with just twenty-five percent of the defining essentials of womanhood. I'd be well on my way if what I wanted was to become a man. I wouldn't mind having a boy's hips again, but that's another matter.

August 20th
The "pre-op" appointment was a waste of time. Blood work, weight — okay, that makes sense. But the nurse wanted me to talk about it with her. She'd have hugged me if I'd let her, but I didn't want her sympathy. I'm not behaving according to the norm, apparently. I'm supposed to be feeling sorry for myself, in mourning for my soon-to-be-gone body parts. I think what people really want me to do is help *them* feel better about their awkwardness over what to say to me. They're projecting, expecting me to react as they would. It's not about me at all; it's about their fear that something could happen to them.

August 25th (noon)
I'm writing this entry on the back of the paper tray liner from last night's uneaten dinner. I'll tape it into my book when I get home this afternoon.

I'm on Tylenol 3 to help with the agitation, mostly in my legs — it was difficult to fall asleep last night, they were so restless. Otherwise, as long as I didn't think about food, I did well for having been under an anaesthetic for so long; unexpected blood loss complicated matters in the surgical suite, I'm told, and a transfusion was required.

August 25th (4:00 p.m.)
Home. Here is what I remember from yesterday (August 24th):

I awaken in the recovery room, nauseated. I hear a woman speaking quietly in the distance. "Hello, Maslen, you're doing great. Can you take a deep breath for me?" It is a friendly voice but belongs to no one I know. "Can you open your eyes?"

I blink a few times and can make out a fuzzy face hovering above me. "Try to lift your head up a little, so you can swallow a sip of water." But a tidal wave in my gut knocks me back. Retching. Dry heaves. A cold metal tray shoved too late underneath my chin. A scratchy paper towel wipes coughed-up mucus and acid from my lips.

The nurse injects an anti-emetic into my IV. Soon the nausea begins to ease. I smell tarnished silver every time I inhale. It reminds me of my grandmother's necklace after it blackened against my skin. "Would you like to see your husband now?" I shake my head, then drift off, imagining it's Ted who is coming to be by my side.

James was at the foot of the bed when I woke up in my hospital room this morning. I was so happy the nausea was gone that I felt euphoric. My lips were dry and tasted like metal when I ran my tongue around them. James found a straw for the Styrofoam cup of water on the table next to my bed and held it to my mouth while I sipped.

The day nurse who came into my room with discharge paperwork was jolly and loud. "Let's take another look at your chest — or at what's left of it!" she said. I laughed, but also thought it would have been cruel if she'd said it to the kind of woman who'd be traumatized by the procedure, and I was glad James had already left to bring the car around front.

The nurse helped me to sit on the side of the bed, my feet dangling far from the floor, and began to peel away layers of gauze. When I looked down at the concavity at the top of my ribcage while she worked, I had the bizarre thought of Gloucester with his eyes gouged out. When the nurse finally reached the wide strips of surgical tape that held the flaps of my flesh together, I saw there were stitches, too — I wouldn't stop bleeding, apparently. "Nice, clean job," said the nurse. Dr. A. came by to check on me, too, before I was escorted to the elevator. Pleased with her artistry, the stitched-up symmetry of my chest, she sent me on my way.

I waited for James in a wheelchair by the hospital entrance. I saw him pull the car into the pickup zone and watched him sit for a few moments, palms held up against his eyes. He looked like a child counting to ten in a game of hide-and-seek, waiting to begin the work of finding where everyone had gone.

August 26th
I slept well last night. I was swaddled, really, the wounds were so tightly dressed.

I wouldn't admit this to anyone, but what I saw yesterday when the nurse checked my chest — what I didn't see, really — made my stomach drop. This was not at all how I'd expected breastless to look, even though I'd planned their departure, agreed to it, even fought for and insisted on it. I felt I'd been excavated. They'd really taken up more of me than I'd realized, those breasts.

September 4th
The home-care nurse was satisfied that the drainage has slowed to a near-stop, so she put the packs of peas James had frozen ahead of time on each side, to numb the pain I'd feel while the tubes were removed. First the left, then the right, she said. Take a deep breath! She pulled and pulled and pulled until the tail end of the first one was in her hands. As she continued pulling the plastic out of me, the sensation produced was like the sting of a rug burn, but it also tickled. Very odd. It was wonderful to be free of the bottles.

I'm free of nipples, too. No more telltale signs of being cold. Just blood-crusted lines with black stitches like a teacher's felt-tip slashes across the page of a badly written essay.

nine

There were times throughout my marriage when I wished I could pack a bag and take off, alone. I was missing the freedom of being elsewhere, or of planning to be elsewhere: of being in an entirely different culture and country and time zone, of hiding out in the open, being invisible to all and unreachable by anyone I knew. A speck on the planet. An individual, not half a couple. Not that I felt subsumed, or that our marriage was complicated; it wasn't. Yet sometimes, with James, I felt that *I* was. Too complicated, I mean. For him.

Life with James started out simply, as a fuck-fest, and that aspect of our relationship remained steady for years. Sometimes when I close my eyes and pleasure myself now, thinking of all the games we played in bed, I pretend James is in the room with me. I imagine him at the end of the bed, watching me, getting hard, while I tell him about my youthful forays and forages — about those times when, bored with the bone-coloured, ridged handle of my mother's ancient and forgotten hair dryer, I'd look in drawers for candles, in the refrigerator for carrots, in the basement for a rubber-handled screwdriver.

We fit so perfectly together, physically, James said; with me, he wanted to keep coming and coming. Simply seeing his face at my door made me wet. We'd rarely make it to the bed, and we'd thrash around on the floor. Because there was only so much newness to be found in each other's bodies, we eventually fell into a routine. It was reliable and fun for a very long time. I might come again if James tied my wrists to the leg of the bed. Sex with Ted had been missionary, mostly, with kissing for foreplay, and it was over when he finished. But oh, how James loved to pleasure me. And with James, for the first time, I was able to think of Ted's escape as my own arrival.

I can't imagine having sex with anyone ever again. I couldn't let any man know my body as intimately as James did. Not now. I don't think I could feel the same way sexually with someone who hadn't known me when I was in my prime, as they say. When I had more parts to me.

Where do they put parts of people to rot, to decompose — to turn into elements, minerals, sediment?

Occasionally I feel a twinge of pain in my chest, like a phantom limb. I've been missing them lately, those pieces of myself. When I think of them, of those symmetrical slices, I still see bloody, lumpy mounds bleeding out into the stainless-steel bowl, punctuated with nipples like brown eyes. A Cyclops, each one, circular sacks of skin-covered fat, the vascular system beneath branching out in fine, spidery lines, spreading toward the outer sawn-off edges like back roads on a map leading to nowhere. I can see them so clearly that it's as if I'd watched the operation happening to someone else.

After the mastectomy, stuck at home and forced into idleness, I thought about how busy my life had been when Ted and I were together — about all the miles I travelled and the weeks I spent away from him, away from home. We'd spent as much time apart as together, but time didn't feel that way as we were living it.

On those work flights, a few minutes before descent, I'd look out the airplane window and see geometric patterns of fields, forests, serpentine lines of water and thin veins with cars following one another in slow motion, like ants, and I'd think *nothing going on down there matters all that much*. It dawned on me that I'd been freed of the constraining hyper-self-consciousness I had been living: I felt myself shrink within the cosmos, and the sense that I was an insignificant element settled my mind. "Sanguine," that was how I'd describe the floating relief that came over me at these times, though when I tried to tell Ted about it he said I wasn't making sense, because "sanguineous" means bloody, and "exsanguination" means bleeding to death. The next time I flew, I thought about those words when the feeling of lightness arose, and I wondered if they made sense in the medical context, too — if bleeding to death would induce a sense of relief at knowing you were about to disappear.

On my way home from one of my last trips to Asia, I fell into a deep sleep and sat still for so many hours in a row that, on waking, my ankles had completely disappeared. My feet were connected to stove-pipe calves that I didn't recognize as my own. Ted met me at the airport and insisted, when we got back to my apartment, that I put my feet up on pillows piled high on the bed. He knew enough about the risk of blood clots to insist I take a baby Aspirin, and he served me salty vegetable broth to get me to pee as much as possible. He stayed overnight, and I felt safe again, secure in Ted's love for me. I couldn't admit that the return of this feeling, and of my being aware of this return, meant that I did not always have it, anymore, with Ted.

Once I'd used up all of my sick leave post-Ted, I expected the travel for work would help to keep my mood on this side of sad, at least in public. I had to take my professional self on the road, to function every day among hundreds of new people, agents and parents and students and hopefuls. I had to keep my numbers up. *Keep moving, keep moving like a shark,* I told myself every morning. *Keep moving or you'll die.* Nancy had offered me an office job, because she was worried and wanted to keep an eye on me, day to day. At first I said no, no way, because accepting it would mean reinventing myself, turning myself into someone Ted had never known, someone he wouldn't recognize when he wanted me back.

ele

I was restless and wanted to go back to work by week two post-op, but Nancy swore she wouldn't let me into the building if I turned up. James had planned to stay home well past Labour Day, though teachers at his school were supposed to be on site for meetings and classroom prep, but on Tuesday morning I convinced him to go. "Gina is coming over today, remember? I'm fine, James, really I am. You need to get back to your regular life. We both do."

While I waited for Gina, I imagined travelling alone again, to somewhere I'd never been — to Morocco or Tunisia, perhaps, where I'd ride camels and be swathed in reams of coloured cotton cloth. And when I got home, James would be his old self again.

The week before, I'd busied myself reorganizing closets and dresser drawers, making piles of clothes that no longer fit me: dresses with darts that accommodated bosoms, scoop-necked blouses that suggested cleavage. When Gina arrived, I asked if she'd take them to the Goodwill on her way home. "I might have to shop in the boys' section for work blazers from now on!" I said. "All that teenage angst I suffered, wanting breasts like yours — and now look at me!" Gina didn't laugh, poor girl, so I tried again. I bent over at the waist, tilting to the right, to the left, to the right, and asked her to guess what I was doing, but she couldn't. "It's the Dance of the Blood Bottles!" I said, but that only made her cry. "You're my hero, Mazzie," she said. "You're so brave."

But it wasn't brave, what I did. I'd taken no risks. What was so brave about being middle-aged and married and facing the world *sans mammaires*? Smart, that's what it was. Brave is something else altogether. Brave is accepting what you thought you couldn't, and finding a way to live with it.

lu

The rugged brown scabs fell off in segments once the dressings were removed, leaving exposed red lines the width of a thick magic marker. But they aren't red anymore; they're more fuchsia, now that they've faded. I hear that for some women, they even disappear completely, but I hope that doesn't happen to me. Compared to what the cyst operation left me with, over twenty years ago, these scars are thin and tidy. They'll gradually become mere echoes of the incisions they once were.

℮℮

Much of my last September with James — what I thought were the early days of returning to normal — is missing. I lived it without the kind of attention that makes an experience stick. My memory faded and now those days have disappeared.

℮℮

Months after James died, I finally surrendered and joined Facebook. I knew I shouldn't look for Ted, but I did. His last name is very unusual; only two matches turned up when I searched, and one belonged to a seventy-five-year-old man who was not his father. The photo associated with the other had been taken from a distance, so it was difficult to make out the person's face. If this was Ted, he was wearing a turban and a djellaba, and standing in the entry to what looked like a cave carved into the side of a mountain.

"Bear, is that you?"

Message sent.

I went on a Message binge, sending Friend requests to Tanis, to work colleagues, to other older friends — people I hadn't thought of in years, like Beau. Notifications from people I'd dated or befriended and then grew apart from, as people do, were not the distraction I needed, because they reminded me of the person I had been when I was young and discovering new writers, ideas, possibilities. The person Ted fell in love with.

Beau looked the same in his Profile picture. He has a deep-brown complexion that he used to play up with his wardrobe of jewel-toned capes and scarves and matching belt-and-boot sets. We had similar tastes and spent more than a student should on things like ceramic wine cups, clear, pale-green Moroccan tea glasses, globe-shaped paper lampshades, and Mexican jewellery. The day we met in the hallway outside our Old English class, he was wearing mustard-yellow jeans, and a shock of thick, wavy black hair covered half of his fine-featured face. He had a curious sexual aura about him, a femininity combined with a sultry voice and the kind of confidence that swivelled heads.

Beau's mother encouraged his fashion experimentation, but she had begun to worry that it stood for other preferences too; she thought I was her last hope, the one to save her son, and she loved me to pieces. But Beau didn't want saving. He *thought* he did, but then he met Tim — whom he seduced right out of the seminary — and confessed it all to me.

After that, we thought that being partners-in-domicile could work. Beau and I talked about living in a big, partially partitioned house, so each of us could have whatever dalliances might come along. I thought that I might be happy in that arrangement: secure without jealousy, nominally traditional. We even talked about raising children, adopted or petri-dished, together. He'd call a baby boy, should we have one, Professor Godbole.

But Beau stayed with Tim, and I met Ted. Ted nicknamed him Bozo. I should never have laughed at that, but I did.

lll

The boys I knew in high school said that Josh was an airhead, though no one had said that about him before he started to model. Josh didn't care what people thought. He often made fun of his newfound profession himself. He'd act out hockey scenes for me, as if reacting to checks on the ice: "No, not the face — hit me anywhere but the face!" At his agent's urging, he had to stop playing hockey — to protect his major asset, he said. Gradually, as his earnings went up, he paid more and more attention to taking care of his body, and gave out a lot of advice on nutrition, skin care, rest.

Josh was especially unrelenting in his campaign to stop me from suntanning. He'd discovered an oil-free lotion in the States called "For Faces Only," and he told me to wear it year-round to protect myself, even on cloudy days. It was unscented, but it had its own clean, fresh smell, like iced tea, and when I said I liked it, he gave me his last tube. I didn't want to use it up, because he was leaving for Europe soon, and smelling it brought him back to me.

I haven't sun-worshipped since university, but I went shopping for sunscreen when I was planning to take Gina's young kids to Ontario Place. I found the same oil-free product that Josh used under a different name; I bought it, though it was five times more expensive than other brands, and it smelled exactly the same. Exactly. I was in the drugstore, inhaling it, and boom, there I was, standing on the driveway at my parents' house, watching Josh as he reached into his car for the tube he kept in his glove compartment, aware that the neighbours would see him handing it to me and giving me a kiss. By the next summer he'd be gone, writing letters from Italy.

eee

I exchanged letters with Prof. L. after I graduated from Western and moved back to Toronto. We lived only two hours apart, but Prof. L. didn't like speaking on the phone, so our relationship became epistolary. His letters, unlike his conversation, were very personal. He told me about his social life and the women he was dating (friends still working on their degrees told me which ones were students); he talked about the complicated bond he had with his elderly mother, who had not yet forgiven him for not becoming a lawyer twenty-five years before. I told him about the relentless trips for work, movies I'd seen, Indian restaurants with terrific tandoori chicken, and my trials with Ted. Writing to him was a very private activity. It felt a little like cheating.

There was a different kind of intimacy in the letters Josh and I used to exchange. It was like keeping a tennis game going: when I opened his latest letter, our connection was in the palm of my hand, but once I let go and sent a reply — lobbing the envelope, dropping it into the red mailbox — the next stroke was his.

Finding an envelope from me in his mailbox could lift Josh out of the bad moods he'd slip into so easily that they frightened him. He said my missives enlivened him, and he needed that. He had "crazy genes" — his mother's legacy. I made him laugh, he said, like no one else. "You're like *meshuga* medicine for me, Mazzie."

I was proud that my pen-and-paper performance made such an impact on Josh. So I confess that I did not throw a life preserver out to him, or wade into those trenches of despair he hinted at. I made him laugh instead, as if that were enough. I didn't tell Josh I recognized the territory he was in, and I did not take those glimpses of his gloom seriously. Each letter I crafted was both a link between us and a piece of the wall I was erecting between us. The invented version of me prevented Josh from getting too close, from knowing me too well.

ℓℓ

Prof. L. told me that he knew when I was depressed because the "I" fell away from most of my sentences:

- "Saw *Interiors* last night. Liked it."
- "Will pack for Beijing after this."
- "Wish Ted had more time for me."
- "Remembering my mother today."

I didn't fuss over wording or set up my sentences for effect in my letters to Prof. L. I'm not sure why that was the case. I pared my words, shared raw shreds of my life in shorthand, like a scientist's log or some kind of anti-diary.

ℓℓ

I found the five-volume set of Virginia Woolf's diaries in a bookstore on Queen West, and it took months for me to finish reading them. I came up with a bio-medical/-graphical theory that I shared with Prof. L. I knew about Woolf's depressions, of course, but in the diaries I noticed a pattern: her worst days seemed to be cyclical, and every three or four weeks she described an immobilizing despair. Over and over again, volume after volume. Did no one ever think of that link? None of those doctors or intellectuals or female lovers of hers? Perhaps she'd thought of it herself but considered it unseemly to connect her moods to hormones, emotions to menstrual fluctuations, to pre- or peri- or otherwise bloody cycles of time — at least in writing.

Prof. L. didn't respond to my diagnosis of Virginia Woolf, other than to say there might be an article in there somewhere.

ею

The July before my double-M surgery, a couple of months after the diagnosis, James showed me an article in *National Geographic* about new discoveries in the Burgess Shale. He'd always taught his students about fossils found in the Rockies, and he seemed eager to work the news of recent finds into the curriculum for the fall. He was grinning when he showed me the colour plates in the magazine: it was the trilobite that excited him, he said, because it suggested the beginnings of an early head.

That day, I thought that James was over the worst of it, whatever it had been: sadness about my health or a mid-life reckoning with his own mortality. I held great faith in the picture of that ancient rock that contained an impression of a life form from five hundred million years ago. It was a sign that my husband was on his way back to me. But he wasn't, not yet. The pounding in his chest and the suffocating panic would fell him, again and again that August and into the fall, well after my surgery had been successful. James likened it to an invisible feral cat that would pounce if you got too close to its den.

James continued to study field stones at the farm, right till the end. Was he seeking something unique in them, looking for subtle variations of colour or striation, to help him decide what to place where? I assume he liked the weight of the rounded rocks, how they felt in his hands. Using a plastic-handled chisel, he scraped off clots of dry, brown earth that clung to some of the stones, which he kept shoved through a belt loop on his dirt-encrusted jeans.

The *National Geographic* issues keep coming. I haven't cancelled the subscription, because I like to see James's name printed on the label. When I open the mailbox and see the golden spine, I can believe for one or two seconds that nothing has changed: the *Geographic* arriving on schedule means that life is continuing as it should. It is crazy, but right now the delivery of a magazine to my mailbox each month is something I am counting on. I've let them pile up on the coffee table. I should move a few of them downstairs, but they are heavy, as heavy as my compilation from Josh's portfolio was.

Josh was wearing new blue jeans and a tight white T-shirt, leather sneakers with their too-long laces undone, the first day I spoke to him. He held one slim notebook in his left hand, a Bic pen sticking out of the spiral binding. It was late afternoon on a sunny spring day, and I wondered what Josh — who rarely attended classes — was doing there. As he approached me in the hallway, I kept my eyes on the bulletin board I'd been reading when he came in.

He said hello in a deep, almost sleepy voice. I turned and narrowed my eyes, then reflected a slow smile back at him. "*Mazel tov*," I said. Josh seemed amused. "For what, showing up?" I found myself pretending annoyance: "No, for making the front cover of the paper today." On my way to school I'd seen a picture of Josh, sitting back to back with a sleazy-looking girl in a low-cut disco dress, in the newsstand. The headline above it said, "Winners of Annual Contest Given a Trip to Florida." "But not together," Josh pointed out. I told him I'd not seen the original prize-winning snapshot of him, published months before as part of the paper's daily feature of especially good-looking people. "Oh, I looked good in that one," he said, "kind of tough, like a young Brando." But his friends were making fun of the front-page colour photo — the makeup caked on his face, the new, shorter haircut shellacked in place for the shoot.

I agreed, it wasn't the best picture. He complimented my sandals and said I had pretty feet. I looked down at them and he asked if I was a ballerina — I was standing in with my feet turned out in position four, more or less. "No," I said, "I'm uncoordinated. I stand this way for balance," and he laughed at that. He might have thought I was Jewish, because most students at the school were and because I could pass. I knew his mother was, so he was. And he'd been dating the Princess for three years, I knew that, too.

A year and a half later, I was at Josh's house helping him pack. After spending an extra semester at our school, Josh still hadn't graduated; but a college in New York State, his father's alma mater, had a Legacy admissions program, so that's where he was going in January. For the few weeks he spent in college, Josh lived with the aunt and uncle who were raising his half-sister. He didn't have his own phone line, so we didn't talk very often, but he wrote to me at least once a week. If the envelope was manila, I knew he had included an assignment. He sent me most of his calculus problems and I couriered solutions back to him, sometimes consulting with my math teachers, Anne and Gloria — not that I needed their help, but I liked to flash my friendship with him wherever I could, now that he'd moved away.

"Calculus, really?" I asked in the note I sent back to him with the first set of answers. "Why, Josh?" Business school was his backup plan, he said, in case modelling and acting didn't work out. He'd need the calculus credit to get in, and with my help, he'd be sure to pass the course. "I know I can count on you, Mazzie."

الله

A few times during the fall after Josh first approached me, he had coffee with Jennifer and me in the cafeteria. Since Jennifer's house was near Josh's, he sometimes drove her to school and picked me up at the York Mills subway on the way. On Saturdays, we'd review everything Josh had said to us the previous week, letting our imaginations skew the meaning of his conversation to our liking. We were silly, but we were having fun. Jennifer's mother laughed at us, told us we couldn't both have him. To me, she said, "And you're not even Jewish."

Josh had broken up with the Princess in August, just before he started to call me at home. He and I had talked a lot more than he and Jennifer had; I soon grew tired of the game I was playing with Jennifer, pretending that I wouldn't mind if Josh paid more attention to her, too. So I betrayed her. How this unfolded isn't important, now, but it worked: she and Josh had a falling out, and I was the one who ended up with him in my life.

ℓℓℓ

When Josh came to my house, I took him upstairs to show him my room, which I'd redecorated myself. The wallpaper was a Laura Ashley pattern, with tiny deep-blue flowers on a linen-white background. I told Josh about the man I'd impressed at the paint store when I taught him how to create a tincture using the colour closest to what I wanted, and adding drops of black — to get the *exact* shade of teal for my nightstand. "Tincture," Josh said. "Like pinching?" He reached toward my breasts, but I pulled away and laughed, then swatted him as he splayed the legs of the blue-and-white china doll that sat at the end of my bed. "I know," he said when he turned around to face me. "Immature. That's me."

That was Josh. When I was home in bed with the flu, he called to see why I wasn't at school. "Would you feel better if I came over and massaged your boobs? Or maybe I could put it in your ear?" My voice was raspy, so when I quipped back — something like "Put it where your mouth is, why don't you?" — he didn't hear me correctly, and he thought I was annoyed at him. So he apologized. "You're the only person who'll tell me if I've gone too far," he said.

My nipples were finally starting to swell. They were so sore that when Gina made fun of them, her finger jab sent a searing ache deep into my nascent right breast. When I complained to my mother, she said, "I think it's time to get you a bra, Maslen." But my development was barely noticeable, and she forgot. Two weeks later, when I asked her to take me to Eaton's, I had to remind her why I wanted to go.

In the store, I hoped no one else heard my mother ask the cashier where we'd find training bras. This sounded embarrassing and surreal, and I pictured breasts as training wheels on a kid's bicycle. We left with a padded lacy double-A teen model, a bra in name only that drew more attention than ever to the flatness of my chest.

By the time I was sixteen, I stopped wearing the regular bras I'd finally grown into. "After all that fuss?" my mother said when she noticed I wasn't putting them into the laundry basket. "They're uncomfortable and unnecessary," I said. "At least in my case." She tilted her head. "Oh yes, I forgot," she said. "You're the *feminist* in the family."

ℓℓ

Josh said it was suffocating, being part of a Jewish family, that the requirement to embrace everyone in the tribe went beyond unconditional; it was inescapable. He was glad he was only half, he said. He wanted a different kind of life — one that would not include a three-car-garage home in the right neighbourhood and a manicured housewife in the suburbs with darling, overachieving children and Friday night family dinners. My family's Sunday gatherings were no different, and I thought I knew what Josh meant about not wanting an ordinary life.

Now I have to wonder if what he was looking for — what we both were looking for, then — was not a different way of belonging, after all. It was more like relief, what we wanted; relief, however brief, from longing of any kind.

℮℮

At the farm, on days that were especially bad for James, I left my door open when I went to bed in my room, so he might feel less alone across the hall, in his. James wheezed in the night like a balloon losing air through a tiny hole, but amplified. I'd turn out my light and listen for the click of the fan we'd bought to help muffle the sound of James's strained breathing; I would hear the blades starting up, their whir climbing steadily with increasing speed until a blanket of nothingness hung in the air between us.

℮℮

Dr. A. told me at a follow-up exam after my surgery that the kind of breast cancer I had is often seen in older women who haven't had children. She also said that a history of cysts correlated with higher risk, which made sense to me. Then she asked why James hadn't come with me to the appointment, since he had been so supportive of me all the way through. In a breach of her usual communication protocol, which was very stiff and formal, she moved the conversation into the personal realm; she spoke quickly, like a teenaged girl, and told me that — though she'd been happy, as a busy single person — she was now dating a man she'd met online, and she was considering moving to Australia to marry him. What was married life like, she asked, and did I think she should do it, did I think her life would be better if she were married? "You have a wonderful husband," she said, not giving me a chance to reply. Immediately she added, "Not all of my patients are so fortunate."

I had deliberately kept the appointment details from James. I felt lucky, but James was still not seeing it that way. The loss of my breasts was devastating for him in some way I still don't understand. Here is how it seems to me now: there was a connection between my successful surgery and James's anxiety attacks that I'd dismissed as coincidence.

ell

Playing the deformity game with Ted: *I would love you if all of your limbs were amputated! I would still love you if you were brain-dead! I will always love you, no matter what!*

Did Ted say that? Yes, yes he did. And it was thrilling; I felt as though I was breathing pure oxygen, and floating above myself, above us both, every time we played that game.

But James said that, too, the day I got the diagnosis over the phone and went home to tell him. And he said, as well, that I could count on him to help me through it.

ell

People can count on me, they say. Ted, Josh, Gina, Nancy. What about James? Did he say ever that to me? No, I don't think so. I don't remember him saying that.

I thought James felt the way I did, or believed what I did: that we didn't need what we didn't have. Maybe that's where I messed up. Maybe I didn't see, or didn't want to see, that James was counting on me — counting and measuring, taking account of what there was between us and coming up short.

ten

James started complaining, after my diagnosis, of a burning sensation in his chest when he jogged. I thought it could be an allergy to something, but James said no, it was more serious than that. "It could be lung cancer," he said, which sounded ridiculous to me, because he'd never smoked. But he countered with the fact that his dad had chain-smoked in the house and in the car throughout James's childhood. "And on the road trips we took every summer, he wouldn't let me open the window because of the air conditioning." We'd recently celebrated James's birthday. "Come on, hon," I said. "You don't really think second-hand smoke is affecting you now, decades later, do you?" James turned his face away from me and sighed. "It's possible, that's all I'm saying. It's possible."

And so it started, what would become James's personality paradigm shift: from highly sexual to self-obsessional, from pleasure-seeking to body-fearing — to fearing what our bodies were capable of doing to us.

lu

When Gina visited me at home a second time after my surgery, she brought bags of chips and chocolate bars and a DVD. We ate our way through *The Way We Were*. As soon as the theme music started, I was sixteen again. The plot, with Barbra Streisand and Robert Redford as the unlikely Jewish/Gentile couple, was the story of Josh and me — the ugly duckling and the stunning boy who'd surprised himself and everyone around us with his interest in me. The feelings that flared up as I watched the movie that day with Gina were fierce, still, all these years later.

Josh and me, our relationship: it was, for a long time, a consistent, persistent connection, and it shaped me. It taught me to know the taste of wanting, the disorientation of relentless unrequited love. I'd left those memories of Josh untouched for so long that I knew, as the film ended, I'd have to be cautious drawing them up again, the way a deep-sea diver has to rise slowly to the surface of the water to avoid the bends.

Gina had probably forgotten about Josh, I thought, but I wanted to say his name out loud, so I brought it up casually after the movie was over. "What a sad story! Kind of like me and Josh. Katie still wants Hubbell, but she doesn't have the right style. Do you remember him, Gina?" She wasn't listening. "Gina," I said again. "What? Oh yeah, Josh was that model guy, right?" She stood up and stretched her shoulders back. "I hate these sagging bags of fat," she said, cupping her breasts. "They give me backaches. I'd rather have a flat chest like yours, believe me. But without the bottles," she added, fake-shivering at the memory of seeing them. "By the way," she said, collecting her purse and keys, "your shower curtain and your Kleenex box are perfectly coordinated. It's *ridiculous*, how well they match."

After Gina left and before James got home, I opened up James's laptop and started to google. There should have been pictures of Josh all over the Internet. A model, an aspiring actor — surely he would have a public profile? I searched online for archived issues of *Vogue*, *GQ*, *Harper's Bazaar* — all of which Josh had appeared in. I knew collectors sold back issues, so I tried eBay: nothing. Craigslist: nothing.

Josh, my Josh, had disappeared.

Months later, a magazine cover I recognized from my lost Josh collection finally did appear on the computer screen. I paid an outrageous sum for shipping the twenty-three-year-old issue of *GQ* from California to Toronto. When it arrived, I turned the pages one by one, until I saw Josh's young face. I knew that picture so well. In it Josh is wearing Italian designer clothes, posing with a blond model who might have been his Norwegian girlfriend; in another photo, he is shot in profile, a melancholy expression on his face, sitting on a patio alone. I'd kissed those moist lips. I'd made that mouth smile so many times. Looking at Josh as he was then made the years spin backwards. Actual pain, not remembered longing, plunged me into a state of mind I could not have explained to James, had he still been there to witness it.

ееее

Falling in love is like being hit by lightning, and there is nothing you can do about it. It's an event, one that turns you into someone new. You fall, you break apart, and you're reconstituted. When it happens to both of you at the same time, parts of each of you slide into the other and overlap, like circles in a

Venn diagram. And if or when it ends, it becomes a remnant, this wrapped-up love, an entity with rings around it for each year of its active life, the final circle a thick contour containing all of who you were when you were together. The rings are a map of where you started from, and where you ended up.

We become chopped up into different versions of ourselves over the course of a lifetime, loving people in whatever way that we do.

At twenty-five, Josh was looking ahead to forty. "Being a model is nothing," he said then. "Nothing." I don't recall how Josh and I managed to let our friendship lapse. When we last spoke, he was still unsure of what and where he should be in this world. I feel sorry for that young man now, and for the young girl I'd been, too, when she fell for him and got stuck there, waiting and wanting, unsure of her worth. We'd smelled sadness in each other, I think, and not known what to do about it.

Thinking about Josh now, thinking back to when he and I stood in his New York loft holding hands, I feel angry at time, and I feel angry at myself — because fear and self-judgment prevented me from cementing the moment by embracing him, from showing him beyond words and smiles alone how much I valued him. I would like to have moments like that one back, to do over again.

What does Josh look like now — still slim, smooth-skinned? Is he still careful about what he eats?

Josh came over to make omelettes for our lunch on a day when neither of us had classes. I cracked the eggs and was relieved there were no red specks in the yolks. When Josh took the butter out of the refrigerator, there were broccoli bits in it from dinner the night before, which embarrassed me, but he just scraped it clean and scooped a tablespoon full into the frying pan, where it bubbled and frothed.

Josh was wearing dress pants I'd never seen on him before. He told me his grandmother wouldn't let him leave the house in jeans, because he was going to "a young lady's house." He seemed a little bit nervous, less relaxed than usual.

I smiled at him, thinking how old-fashioned his grandmother sounded and how sweet it was that he'd obeyed her rules of social engagement, but Josh's story made me nervous. Then he said, "There's five bucks in my pocket. It's yours if you can get your hand in and out without touching me," and we were back to normal. I wasn't brave enough to take him up on it, though, so I said, "In that case, you can keep your money." He laughed and looked at me. "I like that side of you, Mazzie," he said, and blew me a kiss.

Oh, how he teased me. In the school parking lot the day before, he'd said, "Hey, our cars match our eyes. What would our baby car look like, if my green Datsun and your brown Honda fucked?" "Josh," I said, "you know what makes you different from other guys? They think about cars and sex, but you think about cars *having* sex."

One of Josh's shoots in *Paris Vogue* was for a wedding-themed issue. He choreographed some of the shots himself and showed me the one he was most proud of: clad in a tux, with nerdy, round black glasses perched low on his nose, holding a bouquet of flowers behind him, he kneeled before a woman in a white organza gown, her hand held out to him for a kiss. Her expression was hard to read; the word "condescending" came to mind (which wasn't as ridiculous as it sounds, since the model was even more beautiful than Josh), but he said the look she was giving him reminded him of me, of the look on my face when he'd make a joke about sex and I'd tell him to knock it off.

With Ted, the saucy side of me quickly subsided. When he and I were talking about what we'd give each other for our next birthdays, the first we'd spend together, I said, "I'll come up with a list for you, Bear. There are lots of things I'd love to get from you." I kissed him. "You know me — give me an inch, and I'll take six or seven." I thought he'd be amused, but he didn't crack a smile. Nor did he get that rosy flush across the bridge of his nose, the way he did when he started to unbutton my blouse, so I felt foolish. I'd forgotten about that, about the number of times I ended up playing the fool, with Ted.

Last spring, when James and I picked up the keys from the lawyer, he reminded us it was April Fool's Day, and foolish was how we felt when we walked into the house. It had been rented to an old farmhand for years before it went on the market, and it was a mess. We spent a solid week painting and cleaning the kitchen alone, after we took possession. The kitchen walls were spattered with red polka dots of tomato sauce. The bathroom sink was thick with years of dried grime and soap scum, and it took another two full days of scrubbing to make its porcelain shine. My hands were raw from the bleach that somehow seeped into the plastic gloves I wore, turning the powder inside them to slime.

The linoleum that covered the first floor was cracked, curling at the edges, and filthy. It would all have to be replaced and new baseboards put in, too, but I knew James would put that off as long as he could.

lll

The old, cheap flooring at the farm was identical to what the landlord installed in Gina's apartment, where she lived alone while she went to Western. I visited her there a few times in my last year of high school, after Josh went abroad and I'd become lonely again. We spent most of these weekends shopping, watching *Saturday Night Live* with Ben and his roommates, and eating breakfast at a greasy spoon called the Paragon, where students tried to eat off their hangovers.

But one trip was different. It was Saturday night and I was already in my nightgown. I'd followed Gina into the kitchen, where Ben was opening the drawers and slamming the cupboard doors closed. He'd been out with some friends; it was very late, and Ben was extremely drunk. When he started yelling at Gina, complaining that there was no food in the place, my sister grabbed a pound of sugar from a shelf and said, "Eat this, asshole!" She threw the bag in Ben's direction, but he stepped away and it missed him; then he pushed Gina hard enough that she fell backwards, bashing her head on the corner of an open drawer.

After Ben left, I tore sheets of paper towel from a roll and pressed them against the gash on Gina's skull. We sat on the floor next to the split-apart bag for a long time. The red-inked brand name was torn into two words, "Red" and "path," and a river of white crystals flowed between them. Granules had sprayed all over the linoleum, and when I tried to stand up, the skin of my bare thighs was glued to it. In the morning, I told Gina she should charge Ben with assault and get a lawyer, but she laughed. "You don't know anything about men, Mazz. He'll be sorry, you'll see. He'll show up soon with chocolates, and we'll kiss and make up. We do this all the time."

lee

When summer came and James was living at the farm full time, I felt like a hired nurse keeping tabs on a man I didn't know. I was losing patience for my patient. I remember that. I wish I didn't, but I remember that now. We'd been so much more than that for so long, but that summer I'd never been so irritated by my husband.

James would sit on the edge of the bed in front of the fan at night, letting the cool flow crash into his chest. I could see him there, across the hall; he'd be facing the door, his eyes closed, inhaling deeply with his mouth open. I knew without looking when he stood and walked around the room, because the register of the whirring sound changed.

Not sleeping, seeing him not sleeping: yes, I was aggravated. And it was disturbing to me, to be aggravated at him. He had every reason to be relieved — I was well! He should have been happy. He should have been enjoying his retirement. He should have trusted in our life. He was healthy, too: the tests showed nothing wrong. James had not lost weight yet (that happened later in the fall, after he'd spent weeks and weeks working in the field behind the house), so he didn't look sick then, either.

~

The longer Josh modelled, the less well he looked. His agency had him lose weight for a bathing-suit shoot in Capri, and when I saw the spread in *Vogue Italia,* I thought he looked gaunt and pale. By then the newspapers were starting to report that AIDS was striking homosexual men by the thousands, and when I showed the latest pictures of Josh to Gina, she said, "He's gay, all right."

I didn't think so, but I was scared. I was terrified that Josh might be ill and had a sinking feeling that a life-changing fault, something I had no control over, was opening up in the ground between us.

~

There were times at the farm when James was more himself, when we seemed to be close again. One afternoon a bird on the roof slid down the flue and jumped out of the flap on the furnace in the basement; we heard a horrible squawking noise and saw it hopping on the gravel floor when we opened the door at the top of the stairs. We left it open to draw the bird up to the daylight, and it worked; James threw a large towel over it and carried it out the kitchen door to release it. He gently placed it on the deck and when he slowly lifted the corner of the towel so the bird could fly away, I was surprised at how small its body was; after all the racket it had made when it was trapped in the dark, I'd expected something the size of a hawk, or at least a raven.

When the same thing happened the next day, James was less patient. "Again? God, these birds are stupid!" James had never lashed out at any animal, in all the time I'd known him. "I don't know," I offered. "I'd say they're pretty adventurous. Maybe they're bored. Maybe going down the chimney is like a Disney ride for birds." James forced a smile, and we waited for the prisoner to find the light at the top of the stairs.

That night, he was tense again. "I have to do something with that yard. If I don't, you won't be able to tell it apart from the hayfield out back. It's wild." I said I didn't mind wild. "Why don't we leave it?" He didn't answer. "Like the English do," I said. The expression on his face as he paused, just before he answered me: he looked determined, as if he had a problem student to deal with. "This property's too big to be a flower garden, Maslen, English or otherwise," he said. "We have to get a hold on this. Rein it in." I nodded as if I understood James's new need to tame the land, when the whole point of the farm was to let go, to embrace the outdoors without worry. *I hope we don't live to regret buying this place*, I thought.

☙

I didn't regret cutting off my breasts. And I didn't think I missed them, either, until those dreams started: dreams of mouths and tongues and wet, warm affection, my nipples standing at attention. Awake, I missed the weight of them in my hands, slight as it was. They were small, yes, James used to say, but they were eager! He used to pinch pleasure from them with a gentle squeeze, catching them between the knuckles of two fingers, as if holding a cigarette.

In bed with myself, I traced the scars with my index fingers and thought of the first time with Ted, rolling over mid-massage and seeing the surprise on his face, the deepened creases by his eyes when he smiled, the tickle of his fingertips on my breasts. The moment of my self-presentation, the ease of it — of the self, serving up the self. Soon he would say he loved me. He said he'd never felt that way before, he couldn't help himself. The ecstasy of finding each other made us feel like we'd side-stepped our ordinary selves and become two new, extraordinary beings.

Sometimes I think about Ted professing his love to me, asking me to love him always, to promise I would marry him. That need turned out to be a fever that ran its course. But I'd like to know when it was, exactly, during our last year together, that satisfaction and affection started to drain away from him, and for how long he'd had to keep that secret to himself.

That first scar, marking that part of me that Ted had been so worried about until the pathologist determined the cells were normal — it's gone now. As if the scare had never happened to us. I used to touch it tenderly, that wide, whitish symbol of our best intimacy, of Ted's fear of losing me.

I "lost" James. How weak, how soft that sounds. James died. It was not soft. The ground gave way and I fell steeply, landing full force on stalagmites. My entire abdominal cavity felt bruised, for days and days and days.

Weeks into my mourning, when my lungs could expand without my gut revolting, the pain of James's absence became duller. Not less significant, but less like a harpoon between my ribs. A new sensation arrived, an ache that told me I'd lost my way.

lu

"So much loss ahead." James's father said this on the day his house went on the market. And he was right; it was the first of many losses for him. When he moved into the care facility, he'd lose most of his belongings. He'd lose his ability to clean his own clothes, his choice of what food to eat. Lou hoped it would take a long time to sell his house, but it sold quickly — so quickly that he had to take the only room available at the home, on a floor they referred to as "mixed." Lou was one of the few at the upper end of the lucidity scale.

When James and I arrived there to celebrate Lou's eightieth birthday, he was seated at the head of a small table in the activity room surrounded by his "compatriots," as he called the other residents. Many tilted, round-shouldered, in their wheelchairs. They wore food-stained sweaters — layers of them, even in the summer. Especially in the summer, because of the air conditioning. These people had lived whole lives, decades full of events and emotions that no one would guess at, seeing them now: they'd run households, had affairs, broken hearts, and fallen in love; danced and gotten drunk and raised children; held jobs and driven cars, and had favourite foods, music, sports. There they were, reduced to wrinkles and sour smells and familial abandonment.

That day, they waited their turn for a piece of stale, white slab cake and a scoop of vanilla ice cream. We all sang a round of "Happy Birthday" to Lou, and James joined in, though he looked as unhappy as I'd ever seen him. Lukewarm coffee was poured into Styrofoam cups. Its smell floated above the pervasive odour of unwashed hair, wet wool, fresh urine, and reheated gravy. *That's loneliness*, I remember thinking. *That's what loneliness smells like.*

When you're young, you count the days until the date of an event you're looking forward to: Christmas, graduation, reunion with a lover. You can afford to wish your life away when you have so much of it ahead of you. I can imagine being very, very old and wishing I could stop time, stop it dead in its tracks. I imagine going to bed at night worrying that this might be it, thinking *this could be the end*. I think I'd feel grateful, opening my eyes the next morning, for having one more day.

Or not. Maybe instead, if you live long enough, you tire of the limitations, of the sameness, that age imposes on your days. Maybe you begin to detach yourself from time, from its measurement, before you take that ride into nothingness, so that when it begins — the death slide — it doesn't frighten you the way it would when you are younger. Maybe the idea of *non*-life is not so bad, by then.

James couldn't really have been afraid of losing me, at least not for long. He knew I'd be fine, the surgery made sure of that. But maybe he'd been thrown off course by confronting the plain fact of mortality. Mine at first, but also his.

When I was five years old, I saw a teenager die. It was a summer with record-setting levels of heat and humidity that would not break; even the water in the hose we attached to our backyard sprinkler was warm by the time it sprouted thin streams into the air for Gina and me to run through. Our ever-frugal father finally gave in to our pleas one Saturday and took the family to a hotel near the highway that had an outdoor swimming pool. We were going to stay overnight, to get two days' use out of it, but we ended up leaving a few hours after we arrived, because a boy dove into the pool and did not come back up.

The newspaper said he was seventeen years old and that a congenital heart defect had killed him, but it was years before my mother could get me to take swimming lessons. I was nine years old when I registered for a ten-week program; during the fifth or sixth lesson, I saw my mother standing next to Julie, the instructor, looking at the clipboard she carried with her to keep track of the Guppies. "Julie put a nine next to your name and everyone else had a five or a six," Mom said in the car, on the way home. "You're a star, kiddo!" "Those are our *ages*, Mom." I was oldest kid there, but my mother thought that was a coincidence. "You're always so negative, Maslen. I wish you'd look on the bright side sometimes."

Maybe she was right. Maybe I did see a glass half-empty. But when I told James the story and what my mother had said about me, he disagreed. "You were just stating the facts," he said. "She shouldn't have made you feel bad about being right." He started talking about the optics of a glass of water — the liquid surface is not really flat anyway, because of the tension that makes it curve, so you have to account for the meniscus when you measure the water level, etc. etc. etc. James's teacher-talk could bore me, sometimes, but I liked the way he presented that memory back to me.

Once in a while during the long winter before we bought the farm, I thought about what it would be like to lose James — about how I'd feel living alone again, if his symptoms were real and terminal. And each time I imagined being alone, I had to admit that I thought I could manage. *Yes*, I remember thinking, *I'd be fine. I'd be fine without James.*

ℓℓℓ

I would hit James on the back when he started to choke up, and that seemed to help. But one night he couldn't catch his breath, and panic was making it worse, so I tried to distract him. I told him about having the wind knocked out of me once, when I was a kid, and that I knew how frightening it felt. "I was a Brownie, and we were playing something like Red Rover, in the gym. Everyone on our team had to run as fast as they could and rush past the girls on the other team to reach the other side, without being caught. So I ran and ran, and I was so happy that I wasn't caught that I forgot to slow down. I hit the cement-block wall at top speed, and slid to the ground, flattened like Wile E. Coyote." By the time I finished talking,

James was breathing normally again, but he was looking at me as if I'd told him the saddest story he'd ever heard.

"Cheer up, hon," I said, rubbing his back. "I was okay! I thought you'd laugh." I'd told him lots of stories like that about myself before, so I reminded him of a few. "I was such a klutz! I broke my leg on that ski trip, remember that story? And the bruises I always had that made my teacher suspect child abuse? My own mother made fun of me for it, you know that."

≈≈

I often sat with Mom in the evening after I got home, the summer I finished high school. She was still lucid but in serious decline. We'd not spent much time alone together, and like my father she didn't talk about feelings, so we reminisced about safe topics like family vacations. "Remember the time Dad drove us to Marineland?" She certainly did. "Once he found out how much four tickets were going to cost, he almost turned around and went home," she said. "That's why I stayed in the car. Dad would have stayed, too, if you and Gina had been old enough to go in alone." I smiled, and then she said, "At least he left the windows down for me!" I laughed so hard that my stomach muscles locked up with lactic acid and the pain forced me to stop.

"Mom," I said, before I left that night, "these visits mean a lot to me. But they're going to make it harder to say goodbye, too." The pitch of my voice started to rise, as it still does when I speak if I'm upset, and my mother became annoyed, as she always did when I was upset. "Well. When I was your age, I was out with my friends having fun all summer." My mother knew that I didn't go to bars or parties; that Josh was moving to Italy that September; that even Gina was all but gone from my life, since she'd set up house in Mississauga after her wedding in June. "Anyway," she added when I didn't respond, "I didn't ask you to do this. You didn't have to spend time here for my sake."

℮ℓℓ

When I visited Lou by myself, he'd take me on walks to see his friends. "They're dropping like flies," he said on one of the last of our rounds, but not with any sorrow. They named corridors like streets, in Lou's facility, and his room was on "Blueberry Lane." Lou would roam the hallways, hunched over and pushing his walker in front of him like a shopping cart, as if he were going up and down the aisles of a grocery store.

James didn't come with me to see Lou very often. I thought it was because of the grudges he bore against his father. But maybe he felt guilty, too, about having sold his father's house and moved him into the home. Or maybe James avoided the nursing home because he'd simply grown tired of his father, of being responsible for him.

Is it instinctive, this tiring of people you are close to? Perhaps it's a primitive safeguard built into our reptile brains. Elderly parents, aggravating teenagers, long-time spouses — perhaps it's a primal kind of coping, a natural weaning, a gradual hardening of heart before the end comes. Perhaps it makes for a smaller hole to fill after they've gone. I don't know.

III. Beloved

eleven

Prof. L. told me over a glass of wine that he'd been hospitalized the year before I met him. I nodded, thinking, *This is like a Bergman movie*, and quickly changed the subject. I assumed he'd had a nervous breakdown, not only because he was neurotic — he talked about the decades of psychoanalysis he went through, but lightly, mostly in the context of discussing Woody Allen characters — but also because he seemed embarrassed to be speaking of it. To me being neurotic was nearly normal, a source of humour among friends, but a breakdown was another matter. I wasn't prepared to be pulled inside of someone else's vortex. Not Prof. L.'s, anyway.

I moved back home soon after that conversation, to do temp work before my last year at Western. By the next summer, when I was back in Toronto for good, I heard Prof. L. had married a graduate student. I sent a card and a small gift, and he sent back a note to thank me. So began our friendly correspondence.

In one of his letters, years later, Prof. L. told me his doctor had found a melanoma, on his back this time, and he was taking two semesters off to recover from surgery and chemotherapy. *This time*. When I realized what it was he'd tried to tell me that night several years before, I felt ashamed, and childish.

I didn't let myself examine my feelings then, but I am still ashamed when I think about that last evening out with Prof. L. I'd thought, while I was seeing him, that I was so sophisticated, but what I'd really been was judgmental and cold and wrong: I'd distanced myself from a man who'd tried to talk to me about being sick and surviving. Was his need to tell me a test, a means of measuring, through my reaction, how attached I'd become to him? Or was he trying to make sure I knew what I might be getting myself into, if we moved into a romantic relationship? I don't know. I stopped that conversation without understanding what it was about, because I'd taken a hunch for truth. Worse yet, thinking I knew the truth — that Prof. L. was too needy for me — I turned away. That might not have mattered in the long run, because I really was not the right person for him, nor him for me.

But it did matter, that misjudgment. It mattered so much that I couldn't tell Ted about the news in Prof. L.'s latest letter without a fistful of Kleenex. Ted interpreted my tears as sorrow over the sickness of a friend, but it wasn't that. It wasn't only that.

⁐⁐

I am beginning to suspect that James's anxieties had nothing to do with his hypochondria or fear of death. I think it was something else entirely, something deeper. Had James responded to something he'd seen in *me*, something that I hadn't recognized — something, perhaps, that he couldn't reconcile with the person he thought I'd always been?

James and I didn't fall in love at a hundred miles an hour, then gradually slow down over the years; emotionally, we started in stasis, in contentment. We landed where we wanted to be. And it was fine, that place. It was where love existed without worry that there would be turmoil ahead. But James didn't stay there. He slid into a state, without me knowing why, where space and time were fraught with friction, with long days passing, with diminishment.

lu

When I turned forty, I felt I'd reached a peak: I thought I could see the shape of my life behind me. It was a physical sense of place and time, up there, and breathing the air at the height of it was invigorating. I'd stored volumes of my inner self — the people I'd been between ages twenty and forty — in secure, leak-proof vaults.

When James died I was forty-four, nearly forty-five, and I realized that seeing the past is not the same as understanding it, and that the shape of your life is always changing. Your past lengthens and flattens out, as you move forward; the amplitude of major events shrinks the farther away you get from them, like lines on the ECG of a patient with a failing heart.

lu

When James and I had been seeing each other for two months, I handed him a key.

"What's this, the key to your heart?"

"No. Just to my body. For now."

"Okay. I'm a patient man."

Tony's eleven-year-old golden Lab had a tumour on the side of his neck, and in just a few weeks' time it had grown to the size of a golf ball. James was at the farm when Tony called and asked me to take Zed to the veterinary clinic with him. The vet said the cancer was aggressive and inoperable but chemotherapy was an option to extend Zed's life. I didn't blame Tony for saying no.

After Zed was sedated and semi-conscious, the veterinarian shaved some fur from his hind leg and asked Tony if he wanted to stay while the barbiturate was administered intravenously. Tony couldn't speak, so he left to wait in the car alone.

I patted Zed's head and sat with him for a few moments before the final shot took effect. When he stopped breathing the vet donned her stethoscope and confirmed there was no heartbeat, but Zed's eyes were still open, and I was sure I'd seen his chest rising and falling. "It's just the air conditioning," she said. "The current is moving his fur a little." Zed had been breathing, blinking, panting, and then he was not. It was the humane thing to do, to take his life, but it was also a decision that would be difficult for Tony to live with.

The volume of Tony's radio was turned up so high that I could hear Mick Jagger's near-falsetto voice from the clinic door. It was the title song from *Emotional Rescue*, an album Josh and I had listened to on tape as we drove around Toronto the summer it was released. I smiled as I walked to the passenger side of Tony's car, but not with nostalgia. I felt an unexpected surge of strength. I suddenly felt wise, aware of how much people are capable of giving to one another. I was grateful for the chance to support Tony in his grief; I was hopeful that he would visit James more often; and I was optimistic about my husband's new-found pleasure, working with stone at the farm.

ℓℓℓ

When James was at the farm and I was in the city, a glance at the bookshelf where my pottery book sat could bring early times with him back in an instant. I missed the energy that he'd brought into my life. The contrast between then and now struck me hard in these moments, but I believed I'd accepted what was left. I'd adjusted to the new James. He wasn't feeling great, but he was so much better, and that was enough. I thought it would be enough.

ℓℓℓ

It's true that before James died, an old loneliness was creeping back in. Slowly, a little bit at a time. I began to think about close friends who had been important to me at different times in my life, and then not. About how I'd been Auntie Mazz to Gina's kids, but when they hit their teens, I became their mother's sister. About how time alters the nature of human bonds, but so gradually that you might not notice it's happening until they're gone.

ℓℓℓ

Uncle Mark, my mother's older brother, didn't have children. He lived in the US and didn't visit, so Gina and I didn't know him at all, but Mom adored him. She talked about how clever and charming he was, as if he were an old boyfriend. When she called him at Christmas and on his birthday, she'd make herself sound perky, even when she was so sick from the chemo that she could hardly hold her head up. She'd summarize our family news for him, as if Uncle Mark had been dying to know every detail of our lives — as if she could conjure and transfer the intimacy that comes from the dull soup of dailiness by sharing pared-down anecdotes over the phone once or twice a year.

I listened to her talking to her brother, having conversations that could have been with any acquaintance, and I remember thinking, *How can she be so distant from him, after growing up in the same house?* At that time it was unimaginable that my sister and I wouldn't speak to each other at least once a week.

When my mother died, she'd not seen her brother for decades. He came to the funeral but stayed in a hotel, not at the house with Dad. They didn't know each other well enough to have breakfast in their pajamas, as my father put it.

Later, when Uncle Mark packed up his house in Kansas and retired to a condo in Florida, he sent Gina some pictures from his childhood: wee Mom standing two steps above Uncle Mark on the front porch, her arms around his neck; Uncle Mark with his football friends, Mom chasing a ball they'd tossed her way; brother and sister walking the family dog, an Irish setter named Billy, with Mom holding Billy's leash and Uncle Mark her hand. She was looking up at her brother in that one, grinning as though he'd promised her the moon.

She had the same look on her face in another photograph he included in the packet — a wrinkled clipping from the newspaper of the small northern Ontario town where they grew up:

"Local girl marries Toronto executive." Mom was seated, her veil pulled back and resting on top of her bouffant hair-do; he was standing at her side, reaching over to sign the register on the table before them. The long description of every detail — who her bridesmaids had been, who their dates were, the professions of several named male guests, the wedding dress (down to the pearl-trimmed neckline) — it was astonishing, that so much attention was paid to a relatively ordinary event. My sister and I used to laugh at our parents' conventional fifties wedding, but when Gina and Ben decided to marry, she had her own gown custom-made to match Mom's design. She took Ben's name, too. She'd been practising her married signature for years.

ll

Tony remarried in October, a few days before James died. His new wife works in marketing, for a corporation that trades in commodities of some kind or other. She likes to entertain, though I'd not received any invitation from her before the one for Tony's birthday party. By then it had been months since I'd seen Tony — we did meet for coffee one Sunday before Christmas, when he was still a newlywed and I was filled with dread, thinking of the holidays I'd be spending with Gina for the first time in years.

Tony and Kathleen had unplugged themselves from the Internet while on their honeymoon, so I didn't send an email when James died; I left a message on their voicemail, instead. Recording words that I knew Tony would not hear for several days might have been an easy out, but I didn't do it to avoid the pain that his bereavement would inflict on me. I left Tony a message instead of waiting to tell him in person because his bond with James had weakened, of late, and I was afraid that the weight of his sorrow would not be enough.

James and I hadn't seen Tony for weeks when he drove up to the farm last September, to tell us about his engagement to Kathleen. We'd not met her yet, because they house-hunted every weekend that July, and they spent all of August at her family's cottage on Georgian Bay. Tony hoped we would come to the Jack and Jill shower that Kathleen's friends were giving them before the wedding in October. They were going to be married in Hawaii, which was not like Tony at all — Tony, who had flown to Vietnam, Honduras, and Africa on summer vacations, and backpacked through Europe with James after university. A "destination wedding" was not something James or I thought Tony would agree to. We didn't go to the shower.

الله

The birthday party was in May. I was already an hour late when the subway was evacuated due to a medical emergency, so I hailed a cab. The driver told me that when the TTC says there is a medical emergency, it usually means someone has committed suicide. "A jumper, you know?" I *hadn't* known; I'd been taking the subway for more than two decades, and I always believed that those messages meant someone had fainted, or thrown up, or had a heart attack.

A familiar fluttering in my chest reminded me that it had been a long time since I'd gone to a party. I'd never liked parties, which James had understood about me. In my life with Ted, I'd had to force myself to go to his official class gatherings and pub nights, to try to fit in with the other girlfriends. I went to the drinking sessions that followed every exam period throughout his four years of medical school, and then got Ted safely home. Before one of these evenings out, I said, "Stay with me tonight! My nerves are bad tonight!" — joking, but not really. Whenever I complained after that, Ted would imitate my paraphrase of Eliot. I can still hear his imitation of a high-pitched woman's voice, and the sneer in it.

The celebration for Tony was held in the hotel where one of our favourite restaurants used to be — where James and I had held our small wedding-reception dinner. Renovated over the years, it was now swanky, modernized to meet "boutique hotel" standards — grey leather benches instead of armchairs in the lobby, side tables adorned by bamboo shoots in vases with glass pebbles on the bottom, and a clean white counter behind which well-dressed and made-up men and women stood, ready to serve. It had lost the casual, retro feel I had liked so much when James and I celebrated our marriage there. Tony would remember what it had been like; he'd celebrated with us that night. But that was a long time ago. Now Tony was married to Kathleen, and Kathleen was hosting this party for Tony's birthday, and James was dead, and I wanted desperately to leave.

I climbed the wide, curved staircase to the second floor, where the celebration was taking place. Inside the party room, posters dangled mid-air from strings clipped to temporary hooks in the ceiling. These enlarged snapshots of Tony taken at various ages and stages of his life were scattered around the room in no particular order. I recognized the shot of Tony on his restored

Norton motorcycle in the parking lot behind my apartment, that day James introduced us. Tony had brought his camera with him and asked James to take the picture, so he could send it to some woman he was wooing; he still had his full head of hair, then. And there he was in childhood, his blond hair cropped in a buzz cut, standing in front of a garage with his older brother and sister.

There were many photographs that James had taken on trips the two had taken before I met James: Tony in a white T-shirt that glowed in a windowless bar in the Mississippi delta, cigarette dangling, empty jugs of beer on the table; leaning against the wall outside the courthouse in Barcelona, where he'd been caught hot-wiring a Peugeot (the judge believed him when he said thought it belonged to a friend who'd lost his keys — had his bride heard about that?). In these Tony was looking straight at James; I was looking at a moment as seen through James's eyes.

James hated to have his own picture taken, though, and I didn't have very many of either of us. I outgrew the need I had in my twenties to capture memories on film. The day I went to collect the oak box at the funeral home, I saw a brochure about a new trend: emblazoning the tombstone with a glass-sealed, colourized picture of the person buried below. *Buried alive,* I thought, looking at the sample photographs. Perhaps it would be tolerable if an older picture, one taken long before a person's death, were used. At least it would show the person who was already lost to you at a time that you'd accepted was well past. I was glad Kathleen had not displayed any photographs that had James in them.

Tall waiters in tuxes were circulating with silver trays of tiny samosas, grilled tiger shrimp topped with mango tapenade, and Thai tofu sliders. Scores of the stylish chatted in small groups around bar-height candlelit conversation tables. Most of the female guests (who were as thin as young girls, really) were wearing wiggle-dresses, sheaths that a retro television series had made popular again. *Tony's running with a younger crowd now,* I thought, but of course he was — Kathleen was only thirty-four years old.

I noticed a bassinet covered with blue ribbons and bows, next to the gift table, and I was embarrassed that I hadn't known. I was hurt that Tony hadn't told me his news himself, before this. I saw him standing near the bar, his recently shaved head easy to spot above the sea of shorter people with their carefully styled hair. Tony had gained weight since James's retirement last fall; he must have stopped jogging when James did. I had a card for him, with a certificate inside stating I'd donated $560, ten per year of his life, to the Humane Society in his name. I kissed Tony's cheek as he bent down to greet me. "I guess this is a double celebration," I said, trying to keep my voice from rising.

"Birthday, birth — it's all good!" I'd never heard Tony use an expression like that before. Then Kathleen waved him over to a group of friends, and Tony excused himself, and I went home.

ℓℓℓ

Kathleen had selected most of the soundtrack for the party and geared it toward her friends' tastes, but she threw in a few oldies for Tony, including the Stones. When I got home, I played a CD with their greatest hits, and thought of Josh driving us somewhere in his car. Suddenly his sister's name popped into my head: *Leah*. Why hadn't I thought of looking for her before, as a route to finding Josh? When I googled her name, I found an article it appeared in; it was in a newsletter from the synagogue where Josh's mother's family had long been members.

The blurb was Leah's wedding announcement from many years before. Leah's husband's surname was inserted *before* her own, not after, which was a new twist. There was no hyphen, either. I liked that about her; she'd used her husband's name to complement her own, not to replace it. In a later issue of the newsletter, I found a birth announcement for Leah's first baby, a girl whose middle name is Josh. She'd be a teenager herself by now.

I'd noticed Leah's mother-in-law's name elsewhere in the same newsletter, so when I googled Josh after that, I included Leah *and* her mother-in-law in the search, in case I might catch news about him through Leah's extended family. Leah would lead me to her brother.

᷒ℓℓℓ

Cities I travelled to after losing track of Josh:

- Beijing
- Guadalajara
- Seoul
- Tokyo
- Dalian
- Dhaka

– Chengdu
– Harbin
– Caracas
– New York

New York and Tokyo aside, I didn't expect that Josh would have gone to any of the places I did, so I didn't think of him when I was travelling. This surprises me now — now that I've had so much distance from Ted, who had my whole heart in those days. And now that James, who did not, has released me from his.

ell

I'm sure Josh has aged well. I can imagine his mature hand-someness based on the face I knew so well, the way police artists can sketch a present-day likeness of people who were kidnapped years before as children: he'd have greying curly hair, like James's, though Josh might colour it — men do that now; and he would have taken exceptional care of his skin, his physique — his assets. Was I up to seeing him, though? Was I up to him seeing *me*?

In June I was reading a members' newsletter from the AGO, when Josh's sister popped up by proxy again. Her in-laws had donated a small Picasso sketch to the permanent collection, and a public reception was to be held in July, to thank them for the gift. I marked it on my calendar, though I knew it would be hard for me to speak to Leah if she were to attend. I'd seen her just the once, when we were both teenagers, and we'd not been easy with each other — I'd not been easy with her. Maybe Leah would not want to help.

That tiny photograph on Facebook of a person in a djellaba *was* Ted. As soon as he accepted my Friend request, he changed his Profile picture to a headshot, and there he was: silver hair short and bristly, almost buzzed, with a receding hairline; aviator sunglasses; that sharp bump in the bridge of his nose. Clean-cut and still slim. Whoever held the camera must have called out to him, because he was craning his neck instead of turning completely around to look at the photographer. I'd know that smirk of false surprise, that pleasure at being looked at, anywhere. It was chilling, seeing it again, on a face I'd not watched grow older. But I didn't — I didn't — what's the word, swoon? I didn't swoon.

The names on Ted's Friends list were not familiar to me. He didn't seem to have kept up with his medical school classmates, and I wondered if they'd really been as close as Ted always made them out to be.

What I didn't tell Ted, when he asked if I'd run on the beach with him one day, he in a tux and me in a long white dress, was that I would never agree to a traditional wedding. The idea of wearing a white dress and being "given away," not to mention taking someone else's name, was deeply offensive to me.

Gina had had that kind of wedding. (At the reception, which Mom was too sick to attend, Dad said, "Mazzie, I can only afford one big wedding, so you'd better plan to elope.") I was Gina's maid of honour and agreed to wear the frilly, light-blue satin dress she'd had made for me, but I wasn't about to wobble around on the high heels she had dyed to match. I bought some flats, white with a strand of blue woven into them, which I thought was enough of a concession.

We fought about it. My mother insisted I stop being selfish. "It's *her* day, Maslen. It won't kill you to wear those shoes for a few hours." My mother was dying, she would be dead in a few weeks, but my anger was tough to temper. "Really," I said as calmly as I could; I was acting, practicing the script that I'd write out and send to Josh. "I thought forcing the bridal party to spend money on ugly shoes and dresses that will never be worn again — somehow I thought *that* was being selfish. I stand corrected."

They're like disappearing eyebrows, I thought, those scars I wore on my chest. At first, when they were bright red and sharply angled, they expressed anger; then they lightened up to a rosy pink and relaxed, showing mere surprise. Eventually they will fade and become nearly invisible, but I don't want to lose them. Not because they're like an epitaph on a headstone, marking the fact of an existence, making their former presence on my body known: "We were here." They are not memento mori. But they are memories, body memories. They don't say, "Mourn"; they say, "You're still here. You're here, now. So live."

That last summer with James, a sense of unease, a free-floating kind of anxiety, settled over me. It was brief and infrequent, this feeling, and it was nothing compared to James's ordeal, but I knew it meant that I was keeping something from myself.

I know now that at least part of what caused it for me was doubt. Doubt that James would ever return to his normal self. And something else, too, perhaps — an inkling of a slipping-down feeling of my own, of that smooth slide of letting go.

twelve

Tony visited us at the farm only twice. He and James went for a walk out back, the first time; James was proud to show Tony the extent of the property, and the woods behind our acreage. The second time, when he told us about his engagement, Tony asked James all the right questions — "How are you feeling? Anything new from your doctor? Enjoying retirement?" but they were almost by rote. I could see he was losing interest in the minutiae of James's suffering and in the tests that continued to turn up nothing.

ཉ

Fine-fabric dresses worn several times by one person keep the imprint of that figure for decades. Such garments are diagnosed: they are said "to suffer from memory."

ཉ

"You forget all the pain once you hold your newborn in your arms." That's what my mother always told me, but I find it hard to believe. Surely a woman's body remembers that extreme alteration of itself — the stretching of the cervix beyond belief to accommodate the baby's head. "Labour" seems far too gentle a word for what I imagine it must feel like. Gina had difficult, long labours: thirty-six hours for Anna, who was over eleven pounds and whose birth required two hundred stitches for Gina. David was smaller, but no more eager to leave the womb. Ben gave Gina diamond rings after each of their children was born.

ееи

The only jewellery I've ever worn is my wide, rose-gold wedding band, and earrings to match to whatever outfit I put on for the day. Each morning before going to work, I'd feel a small surge of satisfaction as I selected the perfect pair and slid the hooks through my pierced ears. I have a huge collection, some from the countries I've been to, but I also made many pairs by recycling fake pearls in various combinations. These two- or three-bead creations hang on baker's cooling racks that James attached to a wall in our spare room. I still get a synesthetic pleasure feeling their colour when I look at them dangling there.

It's the same pleasure that I got from the clear bottles I filled with coloured water and set in my window, when I lived alone after university. To achieve the shades I wanted, I put each of the basic food dyes — red, yellow, blue — into clear glass lab bottles, which I filled with water; then, using a syringe, I created purple, gold, and green as if by magic. Ted was impressed that I'd used titration to make colours, though he didn't understand what I meant when I said that, for me, they had a tactile quality. I loved the way those jewel tones in jars splashed panels of gemstone-shaded light across the sill and onto the floor, like a temporary piece of art.

I'm smitten with *Yo*, Picasso's self-portrait at age nineteen. Yesterday I looked at the reproduction in a modern art monograph I've had forever. He is posing in a billowy bright-white shirt, and a coal-black hank of hair drips down the right side of his broad forehead. The orange of his cravat blends with the colours on the palette he holds to the side. I imagine that the canvas on the easel we can't see is also a self-portrait, another picture of Picasso painting himself. And in that painting there is another smaller Picasso painted on another smaller canvas, and so on — a *mise en abyme* that makes the abyss seem not dark, but celebratory.

The teal background is made up of vertical strokes in navy and green, which the eye blends. The brush lines create an energy that seems to push Picasso's body off the canvas — as if he is ready to be catapulted, to bounce down and stand, suddenly alive, in front of you.

I'm going to the AGO again. I wander around without following the arrows pointing visitors to this or that collection. Some paintings can stop me dead — a Gabriele Münter or a Kandinsky landscape — and I look at it until I know it, until I can close my eyes and see it. If I stand there staring long enough, a navy-jacketed staff member will start to circle the perimeter, getting closer on each pass. If Josh were with me, he'd probably act out a call requesting backup: "Suspect is wearing a khaki obi belt cinching an oversized maroon T-shirt tunic at the waist, with a pair of sheer grey tights topping black ballet flats, no socks. Strands of fine, pinned-up silvery hair are sliding loose and lining her neck. She's a mess."

I probably do look askew, because I still am.

ece

Gina has always said I look better in pictures than in real life, and she isn't entirely wrong. I've started to build a Facebook album with some of those I kept from work. I looked through hundreds of photos in which I posed proudly with language students after their certificate ceremonies. In most I have an arm around one or two of them. They often looked both happy and sad, preparing to go back home to their regular lives.

One of my favourite students was from Korea. He wore large, black-framed glasses and had uneven teeth and acne, but he was always smiling. Most who came to study English with us gave themselves English names — Lily or Kate, for girls; Joe or Phil, for boys — but this fellow called himself Garden. He liked to talk with me at the reception desk. He'd ask me questions before class, like "What is a Monday-morning quarterback?"

Part of the reason I enjoyed my work was the brevity of the relationships I formed with students, parents, teachers, and colleagues abroad. Even after Ted left and I accepted the administrative post Nancy offered, I kept apart from the people I worked with. I comforted the homesick, assisted struggling learners, reassured family members, and supported classroom managers, but it was easy, since the end had been in sight from the beginning. Those connections were circumscribed, limited. I thought of myself then as a warm person because I was perceived that way. But "controlled" is what I would now, to describe what kind of person I had been.

℮℮℮

Gina had been married to Ben for ten years when she decided to have the sagging skin under her eyes surgically removed. For ten thousand dollars, a plastic surgeon would make slits under her lower lash lines and snip off some of the fatty tissue from the pouch below each eye, before sewing the two raw edges back together. She scheduled it for a time when Ben was away on business, because she wanted to surprise him with the return of her youth.

I was her escort for the day surgery, which took place in a Yorkville office building that looked like a five-star hotel. Just before she was called in, Gina told me she was afraid of being put under, but the doctor assured her the results would be worth it. "You'll look amazing! Your husband will be thrilled by the transformation, believe me!"

I had all of Gina's rings in my purse for safekeeping: her wedding and engagement set and the two stacking, bejewelled bands Ben had given her after the children were born. I didn't want an engagement ring from Ted, and that bothered him for a while. James was happy as long as we wore matching wedding bands. I've never shared my sister's taste for bling, but I was bored and started to play with Gina's jewellery. As I sat under the fluorescent lights, listening to the receptionist provide prices to callers ("You may as well do your upper lids while you're at it, for the extra five thousand"), I was taken with the way the large, bezel-set gems shone when light struck their

some angles they became little round mir-
hatever happened to be in the way — ceiling
wall, a part of my face. Little pieces of clarity,
es made valuable by the sheer weight of the
e.

When Gina woke up from the anaesthetic, I took a post-op
picture of her face for the record. "You're the best friend I've
ever had, Mazz," she said. She wasn't fully coherent, but I was
touched. I promised her I wouldn't put the photo on Facebook.

lee

Ted didn't pay much attention to my Facebook postings. He
"Poked" me once; I didn't quite know what to do with that.
More recently, a notification flag appeared on my Home page,
indicating that Ted had "Liked" a photograph I'd added to an
album. How strange, I thought, to have Ted looking at me but
remaining unseen — both of us remaining hidden from each
other. We were sending glances from afar, playing a game of
hide-and-seek for grown-ups. I was disgusted when I realized I
wanted him to want me again. She was still there, that version
of me, the person I'd been with Ted. I'd kept her locked up for
as long as I'd been married to James.

lee

Tony brought Kathleen to the house after their honeymoon,
perhaps to give his new wife a glimpse of who he'd been for
decades — the man who had spent countless days and evenings
at our bungalow, who'd been so close to James. For Tony, I was
the last link to that James, and for me, Tony was a link to the
younger James I'd never known. When I opened the door and

saw Tony and Kathleen standing there, I realized that the night was not going to go as I'd hoped. It would not be a time for feeling close to Tony or to James. It couldn't be. Because this was the beginning of Tony's leaving.

James used to say that Tony handled problems in his relationships like a magician: he moved people into mental compartments, created new boxes or rooms for them to live in, and then let a mysterious fog hold it all together. Without fully abandoning the person, he'd slowly start to share less about himself, and to recede. He was so good at this that the person he was forgetting about would come to believe that he or she had been the one who initiated the separation from Tony.

Tony had put James in one of these small rooms before James died, and now I had one of my own.

леи

I knew I wasn't meeting James's needs once he retired, but I didn't know what, exactly, they were. I watched James alter course, but I didn't know how to turn him around. I tried to be patient and compassionate, to explain away the concerns he raised, but that seemed to annoy him. If I had known more — known him better, known what else to say, known how to read the signs of his particular kind of despair — I could have been a better wife to James. But I'd married a man who had not been much interested in discussing or exploring feelings; he'd prized clarity, and desired it, and then he changed into a man with indecipherable needs. We were caught in a stand-off that neither of us had the know-how to end.

The scars no longer stare me down in the morning. And during the day, when I stretch at the gym or reach for an ingredient on a shelf in the kitchen, the skin across my ribs doesn't pull as much. My eyes don't go there when I undress at night, either.

As the second anniversary of my surgery approaches, I've been thinking about posting something brief — something along the lines of, "Two years down, three to go!" I think I want to do this to tell Ted, without telling him, what happened to me. To see what, if anything, he might say.

He's still there, Ted, where he's always been. Contained in that spot in my heart, where I left him, once James and I became a married couple. And this, what is this I am feeling now? Is it love, the same love? Yes? No. No, of course not. This must be grief. The old grief resurfacing, slowly seeping out, while my mourning for James carries on. Yes. That's it. That's what it must be.

ℓℓ

Life with James had been so easy, for so long, that I didn't realize how much work a marriage could need — how much of an investment it was, when you pledged your heart to another person. I knew you had to make an effort to keep moving in the same direction, at the same time and pace, even if that speed is zero and you are both trying to maintain equilibrium. There is some art to that. There is probably even a book out there called *The Marital Arts*. I thought I'd seen a book with that title while browsing one day, but when I picked it up to peek inside I discovered it was really called *Martial Arts*.

The last time I worried about being asked whether or not I was married — an awkward question, for my generation — was in the pottery class I took the winter I met James. There were four other women there, and when the teacher asked us to say something about ourselves, three of them identified themselves as stay-at-home moms; the fourth had a husband who'd recently retired — *dramatic pause* — "Enough said!" The teacher had that horrible, snorting sort of laugh, and got the hiccups. I spoke last and said only that I worked in international business, which they had no interest in. They didn't ask why I was wearing a lab coat instead of the recommended apron, either. It was Ted's, the one he'd left in my closet, and it still carried a trace of his scent.

Now, if asked, I would have to say I am a widow. "I've been widowed." That sounds so selfish, doesn't it? As if James's death was an act of violence against me.

On Facebook my status is "Married." I'm still wearing my wedding ring.

        eu

Even though I was thirty-one when I married James, I felt like a child when it came to things like love and loyalty and letting go.

        eu

While James worked on his stone construction — the Great Wall of Nowhere, he knew some men at the hardware store in town called it — he wore jeans and plain white T-shirts that wouldn't come clean without copious amounts of bleach, had he used it. "What difference?" he'd say when I offered to try; he was working alone in the field. I wouldn't have mentioned it, but I thought James might feel better if he put on some fresh clothes once in a while — when he went into the hardware store or to Village Groceries, for instance. It might have given him a lift.

When I'd pull into the long driveway and see him unloading yet more stones behind the house, the brown and grey splotches covering his clothes always reminded me of camouflage. I'd rub my fingers together at the thought of the grit and dirt on those rocks he handled, which dried James's skin so badly that it fissured.

ℓℓℓ

Gina's eyes were bleeding. When she woke up after the procedure, she was delirious and made jokes with the nurse, who dabbed at the rivulets of blood streaming down her cheeks. Her rings were still on my fingers, and she fiddled with them as if they were a rosary. Her nails were chipped and bitten, as they'd always been. They harboured black grime under the crescents, despite the diamonds, and could have been cleaned up with a fifty-cent nail file from the drugstore.

ℓℓℓ

Gina's menopause has started. I'm going on forty-six now, so the end of my cycle could start any time. Gina says perimenopause was hell on earth and just as hot; she set up "pause stations" in her bathrooms at home — piles of clean towels, a few light-cotton sleeveless blouses, a tabletop fan, and a hair dryer — and carried a change of shirt and bra when she went out. Nancy went through the same thing; she told me they call it "the change" because you have to change the sheets most nights for two years running. The only point I can see for hot flashes, evolution-wise, is to deter men from wanting sex with cranky, damp, red-faced females whose eggs are well past their prime. "It sort of makes sense that men go for younger women, when you think about it," Gina told me once. "I want to tell Ben to leave me alone, but you have to pretend you want to, or they'll go elsewhere. That's marriage for you."

ℓℓℓ

When Gina was discharged from the clinic, I had her home before the kids finished school. Anna was nine and David was five, so I'd booked a couple of days off to take care of them while Gina kept to her room and rested. She wouldn't let the kids see her without her wide-lensed sunglasses on. I told them not to worry, their mom had an eye infection but she'd be better soon.

That night, I bathed her sutures with warm salt water to prevent encrusted blood from sealing her eyes shut. In the morning, the bruises were worse than anything either of us had expected, based on the post-op photos of other patients the surgeon showed us: her face looked as though it had been badly beaten. By the time Ben came home ten days later, the bruises had faded enough for makeup to cover them. Gina called me the next day and said Ben hadn't mentioned anything, good or bad, about her looks; but he'd been very affectionate with her, so she thought that the operation had done the trick.

I don't think she has looked the same since. The puffy bags underneath each eye have disappeared, for the most part; but her left lid pulls up at the outer corner as if it is being pinched, and the eye looks smaller compared to the still-round shape of the right. She seems to have an intractable one-eyed squint. James said he didn't really know what I meant, when I asked him if he noticed, but every time I see Gina I think she looks like Picasso's portrait of Gertrude Stein.

‎ℓℓℓ

Early in our marriage, I thought that James might have been better matched with someone like Gina. She skied, she played volleyball, she was decent at tennis. She doesn't do any of those things anymore, but had she been with James, who'd taken his health and physique seriously for most of his life, maybe they would have encouraged each other. Maybe James's legs wouldn't have atrophied after he stopped lifting weights and jogging. Maybe he wouldn't have needed a hobby farm to fill his days.

I'd been in that hospital one other time, long before that night. When I was thirteen, on a school ski trip, I suffered a bad leg break, a spiral fracture. My right tibia twisted as it cracked. Friends and teachers soon found me, but I lay there between moguls for close to two hours, waiting for the busy rescue team to arrive with a sled. I don't remember the pain as much as confusion and immobility, the sensation that my back was frozen to the ground like a tongue on a cold metal pole. Voices were floating above me, telling me not to move (as if I could!), asking question after question to keep me talking and conscious: "Where were you born? How many brothers or sisters do you have? What are your hobbies? Tell me where you live, what your address is. What route do you take to get to school? Do you ride a bicycle in the summer? What's your favourite book? Movie? Dessert? If you could have a big bowl of ice cream, what flavour would you choose?" It wasn't often that I was surrounded by a group of people paying this much attention to me. I thought carefully about each question as if I were taking an exam — as if they were testing me to see if I met their standards, to determine if I was worth saving or not.

ℓℓℓ

"Ben's been promoted again."

"That's great, isn't it?"

"No! We don't need the money. It just means he'll be home even less than he is now. He's not even doing the check-in with me during the day anymore."

"Sounds like Ted in his last year of med school. I hardly saw him. And he definitely didn't check in with me."

"At least you had your job, and your friends. I have to stay home 24/7 with the kids. *His* kids. I hate my life."

"Come on, Gina. You wanted to be a stay-at-home mom. That's what you always said."

"Children screw everything up. Ben and I were fine, before I had Anna and David. You just don't feel the same way about each other, after kids."

ℓℓℓ

When Gina was fifteen, she started smoking in the basement at night after our parents fell asleep. When she came upstairs, I smelled cigarettes on her clothes. "If you tell," she said, "Dad won't believe you. Mom, either. She doesn't even *like* you."

I didn't refute what Gina had said. But I didn't tell my parents about her cigarettes, either. A few years later, when I started smoking in the basement myself, I thought again about the night of my sister's taunt, and I became determined that my mother's coolness, her limited level of affection, would not undo me. By the time she died, I had come to feel exactly the same way toward my mother as she seemed to feel toward me.

For some time afterward, in part because of what had killed her, I used blood clichés to describe her to new friends who asked what my mother had been like. She was cold-blooded. You can't get blood from a stone. There was always bad blood between us. Blood isn't always thicker than water.

My mother said to me once, "You can't know what is inside of my head, Maslen," and I thought she meant that I wasn't as smart as I seemed to think I was. Now I realize she was being truthful, and precise.

Sometimes it is necessary to forget in order to remember a person.

≋

Perhaps a baby will be Tony's means of forgetting himself. Maybe he will name his baby James, or Jamie, if it's a girl. Was that why he changed his mind, at his age, about having children — did James's death have that effect on him? I know this is pointless, this questioning of Tony's motivation. None of that matters now. Besides, I don't need any more proof that people change their minds about things, about major, life-altering things, all of the time.

Tony told me that James would never deliberately endanger himself. But he wouldn't necessarily tell me the truth, either.

One day, maybe after another few months pass, Tony will find that he is severed from James and their shared past. He will also realize, on the same day, that he had no choice but to cut me out of his world, too. We won't see each other again, and Tony will rarely look for the missing compartments where he kept his old friends. From that point forward, Tony will carry on building his new self, creating newer versions that Kathleen will continue to know for the rest of their lives together, the father that their children will know and hear stories about and remember at family birthday parties and beyond, long after Tony is gone. The way I remember Josh, and my mother; the way I will eventually remember James.

thirteen

One recurring dream I had about Josh after James died was so realistic I could feel the tautness of his face when my hand touched his cheekbones. I'd gone to his grandmother's house, and there was a car in the driveway with a sign that said, "Car for Sale: $495." It wasn't his Datsun 240Z, the green one we'd buzzed around Toronto in, but a black sedan. When he opened the front door of the house and told me he was leaving to travel the world, I told him I couldn't stand not knowing when I'd see him again. He put his hands on my shoulders and looked me in the eye and promised he'd come back. But then we were in a hospital, and he was in a private room waiting for test results. He was having severe abdominal pain and was being given expensive bottles of Scotch to drink, to control it. I chased a nurse down the hall asking what was wrong with him. "I demand to be heard! This is unacceptable! I am like *family*!" I was shouting and running after her until a pair of doctors held out their arms to stop me when I reached them.

Suddenly I was back in his hospital room, or in the lobby of a hotel that was also his room — it was a public space, anyhow. He was in a blue chair and I was sitting on his lap, straddling him, my legs threaded under the arms where he rested his elbows, my hands clasped behind his neck. I was trying to talk to him about his medications, and he touched my nipple. He looked up at me and said, "Okay, it's time," and we started to kiss. His lips were so full and soft and then he was inside me and it was wonderful and wet and he filled me with his hard-soft self and we were cuddling and I clung tight and he said he had to go, he was going to a friend's wedding and no, I couldn't go with him, he already had a date.

lll

The weekend I went with James to his father's house for a family talk about safety — about our concerns that there was no one there to keep an eye on him — the front door was locked and no one answered our knocks. We found Lou in the back yard, trimming a tree. James convinced him to come into the house.

I made sandwiches while James began the conversation. "Dad, come on. Be reasonable," James argued. He was losing patience already. "Dad, when we got here, were you or were you not standing on a ladder that was leaning against that dying oak tree behind the house?" "I was," said Lou. "And did you have a chainsaw in your hand?" "I did," said Lou. "And was it *on*?" "It was." "I rest my case."

lll

James was the end of his bloodline. His father wasn't shy about telling me I should get pregnant before it was too late. If James didn't have a child with me, there would be no life after death for either of them. "I'm a practical man, Maslen dear," Lou told me. "I don't expect to live on in heaven any more than I believe in UFOs. We're here, then we're not. But passing the genes on — that's a kind of immortality. Is that too much to ask?" "If that's what matters," I suggested, "then one of you boys can donate to a sperm bank." And Lou laughed! Not James, but Lou.

James became irritated by the rapport I developed with Lou. At first he'd been relieved that I didn't find Lou's personality difficult, as his ex-wife, Andrea, had. Gradually, though my visits to his father alleviated James's guilt about not going very often himself, he became less appreciative; and then, I think, he became jealous. I think James was angry that Lou hadn't been a person he could talk to openly, the way Lou talked to me. He wouldn't have said so, but he probably saw it as a betrayal by both of us.

℮℮

Lou had been a salesman his whole working life. He travelled the province for decades, selling medical equipment to hospitals and clinics, and enjoyed the deference people gave him because of his association with doctors. When his gait worsened, I hunted for a cane that Lou wouldn't find as embarrassing to use as the generic aluminum model with black foam covering the curved handle and a beige rubber stopper on its end. Something stylish. I'd once seen a man in a doctor's office carry a cane made to resemble a hammer, and he told me, when I admired it, that he'd made it himself from a pattern. With my skill set, that was out of the question. But I found a website that sold customized canes, and ordered one.

When the cane arrived it was more attractive than it had looked in the digital catalogue. It was made of a single piece of wood with a whorled grain, stained a golden oak with a clear, glossy varnish. From the base to the top, it widened into the shape of a large handsaw, except the teeth were missing. The handle had carved finger-holds to mimic a saw's grip, and it was painted black. The rubber tip was black, too, and it finished the whole thing off like the period below a question mark.

Lou looked up at me from the chair in his room, where he sat to do crossword puzzles most days after lunch. I held the cane out to him and he stood, unsteadily, to accept it. When he understood what I'd done, he took my hand and held it to his cheek. We stayed that way until his arm started to tremble. "It's from both of us, Lou." "You are a treasure, Miss Maslen," he said.

lu

— I still dream about you, Josh.

— You do, Mazzie?

— Uh huh. I do.

— I must be pretty special then.

— In your dreams, buddy.

— No, really. Tell me about your dreams. How old are we?

— Oh, you're about forty, I'd say.

— Are we happy?

— We drink tea and talk.

— That's all?

— No, not all.

— I didn't think so.

— But mostly. Mostly tea. And talk.

— And we're happy.

— Yes. We're happy. We are very happy, Josh.

lll

I knew when he left that Ted didn't want me anymore, but for some reason I imagined he'd stay a bachelor. I imagined him flirting and flitting from woman to woman as the roaming, proverbial moth-attracting flame he'd fashioned himself to be before he met me. I suppose I wanted to believe he couldn't love anyone else the way he'd loved me.

In a new Facebook photo album he created, called Trip to Venice, there is a picture of Ted in a group of tourists drinking wine on a patio: he is leaning over to put his arm around a woman at the next table, as I'd have expected of him. In another he is standing next to a short, dark-haired, unhappy-looking woman in a low-cut T-shirt that shows off her ample cleavage. Her arms are crossed in front of her, but Ted's left hand is resting loosely at her hip, and I could see that he was wearing a ring. I smiled when my eye caught it and said, out loud, "Good for you!"

I opened a private Message box. "Did I see a wedding ring in one of your pictures?" The next day, I saw that he changed his "Relationship Status" to "Married."

I'm not envious of Ted's wife; I'm really not. But I am curious about his life, about the choices he made and their consequences. Isn't that interesting to everyone, comparing real life to the life we imagined we'd be living?

lll

Perhaps there's no telling why we stop loving someone. Why being with a person you love feels like life itself, until it doesn't. Or why we keep a select few buried in us like stars, alive because we are alive. The soot from the fiery grief that guts you when they leave this world (or, still living, leave you) coats and dulls the glint of them. It unmoors you, the absence of the light, and it breaks time into jagged pieces that take more energy than you can find to put back together, to make a normal moment. To take a normal breath.

I imagine that relief comes when the spark emerges again, when it enlarges, when it warms every bit of you. I imagine it will feel like frostbitten limbs beginning to thaw — the thickness of those prickly stabs of pain in your fingertips, telling you all will be well, all will be well, even if it won't.

Well after I fell in love with Ted, I accepted that I'd lost Josh. It wasn't mourning I went through, then; mourning Josh was what I had done each time he left for another new start. I knew the shape of that sorrow. It was a triangle, it was a shard of glass scraping against the viscera of the hollow that was myself. I'd been so wrapped up in Ted's love, and Josh's disappearance had seemed so gradual, that it was nearly painless.

℮℮

For a long time, I thought what Ted did to me was selfish, and that I made it too easy for him to leave me behind. But I eventually believed that Ted had a right to go, to reinvent himself, to start over, if that was what his heart was telling him to do.

It must have been difficult for Ted, leaving me. Not *deciding* to go; I've never understood people who can't make up their minds, and Ted was not one of them anyway. What would have been hard for him was living in the space between decision and action. He had been in the process of leaving me for some time, though I didn't know it. How free he must have felt, packing up and driving away. Making the choice to keep making choices.

℮℮

Ted posted some more photographs and created new albums in his Facebook account:

- Growing Up
- Europe
- Medical School Graduation
- Morocco
- The Kids

Children. So there were replicas of his DNA out there. The little girl he'd always wanted. And a boy, too. Birthday parties, Christmas mornings, baseball games. He'd kept that wish, then, to have a family. With someone new. Someone who took his name and wore a gown. I bet he ran on the beach in his tux on his wedding day, too.

ꙮ

Before I stopped thinking about Josh, I expected to see his face in magazines at the doctor's office, at Gina's house, in the grocery store line up. I anticipated finding those glinting green eyes looking back at me, and I imagined the letters I'd write to him again. I'd fill them with stories about the travelling I was doing for my job: being strip-searched behind curtains by a woman at the airport in Dhaka; riding in the green Volkswagen Beetle taxicabs driven by unlicensed thugs in Mexico City, because I didn't know enough my first time there to avoid them. And I'd ask about his travels, his career, his girlfriends. I'd say "Let's get together when you're back in town!" and sign it the usual way, "Love, Mazzie," as if no time had passed at all.

ꙮ

My last trip for the language school was to Venezuela. I went there to negotiate a contract with the continuing education director, who wanted to develop an ESL program like ours for their international business students. Nancy was going to go, but she came down with the flu and so it fell to me, as the associate registrar, to replace her.

Usually I fall asleep quickly on airplanes, lulled by the hum of the engines, but sleep wasn't easy for me on that red-eye flight. The humid night air that hit me on the Tarmac in Caracas induced an instant migraine. I was so disoriented that I don't know how I found a taxi to take me to the hotel compound, a few miles from the airport. Halfway there, the driver began to speak to me very quickly, in Spanish, while looking in his rear-view mirror at vehicles following behind. "What's wrong?" I asked, and he suddenly braked hard. "Trouble," he said, pointing to men standing in the road up ahead. "Passports." *This is it*, I thought. *Something is going to happen to me here.*

And then I saw the soldiers: three armed men in full camouflage, aiming machine guns at the car, heavy ammunition belts hanging from their hips. They walked quickly. I handed over my passport, as ordered. I wasn't afraid; at that time, I didn't care if they shot me dead. Whatever was going to happen, whatever the story turned out to be, there was no one at home anymore who held me in his heart, or missed me, or was even thinking about me.

℮℮

What Ted did *not* do after we parted:

- Find a cure for cancer
- Fly into space
- Look for me

℮℮

"You·might be correct, when you say I sound more formal than I used to. I'm trying to avoid being flirtatious. I am trying to show respect for my wife. We both have seen online relationships lead people astray. I guess I'm overcompensating for that fear, sorry. Yes, let's have coffee. It will be fun to share a story or two with you."

Ted's wife's interests: kitchen design, fashion shows, shopping local, yoga.

⁓

When I wake from one of my new Josh dreams, I feel a wash of tingling sorrow settle into my entire body — my joints pain me, and my limbs, toes, and belly all ache. Limb-loosening, that's what the ancients called such longing. It's an earthward pull, a force like magnetism or gravity, but it's specific to me, to my cells.

⁓

Status Update: Two years ago today I was diagnosed. Three years to go, to be in the clear.

Private Message to Ted: Remember that lump that scared us? It came back to haunt me.

Subtext: *Ask me what kind of cancer it was, Ted. Ask what happened; say that you are glad I am okay. Remember me. Our closeness. My body. Us. Ted — tell me. Tell me you do.*

⁓

"Tell": a twitch or a blanching or a blush, something observed that blows the bluff. It "tells" the person looking at you what you are really thinking, what you are hiding. Gina spitting curses at me while denying that she'd stolen my clothes: her "I'm lying through my teeth" tell. Ted's blush spreading across the bridge of his nose while he pretended to talk to me about dinner: his "turned on" tell.

I must have one, a tell. I must give off signals like radio wave-lengths that translate as "Go on, you can talk to me." At the language institute I became the unofficial counsellor, the go-to person for anyone who needed confidential chats about homesickness, a new relationship, school worries — that kind of thing. My surgeon, blurting out that she wanted my advice about marriage, was another incident. And I've heard from strangers about more marital problems and nervous break-downs and delinquent children than I can count. "I feel like I've known you for a long time," they'll say, in the middle of their confession. But usually I just listen.

Yesterday a woman got on the subway at Bloor, sat down next to me, and said, "My god, I'm tired. I wouldn't have to stand on my feet working all day if it weren't for my bedridden husband." I started to say, "Oh, I'm sorry," but she cut me off. "Don't be. He's a mean bugger, and a gambler. He lost all of our savings, so I can't retire. At least he can't do any more harm on his back. If he still had the use of his legs, I'd have to kill him."

Well. What can you say to that?

IV. Bereft

fourteen

There were two uniformed officers at the door when I opened it that night, a man and a woman, both a lot younger than me. I thought there must be a neighbourhood matter they were dealing with, warning residents about break-ins on our street or seeking witnesses to a traffic accident; they'd knocked on doors for such things a few times, over the years.

They stepped inside. What they said was nonsense. I stared as words spilled from their lips, fell to the floor, turned into runes. Obfuscating sounds, pell-mell utterances scrambled in my brain. Language and meaning had been ripped apart like the two rows of teeth in an open zipper.

ellie

The police knocked on the door where Tanis and I were living. It was a three-storey walk-up in London, named "The Deidre-Anne," after our landlord's wife. Waiting for the bus, I'd look up at the italicized gold-scripted letters that swept across the transom window above the front door, and wonder what Deidre-Anne thought about having a squat beige triplex bear her name.

The detective (Emmett something, I think, was the name on his card) told us he wanted to ask some questions about the

had occurred behind our building the night be-
... two policemen assaulting Peter, our landlord, in
.... Emmett said the officers had followed Peter's
car because he had gone through a stop sign; the report they
filed described Peter as drunk and disorderly, and when they
asked him to take the Breathalyzer test, he became violent, so
they had to subdue him.

This version did not describe what we had witnessed. Tanis
and I were both studying for the Organic Chemistry final
and eating bowls of popcorn for dinner when we heard voices
shouting in the parking lot. We looked out the large window
in the back stairwell and saw Peter curled up on the pavement,
knees to belly in the fetal position, protecting his gut. Two
male police officers were kicking him, front and back, and we
ran downstairs. When we got to the parking lot, the patrol car
was already gone. Peter was struggling to stand, yelling, "I have
wi-wi-witnesses!"

We didn't like Peter. He had stringy, shaggy, dirty-grey hair
and wore stained polyester suits that shone in the fluorescent
hallway lighting. He collected rent cheques late in the evening,
smelling like beer, and he pushed his way into the apartment
as though he had a right to be there. But we felt sorry for him,
too, because he'd had polio as a child and he limped; he also
had a stutter, probably from being bullied, and both afflictions
could give the impression that he'd been drinking. Peter was
creepy, and utterly unattractive, but he wasn't violent — in all
likelihood he couldn't be, with those uneven legs and a gait that
forced his full weight to drop onto his right hip with each step.

Emmett asked if we'd ever seen Peter drunk before. In the split second before either of us answered, Tanis and I looked at each other, and I was struck, in that suspended moment, by the knowledge that I could make things go either way based solely on the words that I chose to have come out of my mouth.

ℓℓℓ

Accident. Your. Hospital. Farm. Identify. Ma'am. Are you? Come. Husband. With. Investigation. Us. Neighbour. The. Sorry. Car. Field. We. Drive. In. Found. Will. Name? Tell. Call? No! For. Tony... Gina. No. Lou. Am. Me. Me. Wife. I. His.

ℓℓℓ

LeBlanc, that was it. Emmett LeBlanc.

My father threatened to call the police about another driver once. He was taking Gina and me somewhere — where we would have been going, without our mother? — and the car in front of us stopped suddenly. We were in the back without our seat belts on, so when we hit the other fellow's bumper, we were thrown forward and our foreheads smacked the vinyl seats in front of us. Dad blasted his horn and gestured with his hands before he got out. Then he yelled through the driver's open window, "What do you think you're doing? I should make a citizen's arrest, goddamn it! I should call the police! You could have hurt my two little girls, you see them? You see them? They're crying their eyes out!"

We were only four and eight, and our father's anger frightened us more than the accident. Dad decided we were all right and promised us some ice cream if we'd stop crying. On the way home Gina grabbed the last bit of my cone and punched my arm when I protested. Dad said that if we didn't stop squabbling, he'd get out of the car and slam our heads together like bowling balls.

ℓℓ

Every two weeks, we'd wait at the Don Mills Centre for our mother to emerge from the salon, where she had a wash and set by Leonard, her hairdresser. Mom said Leonard was a confirmed bachelor. He had one of those pencil-thin moustaches and wore a patterned shirt, top buttons undone, tucked into black pants that were too tight. We weren't supposed to joke about the way Leonard spoke or imitate his gait, the way he walked up and down the salon like a girl, because, she said, he couldn't help it.

When Leonard saw us sitting by the cash register one day, he sashayed over. "You girls are growing up fast. I bet you're boy-chasing already, am I right?" "Well, Leonard," Gina said, "I guess you'd know all about that." Leonard turned red and gritted his teeth, but he didn't lose his smile.

When Gina was older, she went to Leonard's salon by herself, to get a permanent using Mom's account. She walked in the front door, stinking of hair spray, as I was coming down the stairs and Dad was walking out of the kitchen. Leonard had turned Gina's long, thick hair into a helmet of frizzy Afro-tight curls. Dad started laughing so hard that he had to lean against the wall in the hall, arms splayed as if he were on one of those CNE rides he'd never give us money to try — the one where ten people at a time stand up, centrifugally plastered to the sides

[246]

of the spinning pod, screaming because you know that nothing but air is holding you in place, laughing because you know the danger isn't real, and squeezing your eyes shut so you can believe it.

lu

When I am exhausted and can't sleep, my eyes won't stay shut. I have to squeeze my lids together so hard that they ignite a light show: swirls of luminescent blue, green, yellow; neurons branching, sparking; cells exploding; stars. *This is like being at the beginning of the world*, I think. Maybe it's like dying, too. Maybe the final release of energy from the neurons in your eyes makes you see stars, as it flares out into the stratosphere. I'd like to think James saw stars. I want to believe his last seconds were not excruciating.

lu

I smuggled in a small illegal kettle for Lou under my coat when he first moved to the home, and whenever I visited, I topped up his contraband supplies: jars of Maxwell House and Coffee-Mate, and boxes of Sweet'N Low packets. The mix was horrible and I couldn't drink it; Lou got used to it, he said, the way you'd get used to the taste of cat food, if that's all you could afford.

His friend Didi grew to like it. Didi was Lou's neighbour from across the hall on Blueberry Lane, and she sat next to him during meals. She and Lou had an instant coffee every morning before breakfast, and another at 4:00 in the afternoon, which they called Crappy Hour. If I was there, Lou would pretend he was a waiter and Didi and I were his customers at a café. One day she rolled in early while Lou was putting the new stock away. I plugged in the kettle and asked Didi how she'd like her coffee. "Black," she said. "Like my men."

Didi was wicked — that's what Lou said when he stopped laughing. He was taken with her. She was ninety and he was eighty-eight and Lou was smitten.

ખ

Lou's skin thinned as he aged, but his nails thickened. He paid twenty dollars every two months to have his toenails clipped with an instrument that would probably have worked better as a tree pruner. I'd arrange to arrive the next day with a large plastic basin, Epsom salts, coconut oil, talc, and a foot rasp, to finish his pedicure.

On a bleak March morning, as I scraped his soles and powdered between his toes, I thought about how long it had been since I'd been pampered. When was the last time James rubbed moisturizer on my back or warmed my hands in his? I couldn't remember. I couldn't remember my husband's touch.

ખ

Me: When we have coffee, there'll be no backrubs involved. Or suntanning, come to think of it. ☼

Ted: I'll bring the sunscreen just in case. ☺

ખ

Gina planned to come over for coffee this morning, after she went to the bank to pay a bill, and she arrived in hysterics.

The teller had paused before passing over the slip showing the balance of Gina's account. "That's strange. Did you know there was a twenty-five-thousand-dollar debit transaction yesterday?" Gina insisted there must be a mistake, the money was taken out of her account instead of another person's by accident. The teller thought that unlikely, and noted the account is jointly held by Gina and Ben. "Could there have been a breakdown in communication with your husband?"

lu

Breakdowns happen to:

1. minds
2. bodies
3. relationships
4. communications
5. language
6. boxes
7. buildings
8. living tissues
9. inorganic objects
10. every known thing in the universe

lu

Just before sundown at the farm, the sky became an air painting. Homer's rosy-fingered dawn had nothing on this dusk. Bright pink slashes mixed with oranges and blues drifted slowly, horizontally, trailing streaks of bruised clouds, and then, abruptly, like the lights on a stage set being switched off, the deep navy of night, with stars gleaming like nailheads, was upon us.

When I saw blue contusions on Lou's white-flaked arms and asked him what had happened, he shrugged and countered with a question: "Are bruises supposed to be itchy?"

James had asked me that once. We were walking to the Film Buff on Queen East to pick up a noir when he let go of my hand to scratch his knee. It was before my surgery but after the diagnosis, and James had already begun to worry about minute changes he was noticing in his own body. I said it would make sense for bruises to itch, since cuts are itchy when they heal, and bruises are from broken blood vessels that have to heal, too. While we watched *Bay of Angels* at home that night, he rubbed his fingernails back and forth across his knee every few minutes, and by the end of the movie it was bleeding.

ℓℓ

Affliction, according to Simone Weil, is irreducible and indescribable. It takes possession of the soul, marking it.

ℓℓ

Lou watched as staff members went in and out of Didi's room all night, checking to see if she had stopped breathing so they could call the funeral home for a pickup. "The nurses don't like us to close our doors," he told me. "That way they can check on us at night without having to come all the way in." He would have been awake anyway, he said, because of Didi's death rattle.

Not long after Didi died, Lou's legs started swelling. His heart was failing, and he wheezed with every breath. When I arrived with my chiropodist's kit, his swollen ankles were hanging over the edge of a footstool, his soles up and ready for grating. I sawed the foot-file back and forth across his cracked heels, and shreds of dead skin fell on a brown paper towel I'd placed on the floor. Lou eyed the mound of grey-white powder, as soft as flour. "If I knew you were coming I'd have baked a cake," he sang, his tiny voice hoarse and off-key.

Ted's wife, Sarah, is short and dark-haired, like me, but she reminds me of Tanis. Her eyes are dark and pinched tight when she smiles, and there is too much distance between her upper lip and nose, making her less attractive than she could be — the way a slight, porcine upturn of a nose can ruin a perfectly good face. Ted once asked Tanis out for a drink at the campus bar when they were lab-mates, long before he met me, but she was busy and he didn't ask her again. (I thought that explained why she became so angry after she walked in on Ted and me, at our apartment, and found us naked on the chesterfield.)

Recently Ted posted a picture from his and Sarah's wedding: under moonlight, in Hawaii, he's wearing a tux and lifting a white veil to kiss the bride. The whole shebang.

In the wedding picture Tony took of James and me before our ceremony, we are standing outside City Hall holding hands; my hair a little longer than usual and flipped up a bit at the ends, sixties-style. James is wearing a new navy-blue boat-neck T-shirt under the jacket of his best suit, in beige linen. I am wearing a vintage lace dress in a coral shade, which I'd bought for twenty dollars at a consignment store, and flats in a complementary colour. The sunlight flashed off my mother's pearls, which I borrowed from Gina for the occasion. They look like a string of stars around my neck.

There was no swearing on the Holy Book for us, no invocation of the Father or the Son or the Holy Ghost. James had stopped going to church as soon as he was too old for Lou to drag him there, and my family hadn't attended since we were christened as babies. Gina, who was married in the church her in-laws attended, told me she didn't *really* promise to raise her children in the faith, despite her vows; while her left hand rested on the Bible, she crossed her right-hand fingers, which were buried in the folds of her gown.

℮℮

Ted and I used to laugh at the notion that God was an old man up in the sky. One of our first conversations was about atheism, which was not so common then — at least, talking about it wasn't. I couldn't imagine staying with a religious person, I said. What would I have in common with someone who carried lessons from the Bible around in his head? Ted agreed, so I found it very strange to see that his wife wears a gold crucifix on a chain around her neck. Especially since Ted's affiliation on Facebook is "Buddhist."

When I noticed that, I wrote a private message to ask Ted if he goes on retreats at monasteries, like Leonard Cohen did. "No," he replied, "it has nothing to do with a deity. I'm just trying to be less materialistic, more mindful of being in the moment." I wondered what that meant. Where was he, when he wasn't in the moment, these days?

❮ℙ❯

"He bought a fucking *house*, Mazz!"

"What are you talking about?"

"It was Ben's cheque, that $25,000 withdrawal! It was made out to Royal LePage Realty!"

"A bigger house? For you, for Christmas?"

"You're not listening! He's moving out! My life is a nightmare!"

❮ℙ❯

Last night I woke up from the dream I had throughout my childhood: I'm being chased through the streets of our neighbourhood by a man wearing a Hawaiian shirt and straw sun hat; and though I know better, I stop to pick up the quarters and dimes that keep popping up at my feet — coins he has planted there to attract my attention and slow me down. It's out of my control, somehow I can't *not* reach for them even though he is pursuing me — and I wake up, my pajamas damp from fear.

When I was a teenager, that dream was replaced by another: I am upstairs in the bathroom, putting on my makeup, and Josh is standing at the bottom of the stairs, waiting for me. I can feel time passing, pulling me toward the door, but I resist, I am not ready; I can't get my eyeshadow to blend properly, my foundation is too shiny, the part in my hair is uneven. One, two, three hours go by, and when I'm done, I find that Josh has gone.

Tony called when he got back from his honeymoon, after he heard the message I left for him about James's death. We didn't stay on the phone long, because neither of us was capable of speaking. The next time he called, he said he'd like to organize a November service so James's friends and colleagues from the school could pay their respects. But I saw no need. James and I hadn't socialized very much over the years with the other teachers; many had already retired and spent winters in Florida, and everyone else had just attended James's retirement party in the spring.

That evening had been hard enough for us both to get through. The principal was there, a man in his forties who hadn't been supportive of James and who was not very comfortable as the MC, either. When Tony noticed James's agitation, he took over. Tapping a spoon against one of the wine bottles until he could be heard, he suggested we all hold up our plastic glasses for a toast to James, wishing him much happiness in a life of ease and leisure — which he knew we were "eager to get back to as soon as possible." James and I were grateful for the early, dignified departure that Tony set up for us.

So I thanked Tony for his offer but said he would have to do it without me, if he went ahead. I think he was relieved that he wouldn't have to. The school staff had already sent me a bouquet with a sympathy card full of brief handwritten notes with the usual phrases. The single statement from Lauren, one of the newer teachers, read like a line of lament in a classic elegy, and I went back to it again and again: "May his memory be a blessing."

It wasn't until last Christmas that I started to think about what to do with all of James's things. I couldn't face his closet yet, so I decided I would open a few boxes he'd labelled "pre-Maslen" that were in the basement, untouched since we moved into the house. My boxes were there, too, but I didn't have as many as James did.

Gina says Ben has packed up and moved in with his girlfriend. He lost his deposit on that house, since his lawyers advised him not to go through with the purchase. If he had, he'd have had to pay Gina at least half its value in a court settlement, in addition to giving her spousal support and the house they'd shared — the matrimonial home, they called it. She has given all of his clothes away; she stuffed them into garbage bags and dropped them at the back door of a Goodwill store, late at night, under a sign that says, "DO NOT DROP DONATIONS AFTER HOURS."

Me: I was sorting through some boxes that I'd not opened for many a year, and I came across the bootleg Springsteen tapes you gave me after we went to the concert in Detroit.

Ted: Wow. I remember. "Santa Claus is Coming to Town" is on there, if memory serves. I think I have an old tape recorder kicking around somewhere…

Me: Hmm, sounds like an "I've got a brand new pair of roller skates, you've got a brand new key" kind of

deal... Speaking of Santa, which list are you on this
year? Naughty or Nice?

Ted: It's nice to be naughty.

lu

Among James's things: cufflinks, sets of keys, matchbooks;
glassware, mugs, a candelabra; a deck of cards, an old address
book, a broken gold chain; a T-shirt from his high-school
basketball team and school newspaper clippings with the
scores; lots of woolen socks with moth-bitten holes in them;
and cassette tapes of Howlin' Wolf, Muddy Waters, Bessie
Smith, Elmore James. He'd bought some of them and copied
others from records. He'd written the names of each song on
the cardboard sleeve in his distinctively cramped hand.

lu

"To remember" in Latin is *recordari*, a word made up of two
parts: *re* (again) + *cor, cordis* (heart). *Again in the heart.*

"Remind" = *re* (again) and *mind*, from the Old English *gemynd*
(memory, thought). *Again in the mind.*

"Remember" = *re* (again) + *member* (members, limbs, body
parts). *Again made whole.*

lu

The police have ruled it an accident. There will be no criminal
charges, no trial. The young man, just twenty years old, had a
valid licence. He was out with his father to hunt that day. They
were on wooded land beyond the legal boundary of our farm.

The insurance company is still investigating, though, one year in. James made a sudden movement, they say. He might have done that. He was not wearing an orange vest, they say. No, he didn't have one of those. So he might be considered partially at fault. They cited a clause about "Personal Injury Causing Death."

"Jesus, are they serious?" Gina said when I called her with an update. "At least James didn't leave you for another woman." It was difficult to get Gina's attention about anything apart from her own crisis, and when I did, she'd find a way to circle back to it. "I just found out that Ben had been seeing her *before* he moved out." Ben now lives with his girlfriend in a rented house, where Gina rings the doorbell once a month. She has no choice if she wants her support cheque, because Ben says he doesn't trust the mail. "*She* opens the door and calls to Ben, and then he shows up and hands me an envelope. I think he likes to see me beg."

Gina has been crying so hard for so long now that the skin under her eyes is sagging again. "It was too little, too late," she said of her surgery. "His girlfriend is twenty-five. I didn't stand a chance."

≈≈

Anna is seventeen. She has large, green eyes, like her mom, but they are not alike in other ways.

Anna has come over to ask me for advice. Is it too soon to tell her boyfriend she loves him? Should she wait for him to tell her first? She can't talk to her mother about any of it, not now. The boy is tender and kind, the complete opposite of her father, she says. He reminds her of Uncle James.

I tell Anna that there are so many varieties of love, it's impossible to write or follow any rules. That for some people, love is a prison, and for others, it is freedom. And that people change their minds, too, even when their reasons don't seem to make sense. I am sincere when I say these things to my niece, but I hope she doesn't ask me to repeat them.

ele

A few of Ted's Facebook "Likes":

- Toronto Maple Leafs
- Norwegian Cruise Line
- University of Toronto Medicine
- Parents Page, University of Western Ontario
- Oakland Athletics
- Riviera Maya
- BMW
- Picture of me holding a neighbour's ten-month-old baby

ele

Ted: Your baby is beautiful.

Me: Well, she is beautiful, but she's not mine! I'm going on fifty, remember?

Ted: Oh right. You look just the same, so I forgot how old we are.

Me: Smooth. Very smooth. Still got it, Bear.

Ted: Trust me, whatever I had, I lost a long time ago.

fifteen

A few days after James was cremated, I sat on the edge of Lou's bed, held his hand, and told him about the accident. I hoped he wouldn't question my version of the story, and he didn't, at least not out loud. He turned his head to the right, and I watched him take it in and silently process what I'd said. He blinked a few times, then said, still facing the wall, "He was smarter than that." I waited, expecting him to say something more — about October being the season for deer hunting, maybe even blaming James for not paying attention when Lou had tried to teach him things. But what he said was this: "He was always such a smart boy. He could have been anything he wanted to be."

I leaned down toward Lou's face and wrapped my left hand around his potato-knob shoulder. "He *was*, Lou." My voice rose with each word. "He was what he wanted to be." My forehead was resting on the left side of Lou's bare skull. With each sob that came out of me, my head nodded, making Lou's bob on the pillow, like a buoy.

lee

When James arrived at the hospital in Barrie, he would have been wearing his muddy jeans and a sweatshirt, bloodied and cut open by the paramedics. I gave the social worker who came to see me there the name of the first Toronto funeral home that came to mind, the one that advertised on the radio. The director called me the next morning and asked if I'd bring over a set of clothes for James to be dressed in.

He must have assumed I'd want a visitation room arranged, I suppose that's why he was asking, but instead of saying no I wondered out loud if fabric from pants and a shirt would bind to the body's cells, slowing down cremation process, or would they speed up the combustion? "I've never heard that question before," the man said. I have no idea if either of us spoke again before I hung up. I wandered into the kitchen, and forgot where I was going. The back door? The mud room? No, the basement. The batch of laundry I started this morning, that was what I'd been thinking of. It was very important that I do that.

Under the lid of the washing machine, twisted around the agitator, were two pairs of James's jeans. I'd brought them home to wash the last time I came back from the farm. I put them on the low-heat cycle in the dryer, so they wouldn't shrink. Later in the afternoon I must have placed one pair in the plastic bag that held a new navy T-shirt I'd picked up on sale at the end of the summer for James to wear next year. He looked so good in blue. The courier we used at the school would pick it up — Nancy told me that, so I must have phoned her to ask her what I should do.

I wrote the name of the funeral home on the bag with a marker. I must have touched the ink before it dried, because after I put the parcel on the table by the front door, I saw fragments of letters on my right palm. I stood there looking at the black marks on my hand, trying to remember how they got there, and wondering how long it would take for them to fade away.

I don't know how much time I spent stuck in that position — the doorbell brought me to my senses when the driver arrived for the pickup, sometime later — but before that happened, I started to hallucinate. That's the only way I can describe what my mind did. I stared at my palm, it was flayed. I'd done it with pumice, it seemed, and the raw flesh stung like a freshly burst blister. There were creases in my other hand, lines that a fortune teller would read, and I thought "legerdemain." Had I heard that word from my mother? What did it mean? I used to know. Rob is wearing that silly hat at the CNE, I can hear the sound of the cards he shuffled in his hands while we looked into each other's eyes. Zed looked in my eyes and I watched the veterinarian make a paw-print by pressing Zed's limp forelimb into a mould. My hands on clay, the delicious slippery texture of it before my skin started to dry out. Moisture. James's hands roaming my body. I was giving myself to him. Our desire is as strong as the need to breathe. We are walking along a sidewalk. How small my hand feels in his. We step aside to let two others by instead of letting go. High-fives in the living room after unpacking the last box. I try to tell him what "palmer's kiss" means and he starts to fumble with the drawstring on the oversized sweat pants I have on. They're not mine! James is underneath the covers and a faceless person in white is pressing my husband's left hand into a soft clay body in a silver tray and I am screaming. *Where is his ring? What happened to his ring?*

After the courier left, I leaned against the closed door and cried until I was light-headed, throat-weary and thirsty, but I hadn't the energy to get to the kitchen for a glass of water. I slept on the floor for a few minutes, maybe an hour, until Nancy arrived to monitor my intake of tranquilizers and stay with me for the night.

~

"We understand James saw his doctor a few times for anxiety," a woman was saying on the phone. "According to his medical records, he was prescribed tranquilizers and antidepressants. Was your husband still taking them when he died?"

"No. Not recently. He did have anxiety, but that was when I was diagnosed with breast cancer. I had breast cancer—"

"And?"

"It was difficult, that's all. He was worried. And he was tired, he was a teacher and so—"

"So?"

"That's why he retired. Because he was tired. And because of me. He wanted to take care of me."

"Of course. That's all there was to it?"

"Yes, and—"

"No?"

"No, not no. Just yes."

~

I didn't want to be there in October. Hunters owned the woods then. James understood.

When deer season started, he was at the farm alone.

Lou's caseworker called me from his room at the home. He'd been hallucinating. He was seeing rain pouring down the walls of his room and dogs running around the bed; a boy was sitting inside the television, sneakered feet moving up and down as if he was on a swing. These visions weren't upsetting to Lou — he seemed amused by the change of scenery, she said — but he was falling because of them, running after these visions. He had a fever, too. They'd called an ambulance. Lou thanked the chauffeur for picking him up in a limousine to take him to the airport. He said he was on his way to visit his son.

When I got to the hospital, Lou was sleeping. His forehead was warm and he'd kicked off the sheet that covered him. He'd lost twenty pounds since James died, about one per week. When he opened his eyes and saw me, he asked if that was James standing behind me.

ℓℓℓ

The last time I'd been in that emergency department in Barrie, it was to identify my husband. I don't remember many details from that night. How I got to the right room. Who took me there. How many people spoke to me.

"Yes!" I screamed. Two gloved hands had peeled back a crisp white sheet stamped "HOSPITAL PROPERTY." Grey-flecked curls, a lined forehead, closed eyes, a still nose. I had to scream to stop the sheet from moving any farther down his face, so I said yes and I screamed and then closed my eyes and said thank god his eyes are shut and I dropped down to the cold floor of that cold room until someone pulled me up and a doctor I didn't know came in and I was on a cot behind a curtain somewhere and nurses were calling out names and phones were ringing and I swallowed a pill and I slept until I heard the social worker's voice asking me if there was anyone she could call to come for me, to take me home.

ℓℓℓ

"I'd like to have my son back. Just for a while. I wouldn't ask what on earth he was thinking that day. I wouldn't say it was foolish to be out in the woods like that."

After many minutes, Lou blew his nose and lifted his head and we looked at each other. "It would be good to see him, wouldn't it?" he asked. I leaned forward and held him, placing my head against the curve of his neck. I burrowed my face into the blanket on his shoulder, and the cotton soaked up my sorrow. "A father should not outlive his son," Lou said. "You have to go on," he said softly. "I'll be gone soon, but you — you'll have to keep going. He'd want you to do that. So do I."

ℓℓℓ

Maslen: We chose not to have kids, but I enjoy being an aunt. I bet you are a good father.

Ted: Thanks. I find it challenging but rewarding, for the most part.

ℓℓℓ

My sister can't stand her son. Now that his voice has changed, David sounds exactly like his father did at his age, so I tell Gina that's all it is: she's projecting her anger at Ben onto David, when she hears him talk. Anna seems to take after me, Gina says. She doesn't know what she'd do without her.

Gina's feelings for David trouble me, and I think about calling him. I could invite him down for dinner or a movie, or ask him to drive out to the farm with me, when I go to straighten things up before it's listed. But I go alone.

ℓℓℓ

I heard the distressed neighing as we pulled in, one weekend in July. The horse, one of two that belonged to the couple who had the place next to ours, was wailing. It was howling, really. It didn't stop. After fifteen minutes I couldn't stand it, so I made the ten-minute trek through the high grass across our property to the neighbour's red brick house and knocked. I turned and saw their dog, Lucky, standing inside the open barn door, his white fur easily visible against the dark interior; he barked in a friendly way and wagged his tail, but he didn't run over as he usually did when he saw me or James outside. Belt-tracks in the dirt from some sort of heavy machinery led from the driveway to the front of the barn, then turned and went all the way back to a large mound of freshly turned earth in the field beyond.

The horse, Sterling, was grieving, said our neighbour, because his companion, Pablo, had to be put down on Thursday morning after breaking its leg. The wife had ridden him through a trail in the woods behind their property, and Pablo stumbled on a heap of stones that might have been a marker for a deer trail. Even if the bone healed, the veterinarian said, Pablo would be prone to further injury. "He'd be worthless, resale-wise," our neighbor said. "Lucky is happy though, because he's got a new best friend out there. He's hardly left that barn for days."

ඏ

I tried to convince the funeral director to give me James's remains without an urn. It wasn't exactly against policy, he said, but in his experience, people who took temporary containers home always came back for a more secure option. He showed me pictures of the urns: a cherrywood hexagonal container with brass hinges and handles; a plain oak rectangular mini-casket; and a glossy dark-green ceramic cylinder with a stainless-steel latch that popped open and reminded me of a flour jar.

When we were kids, Gina and I were not allowed to attend funerals, but once, when they couldn't get a sitter, our parents took us to the visitation for a great-uncle. When I saw the lineup at the coffin, I realized we were there to visit the *body*. The dead man, whom we'd never met, looked like a figure in a wax museum. I didn't know at the time what I was feeling, but it wasn't a fear of or aversion to death. Now I think it was humiliation. That embalmed man was laid out in his best suit, powerless to avoid the gaze of strangers, and I pitied him for that.

ඏ

Before our mother's service, a small affair held at the funeral home, Dad's voice could be heard above the hushed mutterings of the visitors. Scores of Mom's friends and acquaintances came to the visitation — women who were in her book club, others she'd gotten to know in cooking classes, or at the supermarket; gals with whom Mom was exceptionally cheerful and pleasant.

They all adored her and many called her their best friend. A few of our neighbours came, too. I remember how uncomfortable Mrs. Green and Mrs. Fedder looked when they walked in — as uncomfortable as I'd felt at the shiva for my friend Susan's grandmother, the day I stepped into the sunken, silent living room and had no idea what to do or say to those who were sitting for their dead.

ℓℓℓ

Mom was the outgoing one. Dad let her do all the talking when they socialized, and Gina and I didn't expect him be anything but reserved at his wife's funeral. It put us on edge to listen to Dad's chattiness. We didn't want to speak with anyone, so we went down the hall into the Remembrance Room and sat in front of the closed casket, waiting for a brief, generic script to be delivered by a minister we'd never met.

ℓℓℓ

What was found in James's pockets:

- loose change, adding up to $4.63
- his wedding ring
- three used bandages, gauze yellowed from broken blisters
- the cellphone he promised to keep with him, its battery dead

ℓℓℓ

I chose the simple wooden box for James, because it gave me the most flexibility for personalizing it later. James's ashes were in a sealed plastic bag, I was told, which had been placed inside the company's standard blue-velvet sleeve with a gold drawstring tied tightly at the top. This was tucked inside the wooden box. I carried it to the car; it was heavier than I thought it would be. I put it on the passenger seat and buckled it in. Then I buckled myself in.

We sat there for a while.

eee

Gleans from the information I read while James was piling rocks at the farm:

> – A Finnish study of people with depression determined that they had a higher risk of stroke than the control group.

> – In northern Sweden, during the winter, office workers take "sun breaks" instead of coffee breaks. They lean against the outer walls of their buildings, with their faces held up to the sky, to mitigate the risk of seasonal mood disorders.

> – If you answer yes to three or more of the following statements, you are suffering from or are at risk of clinical depression:
>   1. Does the smallest action or task seem to take a major effort?
>   2. Is it difficult to get yourself going in the morning?

3. Do you prefer staying indoors to being out in the sunshine?
4. Have you lost your motivation for finishing a project you've started?
5. Do you feel sad for part or all of each day?

According to these symptoms, James wasn't depressed. Maybe I was right when I thought he had more energy that summer, since his wall had started to take shape. Yes, I thought, he was experiencing pleasure again. Some pleasure, on some days. I was sure that I saw joy coming back to James.

sixteen

To: Ted
From: Maslen
Subject: Last Words

Dear Ted,
I wasn't surprised to get your email this morning —
not after your wife responded to my Facebook
message. No one I know would log into a spouse's
account, unless… well, never mind. She did. And I
suppose if I were Sarah, I wouldn't be happy about
some of our exchanges, either. If cutting electronic ties
with me feels right, then so be it. But first, I want to
tell you something, something I'd have said in person
if we'd gone to that café and become real friends: I am
grateful that you broke my heart all those years ago.
Really. I am.

When you and I met, I was still working out who I
wanted to be — not only career-wise, but in other,
deeper ways. Then, when you started med school,
I tried not to cross that line you'd drawn between
us — the line you insisted be kept in place until you'd
taken the Hippocratic Oath. It was supposed to be

temporary, that barrier, but something changed for you along the way. Maybe you got used to the distance it imposed between us, or maybe you saw me differently, from the perspective it gave you. Whatever it was, you decided you needed more time, time away from me. But not long after you left, I met someone who was ready for me, for "we." So it was the right thing, what you did. For both of us.

I don't know if I can explain why I wanted to reconnect with you, but it had something to do with time passing, with getting older. Despite Sarah's concerns, it was not another beginning I wanted. We *had* our beginning, when we were young. I can still see you standing on the hood of your car to climb up the balcony at my apartment, to kiss me goodnight one more time. (You were full of surprises back then.) But that's an old, finished story.

What I wanted was to hear about the middle of your life, yours and Sarah's. I wanted to find out where your decisions have taken you, and to tell you about the joy I've had as a result of the choices that were mine to make. So part of the answer lies there. I know that this plumbing of depths is not your style, though, so no more explaining, and no more trying to find a time or place to meet, to talk about our lives as old friends would do. Alas, our fate has forked once again. Well. We never did say a proper goodbye, did we? So now we have. At least there's that.

— Mazz

We had a falling out — that's what this electronic split from Ted felt like. Falling in love, falling out, falling apart: people seem quite accident-prone, when it comes to love.

In Jewish creation myth, the world began by falling apart. God created a space in order to make something from nothing. He filled vessels with a divine light so powerful that it shattered and scattered many of them. Every material thing is made from these shards, and sparks of light from the vessels became our imperfect human souls, capable of both good and evil. But if people perform mitzvahs, carrying out works for the good, the world can be mended, and the light made whole again. Time doesn't heal wounds, but light does.

It's hard, the work of mourning. You're building on an absence. You're building on a vacancy, a void. You are making something from nothing.

I thought about veneering the wooden box using chips of the flagstone James had knapped when he built our patio at the farm, but I decided against it. I had to find the right way to honour him.

James knew more about rocks and earth and clay than he needed to, to teach his grade ten Science classes on geology and evolution. I knew very little, and when we started to see each other, I worried we'd quickly run out of conversation. On one of our early dates, James asked me what I found interesting about my pottery course, and I wasn't sure how to answer. So I started to tell him about my trips to China, where porcelain is considered an almost sacred material. I went on about the little I knew: porcelain was not a British invention; the first potter lived in China, thousands of years ago; the word we still use for dinnerware refers to the place where pottery was invented. That part of our conversation makes me cringe even now, when I think of it. But James didn't seem to mind my clumsy misfire; he waited a moment, then used it as a bridge to tell me about one of his own interests, the Burgess Shale fossils.

I loved the words he used to tell me about them, like "varve" and "schist." They seemed to have an inner life, when he spoke them. We fell into an ease, talking with each other after that, which other people noticed. "He gets you, Mazzie," my sister said, after dinner at her house, when James met Ben and the kids. "You seem so comfortable together. He's a keeper."

lee

Memories of Chengdu:

– Touring Sichuan University, seeing row after row of work benches in the ceramic lab to be filled with hundreds of new technical-program students, whose marks on the National Examinations were below the cut-off for academic university study.

– Watching hundreds of people practising Tai Chi in the lush, treed front grounds of the campus, on a day that must have hit ninety-nine degrees in the shade.

– Hearing that the school over-admits by forty
percent because of attrition by suicide.

lu

When I went to our students' home countries, parents took
time away from their labours and travelled for hours by bus to
see me at education fairs. They came to thank me for admitting
their children to our school, which might lead to university or
college in Canada. I'd carry home handmade tablecloths, wall
hangings, rugs, and give most of it away — my apartment was
so small.

One family in Beijing invited me to dinner at an exclusive
restaurant. I was seated as the guest of honour. A large platter
was carried out by three waiters and placed on the table in front
of me. It was a chicken head, a delicacy, and it was for me. I'd
been warned by a more experienced colleague that if this ever
happened, I'd be expected to eat the eyes before the others
could begin to eat, so I was prepared. Unfortunately, I said, I
was a vegetarian, for medical reasons. My hosts did not express
disappointment facially, as they passed the many other dishes
my way. The double treat went to the student's father, my host,
who twice hoisted an eyeball tined on his fork as a toast to me.

lu

Josh became a vegetarian on instruction from the modelling
agency: "Your body is your temple. Be very careful and watch
what you put into it." After a year in Italy, when he came back
to Toronto and had Christmas dinner with my family, he said
he felt like he'd been a homeless person. Dressing up for poses
with pretty girls all day long while living out of a suitcase wasn't

what it was cracked up to be, he said, and we all laughed. I was still determined to be a doctor, then, and he told me to let him know when I got rich, that I was still on his prospect list. He'd quit modelling if I would support him for life.

Josh took me to a popular kosher restaurant on Bathurst near Eglinton a few days later. There was a long lineup out the door and onto the sidewalk, and when we were finally seated in a booth not far from the window, Josh glanced up. "Turn around, Mazz," he said. "Take a look at that woman in line." I expected to see someone from school, or Jennifer, or even the Princess, but she was a brunette, about thirty years old, simply dressed in a blue buttoned-up cotton blouse and a plain white skirt. She wore no makeup. Her hair was messy, not deliberately tousled, and her figure was curvy; I'd have said she was fat. She was holding a sleeping infant against her breast, rocking him, humming to him, kissing his head. "There. That's beauty," Josh said. We both stared until the line moved forward. "That is *real* beauty."

≈≈≈

I spoke to Leah's mother-in-law at the AGO reception, where she was the guest of honour for donating the Picasso. She was very friendly, so after some chat about the sketch, I mentioned that I knew her daughter-in-law's brother, Joshua. I was trying to reconnect with him, I said. Would she mind giving Leah my phone number to pass along to Josh, by any chance? I watched her facial muscles slacken. She did *not* say, "Of course. I don't know his number or I'd give it to you now," or "Certainly. He was in Spain, I think, the last time they spoke." The longer she did not say these things, the stronger my feeling was that something was wrong. "I'm sure Leah will want to speak with you," she said, touching my shoulder.

ℓℓℓ

Josh had told me midway through our friendship about his history — the appointments with psychiatrists, the anger at his mother, the moodiness that would swing so high and so low that he thought he was going insane. So that was why he changed schools — his reasons were emotional, as mine had been. But I didn't tell him about my dark days before I registered at the alternative school. About how I had to claw my way out of the tar pit to daylight most mornings, or the sense of scrambled hopelessness I couldn't shake for months. I couldn't tell Josh how easy it could be for me to slide over to the other side, especially not when he seemed to love me for being his best audience. "I don't know what it is, Mazz, but after I get off the phone with you I'm all sweaty and hyper, as if I've just done a comedy routine..."

ℓℓℓ

I almost did a stint on Seven, as the psychiatric ward at the North York General Hospital was known, about a year before I met Josh. I wasn't there long — just a few hours, while I tried to convince the on-call doctor that it had been a mistake, that my mother had misunderstood. I really wasn't suicidal; carrying one hundred Tylenols in my knapsack helped me to cope, let me think I had an option to get out if I had to. Desperate loneliness had dug in and deepened over two years, but I wasn't at rock bottom, not yet. True, I had swallowed a handful, but I also made myself vomit them up. I was only testing whether or not I had the chutzpah to get that far.

The doctor let me leave only because my mother promised to go through my bag and pockets every day, before and after school. I was discharged into her care with a prescription for Ludiomil that would zombie me into compliance. I couldn't kill myself if I couldn't concentrate long enough to remember what it was I wanted to do.

Gina was in university and my father was at a conference in Saskatoon. Mom and I agreed that it wouldn't do either of them any good if they were to learn about it. I didn't tell Ted about the Tylenol episode because it would have frightened him; I didn't tell James because there was no point, by then; I wasn't that person anymore.

Should I have told Josh? I almost did, once, during a conversation we had about his mother, about her depressions and the multiple attempts she apparently made, according to his grandmother. Josh had said he didn't think he'd have the guts. I said he'd never need guts for that — he was living a glamorous life, a successful life! He could make anyone in the world fall in love with him! That's how young I was: I believed that what Josh had in his life then would be enough to keep his head above water forever.

I also thought that if he knew how far under I'd once gone — that I had come that close to nothing — then he'd turn away. So I didn't tell him. How that haunts me now.

I thought I knew James through and through, too. James and me, together. Would James still be alive if I'd loved him differently?

ℓℓℓ

I stood up as soon as I heard Leah say hello, the day she called in July. I placed the receiver at my neck and pinched it there with my shoulder, and I began to pace, holding myself with arms crossed over my chest, bracing for what I knew she was about to tell me. I had suspected it all along, at some level — there was no other explanation for Josh's absence from the virtual world — but it took a few sharp and audible breaths before I could respond to Leah, after she told me that he had passed. She was patient with me, but when I asked her what had happened, if he'd been sick, she wouldn't answer. "He just... he just passed," she said again.

She did answer my other questions. I asked if he'd been married; he had, to the Norwegian model, but they'd divorced, and it was hard on him, that failure. No, they hadn't had any children.

Because I didn't know her, and because of her gentleness in the telling and her generosity for contacting me, for putting an end to my detective's search for her brother, I tried to explain — in broken, hyperventilated sentences — how important her brother was, had been, to me. I calmed myself just enough to share a few of my memories about Josh, things that I thought she might like to hear: the laughter we could trigger in each other; the pleasure he found, after leaving school, in reading fiction and philosophy; the depth of attention he gave to people he cared about.

When I thanked her for the call, she thanked me — for giving her a picture of Josh she'd not seen before. "When my mother-in-law gave me your message, I remembered your name — we went to a concert together once, didn't we?" Yes, I said, we went to hear Genesis. "That's right. Josh didn't stop talking about his friend Mazzie all summer. Anyway, it's good to talk with you. I learn more about my brother by hearing from people he cared about. It's nice for me to hear what he meant to you, and what he was like when he was with you. It's another piece of him to add to the whole person I'm trying to put together for myself, so I can tell my own children about him."

At the click that ended our conversation, I dropped back into the chair and my head bent down by itself, to my knees. I keened. I wailed. My stiff body cracked, and I bled sound. The lining of my throat was rent. I was silenced for many days.

ееи

Once the official grieving period is over, Jews are to turn back to life, to living well in the here and now. To the light.

But the dead are not forgotten. They are honoured through remembering. Memories are returned to, ritually, and passed on from generation to generation.

Again in the heart.

Again in the mind.

Again made whole.

lu

Rachel, Josh's friend from childhood, is now a professor of English out west. She was the other smart girl back home, and she'd loved Josh for longer than I had. He told me, that morning he called to talk about my Letter, a few intimate details about their friendship: they'd damaged it when it became sexual and complicated. They stayed friends after their failed attempt at romance, he said, but it was different after that — different and difficult. He didn't want that to happen to us.

To us. His voice, saying those words.

lu

To: Rachel S.
From: Maslen
Re: Josh G.

Dear Dr. S. (Rachel),

I am an old friend of Joshua's and have recently spoken with his sister, Leah, who told me that he passed some time ago. But she wouldn't tell me how he died. I know you were very close to him, so please forgive me for opening old wounds — but please, can you tell me what happened to Josh? And can you tell me anything about the last few years of his life? Was he happy at all? He was always searching for something, for peace or contentment or love... I'd like to think that he found it, at least some piece of it, before the end.

After Leah's call, I did an online search for Josh's obituary but found nothing. No funeral notice, nothing. I realized that this made sense, if Josh had taken his own life. Jewish custom meant that no eulogy would had been given at his funeral, either.

The next day I felt a need to speak with someone else who had loved Josh, and the idea of contacting the Princess crossed my mind. She was easy to find on Facebook. She married Rob (their teenaged son looks like he did, at that age). She is friends with many of the people Gina and I knew growing up, and seeing those faces grouped together on her Friend list was like walking into a reunion I'd not been invited to. But I wondered if I should call her. No, not should. Dare. Did I *dare* contact her? She'd shared so much more with him than I had; yet Josh left her when he befriended me. He did. He left her, even though he loved her. He loved me, too, but on different terms. I didn't understand then that he set those terms to make sure he could never leave me.

seventeen

The temple that Leah belongs to has posted its pre-Internet newsletters as PDFs in an archive on its website. One by one, I opened the documents from the late nineties — based on Leah's comments, I'd narrowed it down that far — looking for Josh's name in the *yahrzeit* listings, where the deceased are listed by the date of their death for annual remembrance. I found nothing.

Finally, when I opened the last newsletter for the range of dates I'd entered, there it was: Josh's name, followed by the month and the day he died.

lu

On September 11, 2001, when the Twin Towers fell in New York City, a sudden worry about Josh's safety drove me to the Internet. I felt as anxious as I'd been in 1981 after the earthquake in Italy, where Josh was modelling then, until he reassured me in his next missive that he'd been nowhere near the site. When his postcard, mailed from England, reached me, I was so relieved I didn't think about the fact that he'd not told me he was going on a trip with a model — Tina, or Tanya, someone with another tinkly-sounding name — to London.

When 9/11 happened, we'd not been in touch for many years. I was slightly worried that I'd embarrass myself, if we did connect, by exposing a lingering concern for him; but the magnitude of the catastrophe, I thought, would mitigate how ridiculous I might seem to him for making the effort.

Through online phone listings, I found a Joshua G. on West 57th in New York City. I wrote a brief letter, telling Josh I'd been thinking of him, that I was still in Toronto and happily married. I paused at the word "happily," after I'd written it. Wasn't that redundant? If a marriage wasn't happy, surely you'd be writing a different kind of letter. But I sent it off as written, with my email and street addresses at the bottom, and waited for weeks to hear back from him.

Now I know he'd been gone for over two years by then. My undeliverable note, my dead letter, was likely opened by some other Joshua G., who probably tossed it away.

In August I googled Josh's name once more, this time with the date of his death. Even graveyards have come into the age of the Internet, it seems. "I've finally found you," I said out loud. I stared at the facts that faced me on the screen for several strange moments; there was a fleeting sense of relief, before the grief settled into my lungs, my abdomen. The search was over. If I kept a diary, I would have written this: "Today I found Josh. He'd be fifty-one now, had he lived."

His first name wasn't Joshua, but Lev. I didn't think it suited him. When he told me, I thought he was kidding, so he pulled out his driver's licence as proof.

Lev. I'd forgotten that detail, about his name. Thinking about how it made me feel oddly happy. Seeing it in the listing reassured me that there would be other things I'd remember about Josh, in time. I hadn't expected that, to be comforted.

ee

I'm smiling now, remembering the night Josh and I saw *Young Frankenstein*, when he told me there'd be lots of movies we'd go to that I might like better. He asked me while the credits rolled what it would sound like if "Maslen" were followed by his last name, instead of my own.

ee

Need tarnishes friendship, said Weil. I still wonder, now and then, if Josh might be alive if I hadn't coveted him so. Not that I was so powerful a person in his life that I'd have been able to keep him afloat — it's clear by now that I'm not capable of doing that for anyone. I mean that perhaps our friendship would have lasted longer, without the Letter; and if it had lasted longer, then a different chain of events would have unfolded. Not necessarily leading to a different outcome, but possibly. Possibly.

When I am having one of my bad days, when I am sundered and inconsolable about life and James's death and what choices I've made, or how I've behaved, I decide I am responsible for poisoning what we had, Josh and me, with greed. On better days, though, I know that without that confession to Josh, I might not have loved Ted and therefore probably would not have met James. On better days I can forgive my young, passionate self for sending my honest, desperate plea to Josh. In between I am melted by the thought that because Josh drifted away, I had James in my life for as long as I did.

lee

Rachel did not respond to my email, so I didn't persist. We'd been long-time competitors in a way that the Princess and I never were. Her demons could be much worse than mine.

Recently I've looked at old photographs that my university friends took during our trip to New York. Lise even snapped one on the patio when Josh arrived to pick me up. It might be commonplace for older people to be reminded, when they compare a picture taken decades before to what they see in the mirror now, how attractive they were their youth. But when I look at my young self, I'm shocked — not because the lineless face of the slim girl I see in the photo is so different from the woman I am today (though that is true, too), but because I see a beautiful young woman who thought, without any doubt at all, that she was unworthy of the young man who stood next to her.

How sorry I feel for having caused her so much suffering. She wasn't ugly; she wasn't even ordinary-looking. She was, as her mother had told her, interesting-looking. Striking, even. Maybe Josh could have loved that twenty-two-year-old face.

I was never the kind of wife who took an interest in dressing her husband, but James hated to shop, and he never wanted to try on clothes; so on occasion I went to the Scarborough Town Centre on a Saturday, to pick up jeans or jersey shirts from the one men's store he seemed to like when they went on sale. When I did, I took the bus up Brimley Road from Kennedy Station. I don't know why, but on those trips I'd close my eyes and become that seventeen-year-old girl who heard Josh approaching her in the wide hallway at school. Or Josh would be standing in the front hall of my house, handing me a silly stuffed animal he bought for me in Florence, for Christmas. Driving in his car, "Born to Run" blasting and the windows down, and I'm watching the wind blow back his hair. Sipping tea in a Japanese restaurant in New York.

There was no voice saying his name, on these bus rides, telling me Josh was close by — I wasn't as crazy as that; but I do wonder if I was sensitive to a signal, an energy of some kind that emanated from the burial ground as I passed it. Maybe spirituality, that belief in the existence of a life beyond and the feeling of connection to otherworldliness, can be traced back to energy: to light, to atoms and neutrons and electrons, to earth and to water and the elements.

There he is, I thought as I pulled the car over to the side of the narrow paved lane. The cemetery is on Brimley Road in Scarborough, in what would have been the far outskirts of Toronto, back when Jewish people were not allowed to join country clubs or golf clubs or yacht clubs, or bury their dead on prime real estate, or go to medical school once those five slots reserved for their race had been filled. Not very long ago.

I walked up and down the rows of tombstones, reading brief biographies that sounded like abbreviated eulogies: "Seeker of justice, elegant, kind." "Charming, witty, charismatic." "A pioneer in his field." "Aunt and dear friend to so many." Josh's family had not provided a description that would allow future generations to grasp the kind of person he had been. As it is, the blank space speaks to his vanishing. Life had driven him away from the light; his mind had betrayed his being, trapped him in a silo others couldn't penetrate, where he sentenced himself to death.

When I went to him that bright August day, I was the only visitor. The grounds had been freshly mown and the tombstones were very orderly, even in the older sections where parts of names and dates were worn away and harder to read. The back of each marker bore, in large block letters, the last name of the deceased. As I looked for Josh's plot, I recognized surnames of childhood neighbours and acquaintances: HIRSCHFELD. BLOOMBERG. SILVER. ALTER. GOODMAN. FEDDER. ROSEN. Josh's was the only gentile name there.

I stood petrified in front of his tombstone. Carved on the front was his full name in English, but it was also carved in Hebrew script in the line below, followed by his dates of birth and death. There were a few pebbles on top of the headstone. How perfect that custom is, I thought, marking a visit to the dead with a rock, a piece of time.

I stood there for twenty minutes or so, holding my sides like a swimmer with muscle cramps. I grieved for Josh, for our lost friendship and the loss of our youth and the brevity of his life. I grieved the fact that I hadn't known how badly beaten down Josh had been by life, so badly that he chose to leave it.

I touched his name. I ran my fingertips from right to left along the script as if the engraved letters stood out, instead, like Braille. I told him how much he meant to me. I told him I was sorry for our estrangement, and that I knew estrangement can happen within a person, too, and that I should have said so. I said I did not think he'd betrayed or abandoned those of us who loved him, and that I understood. That I will always regret not being strong enough to let him know how much I understood, when I'd had the chance.

I stood at the grave for a long while. My grief roiled from the place where I'd locked in so much feeling before I'd even met James. I mourned anew for my husband and our lost future, for the life we'd had and the life we'd not. I howled silently into my hands, while three staff gardeners gathered near the gate at the entrance at the end of their day's tending, speaking with each other in a language I didn't recognize.

When I was spent, I lifted from my purse the several small stones I'd collected from the farm. I had not seen Josh in many years, so leaving only one marker to note I'd been there, and that he mattered to me, did not seem enough. I took my time and placed them, all of them, one by one on top of the headstone. I considered where each seemed to fit in terms of colour, texture, shape, before I put it down. I thought about the way

James selected rocks for his wall, too; it was like choosing the right words to build a sentence that means more than its components. The stones I left for Josh that day tell the story of a deep adoration that will not be dispelled or dismissed.

I snapped off a bloom from the pruned plant — a begonia, I think — that was growing in the ground that covered his bones, and I took it back to the car with me. I pinched the stem between my finger and thumb, as if I could imprint myself onto it, onto those green cells grown from the earth that sheltered the sweet, decayed, silent love of my youth.

I hadn't visited Josh's relatives during shiva. I hadn't kept his soul company for twenty-four hours before his burial. But I communed with Josh that day. Communing with him in my mind was something I'd become so expert at, while we were close friends, that it seems almost a reunion of sorts, to go back to him that way again. And it will go on. When I'm an old lady, I told him, I will still be standing here missing you, whether I visit your grave again or not.

r. Blessed

eighteen

James was a genius at making my taste buds sing. His sweetened rosemary quiche, for instance: my salivary glands would hurt from the surprise of sugar, and then the savoury pastry dissolved on my tongue like liquid velvet. I couldn't help but put on a few pounds over the years. James pushed me to jog, to run, to walk at least, but I didn't listen. I thought I'd be able to go for long walks when I was stuck at home for weeks, after my surgery, but my focus turned to James's health, to his panic attacks and anxieties, his adjustments to retirement.

And then there was the farm. I drove up there every weekend, and I spent weeknights after work checking in with James on the phone, laundering sheets from two households, and feeding myself with whatever I could scrounge from the fridge. When I walked in the door on Friday nights, James used to look at me and say, "You're not taking care of yourself. You need to eat when I'm not home." It didn't matter, though. After years of sitting behind a desk, my rate of metabolism was barely above a cadaver's.

One Sunday when I was on my way home, I made an impromptu visit to Lou on my way to the city, and Didi was in his room. "Hmmm," she said when she looked my outfit up and down. I was wearing my farm clothes, an old sweatshirt and jeans. "You're not as thin as you look in your regular clothes." I hugged her for making me laugh, and she pushed me away.

James had spoiled me, doing all the usual household chores after his day ended. We'd eat the dinner he'd prepared — gorgeous risottos, handmade pasta dishes with that spicy red-wine tomato sauce, kormas or jambalayas on basmati rice — along with a glass of the wine he'd chosen to accompany it, and then he'd clean up (I would offer every night, for the first year we were married, but I don't think the result I achieved ever met his standards). For the rest of the evening, James would mark assignments or watch the sports channel, and I'd read a novel or the *New Yorker*. Sometimes — less often as time went on — we'd make love before falling asleep.

Life seemed so full to me, then: busy, but relatively calm, and full. Was it for James, too? I thought so, but I never asked. Not that I didn't care, but you don't pester the other person with questions when you think that you're happy. That you both are.

⁂

In the express line the other day, I heard a man several people back say my name as if it were a question. At least I thought I heard my name. I was counting coins from my change purse and was annoyed at the interruption; and since I wasn't completely sure I'd heard right, I only half turned to quickly scan the male faces behind me. I didn't recognize anyone, so I paid, took my bag, and walked out.

All the way home I thought about that man's voice. I tried to attach it to someone, some place, sometime in my past. Was he a former colleague of James's? Was he someone I knew years ago, who hadn't aged well, who'd changed beyond recognition? Maybe he was a former teacher from the language school, who'd had his adventures abroad and then come home again to live an ordinary life, like the rest of us. If he had known me and I'd forgotten who he was, then my dismissive response would have embarrassed him. I'd spared myself from feeling foolish at his expense. Now, whoever he is and whether he knew me or not, he'll think I'm a shallow, unkind person. And he'll be partially right. Impressions are all people have of you.

Putting the apples, yogurt, peanut butter, and spinach away, I felt overwhelmed, the way I used to in university, when putting a meal together was beyond my capabilities. Tanis and I ate junk food, mostly, and every few weeks we would subject ourselves to extreme dieting regimens: we'd drink black coffee on campus all day and eat huge bowls of unbuttered popcorn when we got home, for days on end. James was horrified when I recounted those days to him. "What'd you think, you were a plant that could live on sunshine and water alone?" No, I answered, reminding him that I'd studied physiology and cell biology. I'd starved myself despite knowing about mitochondria and hypoglycemia and ketosis. "I know it was stupid, but I refused to learn how to cook because I didn't want to be like my mother," I said. "Good thing I found you, to keep me going."

ʝ

Sometimes I still lack the energy to haul myself out of bed in the morning. I wake up late and think the day ahead of me is still long, far too long. I tell my doctor that it's too much to expect me to face it, but he is an optimist. He says I need to exercise. The endorphins will help, he says. "It won't happen overnight," he adds, as though he is a wise old man. He is perhaps thirty, thirty-five at most. My personal trainer — I have one now — agrees with my doctor. "You have to get your metabolism charged up again, which takes time." So I will try.

I registered at a gym near the house, dreading my entrance into the wilds of sweat and youth and ruthless self-improvement. Trim blonds prance about in sleeveless spandex T's and capris that they may as well leave in their lockers, they're that tight, and I think, *What are they doing here, anyway?*

I hated phys. ed. in junior high school, and was relieved when I broke my leg to be let out of gym class for more than two months. The teacher made me change into my uniform as if I were participating anyway, and I stood against the wall with my crutches, watching everyone practise volleyball or tumbling, or do the Canada Fitness Test. Gym was coed, and the boys could wear whatever they wanted, but we had to wear shapeless, short-sleeved, one-piece numbers in royal blue. They buttoned up the front; they were called rompers, I think, and they had elastic around the leg holes like old-fashioned underwear. Most girls wrote their names across the back in red Magic Marker, but I stitched mine with multiple strands of silky embroidery thread, the kind women used to monogram pillow cases for their trousseaus in my mother's day.

My new workout clothes are extra-large men's T-shirts and below-the-knee leggings, both in black. I indulge in matching sets of tennis socks and headbands. James always said I looked good in black. Not that anyone's looking; at my age, women become practically invisible. But I like to think, when I glance in the change-room mirror, that James would approve.

Lou is in decline. It wasn't two weeks ago that I sat at a guest table in the home and had dinner with him. I suppose I've not paid enough attention to the little changes in him along the way. Lots of little changes.

It seems ridiculous that our days simply stop. All of this — the years of loving and wanting, of being and giving — and then the light goes out, poof — you're gone. You go from being something, and turn back into nothing. Nothing.

James put the family house on the market when it wasn't safe for Lou to live alone anymore. Lou had given him power of attorney as a matter of course, but he didn't think his son would use it. "Why do you get to decide when it's time? What am I, vapour?" But James refused to discuss options with his father. "I'd like to know who made *you* God," Lou said. That was a difficult day.

I tell Lou I love him, and kiss his cheek. His sockets are sunken. His face is shiny where his cheekbones have stretched the skin taut. His lips are cracked, and dried saliva is caught in the corners, which I wipe away with my thumb. He closes his eyes.

When Lou takes a breath, the oxygen tank hisses, and every few seconds it clicks, recording the hours the machine has been running. That's important for some technical reason, this tracking of machine-time. I think of the apple-shaped timer James set when he baked chocolate-chip banana bread, my favourite, on a Sunday morning, and of the way our granite kitchen counter amplified the minutes ticking by, streaming the sound into the living room, where we sat reading the paper. Both of us would startle when the bell rang, even though we'd started to expect it as soon as the sweet, warm air began to waft its way from the oven toward us. I close my eyes and inhale deeply as if the loaves are close by, settling a little in the middle as they cool, and I smile.

I look back at Lou and see that he's been watching me remember Sunday mornings with James. He smiles, too, and I squeeze his hand.

lu

Lou's friend Didi became angry near the end. The charm, the jokes, the outrageous self-presentation — all of that disappeared, and she was furious, just plain mad. People in their wheelchairs would get in her way, and she'd spit at them. Lou would ask if she wanted an instant coffee, and she'd say he must be stupid if he didn't know her well enough by now to boil the damn kettle without her having to say so. At dinner, when a woman spilled a glass of water on the table, Didi said the worst thing she could think of: "You're a nothing! A nothing!"

lu

A few other women at the gym belong to the subset I find myself in. They create their artisanal looks with unusual earrings, slant-hemmed skirts, ochre and plum handbags in oblong shapes, and wardrobes with depth in their palettes. Their dresses have waists. They half smile at each other, too self-contained to stop and compliment a hair style (the natural silver streaks like a licorice candy cane, angled bobs that swing and sparkle).

But they know. They glance, and they know: they've escaped the bloated blurriness that befalls so many who are past their prime.

I see one of these women and think, *We should be friends*. But we won't become friends. It's too much effort once you hit middle age, choosing which story you'll tell to someone new or deciding where you'll start the tale. You've lived so many of them, by then. Besides, speaking to strangers is far beyond my capacity at the moment. Getting myself to exercise in clean workout clothes is still enough of an accomplishment.

Breaking the day into single steps is what it takes. *Wash your face*, I think. Paralysis so easily sets in, without these directions. *There now, that's done. Brush your teeth next. Good. Drive to the gym, tread on the mill, and drive home again.* When I get home, I give myself permission to collapse. *Put on your pajamas. It doesn't matter that it's only three p.m. Don't vacuum tonight. It can wait. Pay the phone and the power bills later, pay them tomorrow, or next year. Put them back on the table. If you get hungry, order spring rolls or pad Thai, or eat a box of cereal. You can do that. You can.*

This is still the aftermath. It began last October, when James died; it carried on through November and straight into December; it baptized the new year, and it welcomed the summer solstice. A year later, "after" is all there is.

nineteen

A documentary about the Chauvet Cave was on PBS last night. What I thought when I saw the image of the hand-prints was this: *Thirty thousand years just collapsed like an accordion.*

Had I seen the film with Ted, I would have tried to start a conversation about the ancient need to leave a mark, to say "I was here." Ted would have acted like a cartoon caveman, pulling at my hair and grunting, and we'd laugh and roll around the floor and try to tear each other's clothes off with our teeth. Had I watched the film with Josh, we'd have discussed the intelligence behind the art, the painter's effort to portray the movement of animals through time and space by drawing a series of overlapping horses. I would have described for him the sensation that looking through ancestral eyes gave me — "It's like a bellow's breeze and it gives me the chills" — and he'd say something about blowing him, and we'd laugh, and then he'd make us a cup of tea. With James, I'd have said, "It's like looking directly at the past — it's right there on that wall!" and he'd smile and agree but not talk much, while I thought about what history means; how major changes to life on earth across huge swaths of time are so difficult to grasp; and how learning evolutionary facts can make less of an impact on us than seeing a single handprint made by one ancient human being. And about how easy it is for time, in one flinted moment, to evaporate.

ՏԱ

Sometimes the fact of James's death blasts me full in the face, and I gasp for air as if it happened only yesterday; at other times, a sadness seems to sprinkle down like a shower of sifted flour — when I'm watching the news, or writing an email to Nancy, or thinking about calling my sister. At those times, it seems as if it's an *echo* of grief, what I feel. The real grief is still there, and the memory of its initial impact — the flaying, the visceral ripping of my husband from my life, gutting my days — that is still there, too. But I don't always respond in the same way. I might hear an inner shrilling, a shriek of tinnitus, for instance; more often, profound silence settles around me, and I become oblivious to sirens or children yelling outside on the street for minutes at a time.

The world is emptier without James. It looks emptier, and it sounds emptier. I miss his voice: his good-nights and good-mornings, the love-you-Maslens. His hugs. I miss the CDs he played while he cooked, his singing "Come On in My Kitchen" with Robert Johnson, his bad Robert Plant impression of "Whole Lotta Love." They don't sound the same when I play them, those tunes. The house is so quiet now.

I miss his voice the most, I think. Especially at night. I'm afraid that I'm going to forget what it sounded like.

The first few nights we spent at the farm, the intensity of the coal-dark sky pierced me. Without pollution from lit-up office buildings and streetlights dimming the stars, I seemed to meld with the air while staring up at them. At night on the farm, there was just one thin sheet of skin, a single scrim of cells preventing me from evaporating into the universe.

James tried to teach me the names of constellations, but I couldn't remember them or identify the different groupings with certainty. I saw only sparkle, not patterns. No images of familiar objects or animals. And when I looked up on humid nights, I could make star halos if I blurred my eyes.

The barometer was all over the place this summer. When it is so humid in the city that walking the asphalt streets is almost like wading, dawn and dusk play tricks on my eyes: clouds heavy with water seem to leak drizzles of fog, or to spit out white threads, like thrumming; rooftops seem to have a grey haze rising from their surfaces, like water ghosts.

James said the Big Dipper is so far away in light-years that what we are seeing, when we look at it, is really a *picture* of its stars as they were *eighty years ago*. It's a trick of time or light or space; I can hardly get my head around it. Now, when I look up at a night sky and see stars, I remind myself that I'm looking at the past. And even though the past I'm seeing happened long before James was born, I think of him, and I feel as though I'm looking up at him, and that he is still teaching me about light.

James and I had gotten a deal on the property because it was an estate sale. All I wanted, a year later, was to break even. In April I went to the farm to clean the house before it was listed, and I asked the realtor to meet me there, to discuss its market value.

The area had been identified by town council as ripe for development, he said, and a contractor he knew was already interested. He wanted to tear down the house and barn, and subdivide the fifteen acres into estate-size lots for commuters. The neighbours with the broken-spirited horse were considering a buyout offer, too. "Family farming is going the way of the dinosaur," the agent said. "Lots of opportunities for investors up here now. Your timing couldn't have been better."

ℓℓ

I sit in the wingback, the green one that has always been mine. I sit in the other wingback, the blue one that has never been mine. I stretch out on the couch that is no one's couch. Immediately I think of leaves, bronze and brittle leaves falling, in a rush, but never touching the ground.

I close my eyes and imagine that crisp fall day at the farm. I imagine being James. I am looking through his eyes now.

It hurts, that sun glinting off the quartz in the stones on the top of the wall. Almost done. What about the rocks at the end of the property that I haven't looked over, though... should I start the car and load some empty buckets to bring them in? First I'll use up the few I've left scattered about the courtyard.

"Courtyard." That sounds pretty grand for grass surrounded by a handmade stone wall. Mostly dry-laid. I dug up some clay near the edge of the pond, but I only used it in a handful of spots, where a loose join needed fixing. I scraped off the mud that oozed out as I worked, so you'd hardly notice there'd been a need for it.

The farther away I get from it, the more perfect it looks. I'd like to look down at the wall from the sky, from an airplane or helicopter, to take in the whole of it — its curves and undulations and the land in the middle.

Might as well do an inventory of the rocks I've missed back here. I'll carry any I like back by hand. Where was that pile — which side of the property line? So much garbage has blown into the brush. You could trip on these tangled pieces of plastic. No wonder that horse got into trouble.

Nothing here. Must have dreamed it. How long have I been back here — where's my watch?

Feels good to stand and stretch. The cool fall air in your lungs is bracing. The wall looks fine from back here —

His heart stopped precisely then. His body dropped to the earth, thudded to the ground he'd spent so much time thinking about. In that split second before the bullet cracked him open, I imagine my husband happy, content.

I rehearse the story with my eyes closed, night after night for weeks, until it begins to feel like the truth.

லம

Forever, it seems, we've wanted to believe that stars are the spirits of the dead shining down on us.

On a dark night in April twenty-three years from now, if I am still here, I will be able to look up and see the fires in the sky that burned on the day my husband was born. And forty-two years after that, when I will be long dead and gone, light from the day James and I met will beam down to earth, unrecognizable to seeing eyes but seen, nonetheless.

What will I think about when I am dying? Not an afterlife, not meeting those who left me bereft. There is no heaven to look forward to, I've known that since I was a child. Maybe I won't think; maybe I'll just sense, take stock of the moment. I think I will be greedy for the world, and will be sucking in all the colour, texture, sound I can get.

லம

When she was dying, my mother's conversational range became very limited, reduced to confused imperatives. She issued instructions, and they had to do almost wholly with my father: Don't feed him too much beef, for his heart. Take him to a movie at the dentist once in a while. Remind him to separate the whites from the waste, the organics from the colours.

It annoyed me that my mother was about to disappear, but all she wanted to talk about was garbage. I had come from her, and part of me — the version of myself that no one on earth could know the way she did — would be going with her, too. Was there nothing more important to say to one another, before she left? Perhaps not. I can't think of a thing that she could have said from her deathbed that would have made a difference to the life I've built for myself, anyway.

ееи

"He had an eye for it," the real-estate agent said when he looked out the kitchen window to the field beyond the house. "That is an impressive achievement. Your husband built it himself, you say?"

"Yes. From the field stones that were around the edge of the property," I said. But I could see that the wall was in disrepair. James had banked earth behind the wall to stabilize it, but the freeze and thaw of winter ice and spring rain had damaged parts of the foundation. Rocks were sticking out in a few places, like herniated discs in a spine. *What was it for, James?*

I doubted that whoever bought this place would leave the wall standing. "Do you suppose the stones will be pushed back to where James found them, once the builders move in?" I asked the agent, but he was on his phone and hadn't heard me.

He drove away from the farm before I did. As I started my drive back to the city, a burst of birds filled the sky a half mile ahead of me, like flecks of floating black pepper. I pulled the car over to the shoulder so I could watch. They swarmed together then pulled apart, came back together and pulled apart, several times, as if choreographed. "Look at that!" I said, as if James were beside me. I sat behind the wheel, shuddering.

Those birds were too small to be crows. A group of crows is called a murder, I knew that, but James would have known the name of this species, why they clustered that way in the air and what the flight pattern was called. He wouldn't have told me unless I asked, which I usually did, because I liked to have answers to questions. James knew so many things that I did not.

twenty

Lou is buried next to his wife. He'd prepaid for the casket and made the arrangements himself, many years before, as people of his generation tended to do. "To know it's done," Lou said. "To make it easier on the family."

The obituary I placed in the *Star* on Lou's death included his brief autobiography, which he'd readied for the newspaper and kept, with burial instructions, in the drawer of his nightstand.

> Louis Charles (Lou) H. was born near Barrie, Ontario, as was his wife, Adele (née Healy), who predeceased him in 1970. He became a farmhand at age eleven to help his family during the Depression, and was paid in beef and milk. An accident at age eighteen cost him a kidney, and kept him out of the military. He went into sales, where he stayed for the rest of his working life. On retiring from Schmidt's Medical Supplies in 1975, Lou made and sold fine wood furniture at local markets. He also enjoyed playing cricket, ice fishing, and hunting. He is survived ∧ *was predeceased* by his son James (Maslen).

I hadn't heard the story of Lou's accident. There is so much about people, even those you are close to, that you have no idea about. No idea at all. Our minds are like invisible civilizations, full of complicated lives. We carry worlds in our head, and we people them with everyone we've known, making characters out of the bits and pieces they show us.

The cemetery is in the town where James grew up. When his mother died, the face of her tombstone was divided in two by a vertical line. Her name and dates of birth and death were engraved on the left side, Lou's name and birth date on the right. The blank would be filled in soon by the caretaker, a short man with broken, brown teeth who told me the adjacent plot was paid for, too. I hadn't decided yet what I was going to do with James's ashes, but I did know that I was not going to leave him next to his parents.

ℓℓℓ

I woke up one Saturday morning in October ready to do it — to create a crypt of clay. I turned to *Finding One's Way* for design ideas, and I chose a footed sphere. It will have my fingerprints all over it, and through it, and inside it. The top half will, one day, hold me.

The book explained how to make the shape I wanted using pinch-balloons, a variation of the pots I'd learned to make. I bought the clay at an art supply store. I left it on the floor of the pantry, by the back door, for a few days. I needed to get used to it. I needed to walk past it, to live with it. To see it sitting there, solid and waiting, until I could pick it up and begin.

I donned one of James's aprons. He had six, all of them red, his favourite colour. Then I put my wedding ring in the hard-boiled-egg cup I keep on the kitchen windowsill, where I put it when I do the dishes. In the quiet of the house, the amplified ping of the metal hitting porcelain startled me, and I knocked an empty tumbler to the floor. I could hear my mother saying, "Maslen-itis strikes again."

The cellophane package of the large block was airtight, and when I opened it, the smell of clay instantly took me back to the pottery classroom. I saw James looking through the window at the collapsed mess I'd made trying to throw a bowl. Smiling at me.

I sunk my fingers deep into the clay body, and it was a physical pleasure. My hands hummed.

ຕ

To make pie crust, James always used an old hollow glass rolling pin that he'd picked up at a yard sale before I knew him. It had a cap on one end and could be filled with cold water — the water for its weight, the temperature to prevent the flour mixture from sticking to it. I thought the principle would apply to rolling clay, too, and it worked well. Soon I had enough kneaded and rolled to make a half-inch-thick wall. I shaped it, pinch by pinch, and as I worked I decided that I didn't want the container to be smooth on the outside. I wanted to see ridges, bumps, crevices. I wanted texture. I needed touch.

I had no proper tools, so I improvised. To get a level rim, fine waxed dental floss worked as well as cutting wire. With the bowl upside down, I attached four palm-rolled balls for feet.

The velvet bag was now lying inside the open clay vessel, the plastic one inside it. When I looked at the velvet, I could taste whisky. In the seventies, when you opened the box of a certain brand of whisky — Crown Royal, I think it was — the bottle inside was in a smooth purple sleeve of the same colour. My parents kept one on hand for their bridge and cocktail parties, nights when Gina and I would hide in the rec room with the TV volume turned up high to block out the sound of women's laughter.

I knew I wouldn't be able to empty the bags' contents unless I could do it without looking. So I rolled a square piece of clay and laid it on the top of the bowl, leaving a two-inch open-ing — enough room for me to reach in with my thumb and forefinger and work the velvet sack free. I pulled it out, empty, and put it back in the wooden box from the funeral home.

I reached in again. When my fingers found the plastic sack, I pulled just enough of it through the narrow opening to slice off a corner. I pinched another corner of the bag and spun it around, shaking the ashes into the bowl.

But "ashes" is not the right word. We don't burn into flakes that could fly away in a breeze, like ashes from parchment or fire wood. What I am keeping of James is pulverized bone, skeletal gravel.

A silver-grey residue as fine and as soft as baby powder clung to the plastic. I had an urge to touch it. I put my hand inside and drew my index finger across the dust. There was no smell. It tasted like water, like air. Like nothing.

Starlings. Those birds, dancing across the sky, they were star-lings. And they were murmurating. That is the word that describes those particular actions. I don't know where I got that word from, but I'm sure it is right.

To keep the walls of a clay container from sagging as they dry, the pressure inside of it must be kept constant. So I punctured a hole in the side of the closed bowl with a steak knife and brought the vessel to my mouth, blowing air into it the way you would a balloon. The cool, firm clay was soft as flesh against my lips. I stayed there and held my breath until it hurt. When the tension of the wall was solid enough to withstand my palm pushing against it, I pinched off the blow hole with my lip-covered teeth, kissing it shut.

To make the opening through which my ashes will be poured, I carved a small square into the top convex wall of the globe. I was careful to angle my knife's approach; the outer edge of the lid had to be wider than the inner, to keep it from falling in. When I pulled the paring knife back out and saw still-wet clay smeared on the blade, I thought of the dissections we did in biology labs, and how peeling back the peritoneum in those pickled baby pigs made me want to throw up.

With the knife tip, I lifted the cut-out just enough to get a purchase on it with my fingers, and gently removed it. It had to retain its exact curved shape while it dried or it wouldn't fit in place later, so I used a paperweight I found in a box in the basement — one of those clear domes with colourful acrylic swirls captured inside, an imitation of expensive Venetian glass, that had belonged to my mother — to rest it on.

Washing dried clay from my hands at the end of the day, I glance into the egg holder by the sink and see my wedding ring. I wonder if Anna will want it as a memento one day. My mother's wedding ring was buried with her, as was her wish, and Gina was disappointed. "What did Mom think," she said when Dad read us the will, "she'd need gold for the afterlife, like King Tut?" I can see Mom's ring mixed up among the broken necklaces, single earrings, and hair clips sitting on top of Gina's messy bedroom dresser. The band would have been lost eventually, had Gina gotten it. Gina or Anna or maybe Anna's children would lose track of it, and by then there would be no living person who knew what that ring had meant to any of us.

In our back yard a few days later, I found a small branch that had broken off the old maple tree. The twig I snapped was the right thickness to use as a tool for decorating the urn. Its pith was like the bristles of a stiff, ragged paintbrush, and as I dragged it up and around the curved, leather-hardened clay, it made faint cursive-like lines. The bark at its edge gouged deeper marks into the pot when it made contact with the clay.

No pattern — I didn't want symmetrical shapes or suggestions of any recognizable image, like a leaf. Just random scoring, etchings and dips. I used my double-jointed ring fingers, which failed me on the potter's wheel, to add the odd depression, dimples barely noticeable unless you traced your fingertips lightly over the surface with your eyes closed.

The markings remind me of the variegated lines for rivers on an old spinning globe, the kind that sat on every father's desk in those wood-paneled suburban rec rooms of the sixties and seventies: pale green, pink, purple, and orange countries with cobalt oceans and cerulean lakes made the planet look both beautiful and ugly. It felt good to hold the whole world in your hands, while being able to pinpoint exactly where on earth you belonged.

I'll let the vessel air dry to a bone-white finish. I've decided not to fire it. The extreme heat of a kiln gives clay the permanence of a fossil, and that's not the way I envision this story ending, for James and me.

I pressed an imperfect, oval pebble of clay onto the lid of the orb, and then peaked it with a pinch. *Anna's thumb and forefinger will fit there, one day*, I thought, imagining her lifting the lid from this crypt to fill the top half with my ashes. She'll need instructions. I'll put a folded piece of paper inside the top of the urn, once I've decided where James and I should be set down and left to the elements.

twenty-two

Sometimes when I can't sleep I reach for the clay globe, and in the morning I wake up on my side with its hardness pressed against my flat chest, an arm underneath, cradling it there.

The bed is flat and smooth and null. I miss the swale James's body made next to me in the mattress. It has forgotten his shape.

༄

Healing hurts. You want it to. Because you keep touching it, don't you? The way you touch your tongue to a canker, to feel the sting. You probe it to summon the pain, to exacerbate it. If you can make it worse, perhaps you can make it better.

༄

I used to think all true love would feel the same, but I was mistaken. I misread my marriage, my husband. Myself. My love for James was of a different order than what I felt for Ted, and different again from what I gave to Josh; but it was true, as true as I could make it. It wasn't enough, perhaps, but I couldn't help that. I could not have loved James any more or any differently than I did.

I think I was wrong, too, about all of the selves we create throughout our lives, about the discreteness of the self-in-love. Even that self is an accretion, not a circumscribed, calcified entity. Time does not chop us into bits, or undo us piece by piece; each self is not separated from all the others, like a photograph in a frame, encased and preserved when ardour or life ends.

No. Time paints us in layers, I think. We are composed, built on top of a charcoal sketch; the oils comprising one likeness influence the shade, the texture, the shape of the next. Each portrait is entirely new and fresh, yet inseparable from the one underneath. To see what lies beneath the surface requires a careful, almost surgical peeling back. Or maybe a slicing, a cross-sectioning would be better. That would reveal everything in an instant: the whole gamut of human want and need, of love and betrayal and sorrow and happiness.

There was lots and lots of happiness, James. Squads of it. That's what you gave me, my love. Because I did love you, you know that I did. I vowed it, and it was true.

ee

This is what I know: it wasn't a fear that ill health could take me from James that got to him. And it wasn't a fear of his own death, either, that pushed him into that airless space where he huddled. But it did have something to do with my diagnosis — I was right about that. Because James fell apart, and I didn't. That was the key: I didn't. And in those moments when we confronted the fact of my illness for the first time, James imagined a life alone but saw me standing in a particular spot — over there, in the place where I knew I'd be fine, whatever happened. I'd be fine without breasts, or with a serious illness. I'd be fine with a shortened life, or a life without a partner. Without him. Because this is what I missed: James had seen something hard in me — something heavy, like a refusal that would not be moved.

"Mom is cracking up. I think it would have been easier if Dad had died, instead of divorcing her," Anna said, her wet, webbed, mascara-coated lashes sticking together. "I'm sorry," she said, "I shouldn't have said that."

"It's okay," I told her. "You can tell me whatever you want. It's just us here, honey."

"Mom says life is ninety-five per cent crap, and five per cent joy."

Oh, Gina. "It feels that way sometimes," I said, "but you get through it. Happiness is something you have to make for yourself." Anna quickly glanced up to read my face. I know I didn't radiate happiness in that moment, but I was trying. "I really miss Uncle James," she said.

"I know. Do you remember how much he loved to play badminton with you in our back yard when you were little?" Anna nodded, but she was looking at the clay sphere behind me, on the shelf. "What's that?"

I hugged her before saying I'd made the urn for Uncle James and me, and that it will work like a garden-kit after I'm gone. She was puzzled. "Uncle James is waiting in there, on standby." She was now uncomfortable. "And eventually —"

"Don't say it, Aunt Mazz!" Anna covered her ears and closed her eyes and hummed like a child blocking out a scolding.

"Eventually," I continued, "it will hold me, too. And one day both of us will go back into the earth. The clay will break down. What's inside will break down and be absorbed, too." I raised my voice. "On and on it goes." She wasn't listening. I almost yelled at her, but I didn't.

It will be years, I thought, *decades, before she'll know what I'm talking about.*

Anna opened her eyes. We were silent for a while. Then, abruptly, she smiled. We both started to laugh, and I couldn't hold back how much I loved her then. My love for Anna flowed out of me like an estuary, and the flood of it kept coming and coming, and it carried with it my feelings for James, too — and I couldn't stop crying with the joy of it, the sad, saturated, bloody joy that loving people forces into your heart.

twenty-three

Light streamed through the open blinds in the living room. Dust coated the coffee table, the windowsills, the bookshelves; I hadn't cleaned the place in weeks. *What time is it?* I wondered. I was still wearing my pajamas. I hadn't slept well, but I'd slept late, and my sense of time was skewed. Was it late morning or early afternoon? There were too many hours in the day, and they were all the same. *Where did I put James's watch?*

Nothing felt right. I picked up the urn, I don't know why, and wandered into the darkness of the bedroom, its curtains closed tight. I could have been in one of my recurring dreams. I could have been levitating, hovering above the ground.

The urn grew heavy. I went through the kitchen, out the back door, onto the patio. I walked through a dune of snow. Ice glittered the diamond mesh of the neighbour's chain-link fence. My stockinged feet took me to the ancient maple in the corner.

The urn became lighter. I raised it high and it blocked out the sun.

What would James want? I closed my eyes. *Where would he want us to be?* I didn't know. *Would he want to be mixed with me?* I shivered, but not from the cold. The urn was weightless now.

I almost let it go.

⁓

I put the urn in the passenger seat, wrapped the seat belt around it, and drove to the farm. It wasn't my farm now, but it never had been. The sale was quick and final; everything would be demolished come spring. Yet I felt I had the right to trespass.

I walked toward the long white mound of James's creation, the clay globe cupped in my hands. I moved like someone who knew what to do, and why. When I came to the wall, I felt James with me; I paused, and then he was gone. No, not gone — he was up ahead now, and I was following, slowly.

I watched him grow smaller and smaller, and then, before he reached the far tree-line, my husband stopped. James stopped and for a moment I saw him there, standing whole against the wild, wide sky.

ACKNOWLEDGEMENTS

This book has been a long time coming and many people have had a hand in making it happen, both directly and through a kind of magical, osmotic influence. My gratitude first goes to my mentor, Diane Schoemperlen, for her expert guidance while I was writing the first draft of *This Side of Sad,* and for her ongoing friendship. Thanks, too, to Antanas Sileika at Humber College for encouraging me to aim high. Stephanie Sinclair, my agent, believed in my book and its potential, and I greatly appreciate her commitment to my work and her efforts on its behalf.

It has been my great fortune to work with Bethany Gibson, who is an exceptional, insightful, and intuitive editor. Her support for and work on this novel inspired and energized me to make it better and better. A kindred spirit, Bethany is someone I'm sure I was destined to meet. And thanks to Peter Norman, who copy-edited the book, for his astute suggestions and careful readings, which made the process a pleasure for me.

My appreciation goes to many writer and professional friends, old and new, who have been supportive along the way: Lynn Henry, Joan Givner, Stan Dragland, Adam Lewis Schroeder, Miriam Toews, Ian Colford, Dawn Promislow, Danila Botha, Mark D. Dunn, David Doucette, Kasia Jaronczyk, the late Tish Pacey (Thornton) Bird, and the late Gwendolyn MacEwen. My deepest gratitude goes to Donald Hair, Professor Emeritus at Western University, who was the first to read my earliest work; he made me believe I could be a writer, and thus myself — a gift for which no words of appreciation will ever suffice.

Thanks, too, to close friends who stood by me and my writing at critical crossroads: Jan Richardson, Janis Rosen, Denna Benn, Susan J. Carlyle, Janet Helder, Mary Wyness, Michael Groden, Parrish

Balm, Marco Balestrin, Sarah Hechavarria, Nancy Gruver Van Wagoner, Lydia Makrides, Maria Parrella-Ilaria, Mala Darshanand, and the late Karin Prior.

Gratitude galore goes to my parents, Margaret Ann Smythe and Dr. Clifford Smythe, for engendering a love of reading, writing, and learning in me — and for their continuing certainty that I can accomplish whatever I set my mind to. To Gretchen Betts, mother-in-law extraordinaire and writing-shed landlord, I also owe much.

And finally, boundless thanks go to my husband, G. This book could not have been written were it not for his constant support, understanding, patience, and encouragement, not to mention his brilliant wit, curiosity, and creativity — a mighty mix indeed.

John Wills Photography

Karen Smythe is the author of *Stubborn Bones*, a collection of stories, and *Figuring Grief: Gallant, Munro, and the Poetics of Elegy*, a work of literary criticism. She lives in Guelph, Ontario. *This Side of Sad* is her first novel.